Solsbury Hill

Solsbury Hill

Susan M. Wyler

RIVERHEAD BOOKS, NEW YORK

RIVERHEAD BOOKS
Published by the Penguin Group
Penguin Group (USA) LLC
375 Hudson Street, New York, New York 10014

USA • Canada • UK • Ireland • Australia • New Zealand • India • South Africa • China

penguin.com

A Penguin Random House Company

First Riverhead trade paperback edition: April 2014

Library of Congress Cataloging-in-Publication Data

Wyler, Susan M., date.
Solsbury Hill : a novel / Susan M. Wyler.—First Riverhead trade paperback edition.
p. cm.
ISBN 978-1-59463-236-5 (pbk.)
1. Heiresses—Fiction. 2. Americans—England—Fiction. 3. Heathlands—Fiction. 4. Bronte, Emily, 1818–1848. Wuthering Heights—Fiction. 5. New York (N.Y.)—Fiction. 6. Yorkshire (England)—Fiction. I. Title.
PS3623.Y6285S65 2014
813'.6—dc23
2014000038

PRINTED IN THE UNITED STATES OF AMERICA

10 9 8 7 6 5 4 3 2 1

Book design by Kristin del Rosario

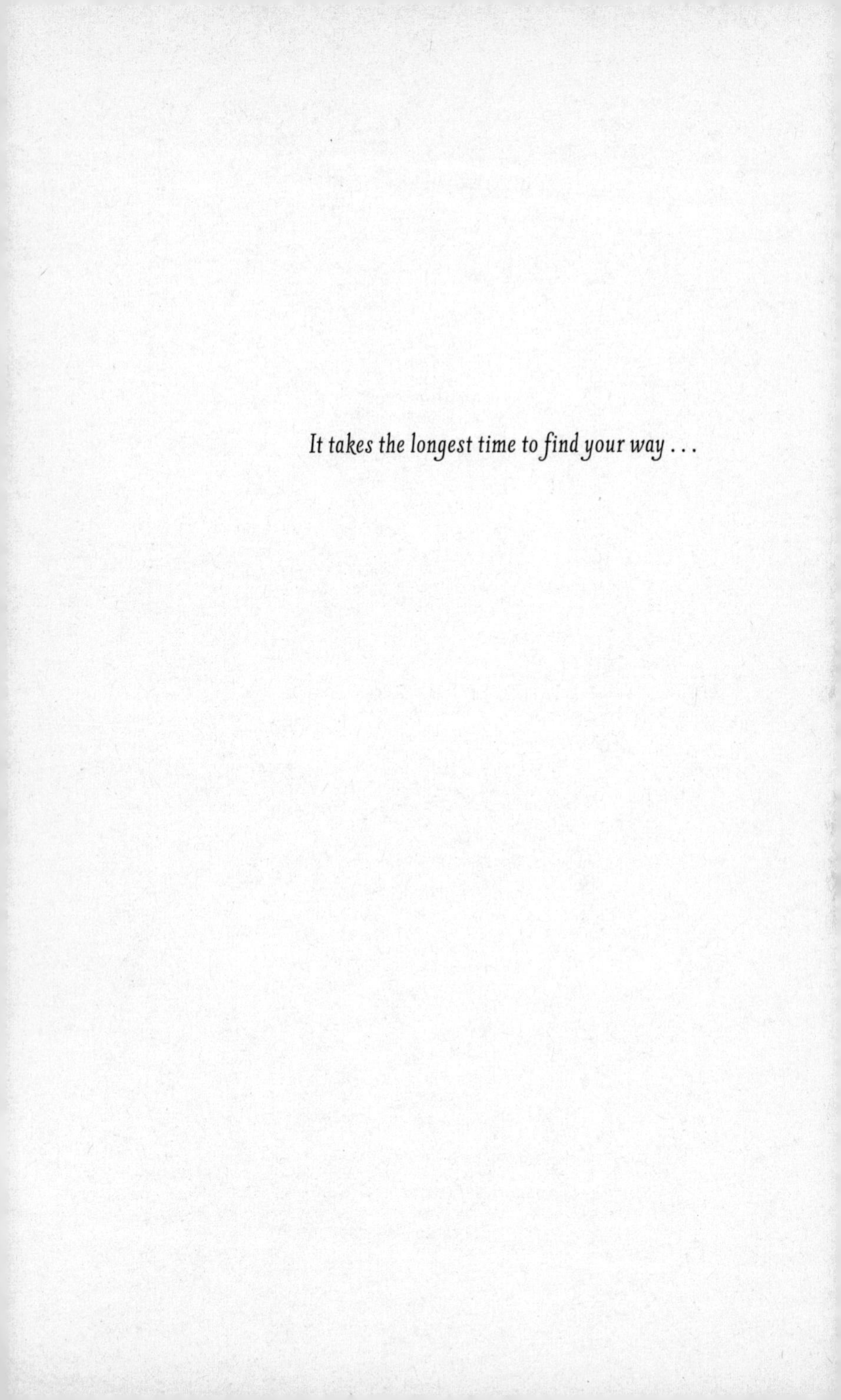

It takes the longest time to find your way . . .

This is for Timothy

PART ONE

The phone rang off the hook, she read. As she poured milky coffee from the saucer back into the cup, she wondered if old phones had startled with electricity, if they'd jumped right out of the cradle from the shock. With a blister on her heel from the recent heat and humidity, she folded down the back of her ballet flat. The café's air-conditioning was up too high and she had no sweater to cover her bare shoulders. She was trying to read a book her friend Tabitha had lent her, but it was filled with a tedious cast of artists in turn-of-the-century Paris, so she set it aside.

Eleanor pulled her hair into a ponytail and swirled it into a bun, which she punctured with the stem of her glasses to hold in place. She pondered the word *cradle*. The café air was thick with roasted beans, and the waiter, who set her plate with a clatter on the zinc table, reeked of coffee from his pores. She thanked him, sat up in her chair, brought the cup to her lips, and sipped. Eleanor had elegant limbs and three feet of straight spine to the top of her head. Despite the challenges of being tall, she refused to stoop. Even in high school, once she got over the drama of being taller than many of the boys, she wore heels whenever she wanted to. These days, she wandered about the East Village in five different versions of ballet slippers, one for almost every day of the week. She checked the blister and resolved to stop by the pharmacy for some liquid bandage, slipped the leather slippers off, and sat on her feet to keep them warm as a blast of thunder clapped and a downpour exploded outside.

Miles swept in and shook out his umbrella. He would be irritated by the rain, she knew. On the lake at Christmastime with pine and cinnamon in the air, he liked the rhythmic backdrop of rain, but at the end of a busy day in the city, with the outdoor tables pulled inside, he wouldn't be able to smoke a cigarette with his coffee. She watched as he shook his wet hair and scanned the place for her profile: the angled nose, creamy cheeks on pale skin, the self-assurance in the length of the back of her neck, and then the quirky red glasses stuck in her tangle of hair.

Miles bumped through the tables on his way toward her, excusing himself to the other patrons till a young woman stood and said his name in a husky voice that carried to the back of the room and the table where Eleanor was reading. She looked up. The pixie was pressed too close against him. There were gray bentwood chairs and metal tables urging them toward each other. The girl wasn't trying to move away and neither was Miles. His face was flushed and the girl said, "Call me," as Miles looked caught in a tight space between pleasing the dark pixie's pleasant smile and tossing glances at Eleanor to say, "I'm on my way, babe. I'm trying to get there, honey."

She studied his face, how he'd changed since they were in high school when he was awkward and stood too close at parties, popped up behind her locker door, and was hesitant to drop his tray across from hers in the lunchroom. Miles had grown into good looks over the years. His slight build had filled out, his bright hair had darkened to a curly, tousled gold, and he had stretched to six feet, two inches tall, but more than that, he had grown into charisma, and she smiled to herself to see the boy she'd known since sixth grade exercising his newfound magnetism.

"Sorry, El," he said as he got to the table.

He kissed her.

She kissed him and offered a sip of her coffee. "It's a latte with whipped cream." She licked her upper lip to catch any remnant sweet.

His legs wrapped around her legs under the table and he took her hand, kissed the tips of her fingers and took a tiny nibble, then a tender suck of her forefinger. He could be gentle. Raised genteel, from an old Connecticut family with money and manners to match, Miles wore smart shoes and tailored suits in fine wools. Still, he tangled his body around hers as often as he could.

"What was your day like?" he asked.

"Amazing."

His hand rested above her knee on the inside of her thigh. He was distracted.

Eleanor nibbled on a corner of lemon tart as her eyes shifted to the girl who was watching them, then back to Miles. "You?"

"Average day. Mostly looked forward to seeing you at the end of it." He pulled the glasses out of her hair and ran his fingers through the long strands, his eyes soft with affection. "What's this?" He picked up her book. "Is it good?"

Eleanor scrunched up her face and shrugged, and just then the light in the café changed and they both turned to see what had happened outside. The burst of brilliant sunlight from a break in the stormy clouds was enough to silence them for a minute. He reached for her hand. Whenever the sun broke through the darkness of clouds in this particular way, it reminded them both of the day of her mother's funeral, when she and Miles were twelve years old.

"Let's get out of here," he said. They were expected for dinner at her friend Violet's apartment. Miles took Eleanor's hand and led her through the tangle of tables, right past the pixie, out into the silver light of a tropical storm in New York City.

❧

VIOLET, WHOSE BONES WERE BEAUTIFUL BUT WHO'D grown too thin, liked giving elegant dinner parties so she could watch her food eaten, so she could dress in tiny, sleeveless, backless dresses that displayed the pale scars of cuts along her forearms. It was hard to take your eyes off her when she walked through the room: she was crystalline, sparkled like a clear glass lightbulb. Eleanor could only take small doses of Violet these days. She enjoyed the beluga in soft eggs, also the chilled, modern blend of Pinot noir and Riesling, but it was always good to leave and get home.

Eleanor's apartment was six floors up a tight stairwell. Wet from walking in the pouring rain, they tumbled up and kissed at every landing.

"It's great not being your buddy anymore," he said.

She took his hand and led him around the last curve, up the last step, fumbled for her ring of keys, and let them in.

"So you're not my buddy?" She unbuttoned the first two buttons of his soaked black cotton shirt. Unbuckled his silver belt buckle and dropped his pants. "Say you're still my buddy, honey, sweet Miles."

Miles stepped out of his pants, and Eleanor led him into the kitchen, where she opened the fridge and pulled out a bottle of champagne. She popped it open and poured two flutes. Held his eyes, took a deep breath, and stopped time for a moment.

"Ah, your amazing day."

She clicked her glass against his. "Barneys bought the collection." She raised her glass above her head as Miles whooped, howled, picked her up off her feet, and spun her around. "My wunderkind!" he said.

"To you, to me, to us!" She was bubbling over.

He kissed her and his hand slipped up the back of her shirt. He tipped his glass for her to sip and then he took a sip and then he walked her backward and lowered her onto the bed without losing contact, without for a moment letting his eyes slip from hers. He didn't let her feel the floor but kept her body lifted toward him.

She remembered when she'd fallen from a low limb of the tree in her back garden, a week after her mother had died. She had climbed the tree to get away from the visitors inside the house, and she remembered feeling high and separate from her sadness up there, and then climbing down she slipped on a low branch and somehow Miles had been there to catch her before she hit the bricks below. Now, in the ceiling overhead she saw the face of the boy Miles had been. She looked into his eyes, into this face so familiar.

IN THE MORNING, THEY LAY IN BED WITH THE BLINDS cracked enough to watch the rain that had resumed, a wind so loud they heard it through the window, a rare hurricane warning for New York City. Miles smoked his cigarette at last. Eleanor didn't mind. She had quit smoking when she was eighteen but loved the smell of it, loved the taste of it on his tongue. She inhaled what he exhaled and it made her woozy, loved it after they'd made love, loved it like she loved licking frosting off cupcakes, eating olives from martinis.

She climbed out of bed. "I'm gonna shower." She closed the door then opened it again. "I've got to sleep alone here tonight, right?" she said. He was going out with guys from work.

"Yeah, is that all right still?"

"Of course." She closed the door.

The water poured over her body and she squeezed some almond scrub onto a glove to scrape a crust of city dirt, sweat, and sex off her skin. When she shut off the water and pushed the curtain open, the small fan in front of the open window blew a chill across her nakedness. She heard the linen closet open and imagined Miles changing the sweaty sheets, snapping the fresh top sheet till it floated to rest. She wondered if he'd be able to stay for the day or whether he'd hurry away to get some work done at home.

She felt strange and she couldn't shake it. Everything seemed odd and she didn't know why, but this happened sometimes. There were days when she didn't trust what she saw and couldn't fathom how she felt, but the simplest thing to do, she'd found, was to assume that all was fine.

The bedsprings creaked in the other room. With vigor, she rubbed her hair till it was almost dry, rubbed her scalp and then her face with a rough hemp towel, then ran a thick comb through her hair.

Miles came in and moved the fan to pull the window shut. "You smell so good." His nose in her neck. "What is that? It's new," he said.

"Lavender," she said.

He shook his head.

"Almond."

Shook his head again.

"Karma." A sticky balm of flowers and herbs.

"Ridiculous good," he said.

Wind rattled the windows and the sky let loose an annihilating downpour. It drew them to the window to look up, to look out.

"Jeez," he said, watching the storm crash down. "I guess I'm staying." He smiled.

"You might have to." Eleanor pulled on her blue kimono but didn't tie it shut. "I've got bear claws in the freezer."

❧

IT WASN'T PLAIN BLUE, THE KIMONO. THERE WERE IVORY cream branches and vines with leaves and flowers, all on slippery silk that skimmed her body. Her skin was pale in the winter, almost blue, but in the summer turned to the color of caramel. Eleanor licked the stickiness of bear claw from her fingers, then from his. Her kimono, draped carelessly, exposed part of her breast, her hip. "I feel kind of weird," she said.

"How weird?"

"Not very." She smiled mischievously and sipped the yerba maté she loved. Miles found it too sweet.

"I mean, weird, how?" he asked.

"Don't know. Uneasy." She looked outside and thought a bit. "It's the weather, maybe."

He kissed the mole on the inside slope of her right breast. Her mother had the same mole. When she was small her father had called it a beauty mark, told her it was a sign of a destined and great love, winked at her as if to let her in on a secret.

Miles licked the scar on her arm that looked like a souvenir from a knife fight but really came from a cookie sheet coming out of the oven, then he scooted down to kiss the circular scar where the engine of a motorcycle had burned the inside of her right calf in high school.

Even though Miles' place was uptown and grander, an apartment his parents had kept in the city since she could remember, they liked to stay at her place. She could count on one hand the times they'd been at his place. All day they stayed in. They wandered about half-dressed, listened to music, sat side by side and read the papers to each other. Miles ordered Thai food as Eleanor went through pictures of a red-haired beauty modeling Eleanor's sweaters on street corners all over Manhattan. They curled into each other on her deep couch and ate tom kha soup and red devil noodles. Suddenly, he stepped out of the bedroom in a smart-looking jacket and tie.

"I forgot you were going," she said, feeling disheveled.

"Wish I didn't have to. You okay?"

"Go." She extended her leg, touched his thigh with her toe. "It's okay, go."

"I'll be running in the morning, if the storm lets up."

"I know."

He turned from the door and leaned over the couch to kiss her. She dropped her head back and took his face in her hands. "See you," she said.

When the door closed behind him, the strange feeling swept through her again.

She had just pulled a pint of mocha chip ice cream from the freezer when the princess phone rang. It startled her. Her home phone almost never rang and she had no idea who'd be calling. The sweet blue vintage phone didn't identify the caller.

"Hello?" Eleanor's tone was uncertain.

"May I speak to Eleanor Abbott, please?" An Englishwoman's voice.

"This is she."

"Eleanor, this is Gwen, Gwendolyn Angle. I *am* glad to have reached you. You probably don't remember me, but I'm a friend of your aunt Alice and, well, I have rather bad news, I'm afraid."

Eleanor hardly knew Aunt Alice, who sent her birthday

and holiday cards and recently, on her twenty-seventh birthday, a ring: a striking jet cameo, which Eleanor always wore.

"She's quite ill, and she asked me to call you."

"I had no idea . . ."

"No, no, you wouldn't have. It's been recent and terribly sudden."

Eleanor had written a thank-you note on a beautiful card, but she hadn't given it another thought. She remembered meeting Alice only once. Eleanor dragged herself back to the quiet voice from far away.

". . . Alice would be so pleased if you could come. The doctor thinks she won't be with us for long, and, well, I have the sense she's in some way almost desperate for you to come."

"I'm so sorry."

"I hate to impose, my dear. I know you must be busy."

"No, not at all." Hesitant. "I mean, I could come . . ."

"Could you?" There was measurable relief in Ms. Angle's voice. "We'd arrange a ticket—I can do that right now."

"Umm. I think I should be able to come . . ." Her mother's sister, an aunt she'd forgotten. It was inconceivable. She'd had no family for so many years.

"I'm sure you have things to arrange. Your job . . ."

"I work for myself. I could come."

"If you would, it would be wonderful. I'll tell her, then, shall I? Thank you, Eleanor." She waited. "No, I won't tell her yet, but she'll be so pleased if you come. Do you think you really will?"

Eleanor ran through the plans she had for the next few days and realized she was, for the first time in a long time—free. She'd need to speak with Gladys and maybe it would be possible for Miles to arrange things. "I absolutely will. I'll come."

They exchanged information and Eleanor put the phone back in its cradle. It was stifling inside the house, and she wanted to get out. She called Miles, but he didn't answer his phone, and she didn't leave a message. She opened the kitchen window and climbed onto the tiny balcony there, thought about what she knew of her aunt.

Alice lived on the Yorkshire moors, in the home where Eleanor's mother had been a girl. Eleanor had never been to visit, for some reason her mother had never taken her, but she knew a bit of the story, knew that her mother left England when she was fourteen or so, that her sister, Alice, was fifteen years older and had stayed on. Already a professor at Cambridge when their parents decided to take their young daughter Anne to the United States, Alice had stayed in England on her own.

In the front hall her mother's trunk had sat for years. On it was a Chinese bowl Eleanor dropped her keys into at the end of every day. Now she took the bowl off the trunk and opened it. She pulled things out one at a time. As she unwrapped tissue from pieces of a silver tea set, she grew curious. She'd lived her life without cousins or siblings, the last ten years without a mother or father, and suddenly she was part of a family. She took a box of letters her mother had saved, letters she'd once started to read when she was thirteen but hadn't been able to finish, and put them in the bottom of her suitcase beside her old brown Uggs and wool sweaters.

She called Miles again. There was no answer.

She found her mother's copy of *Wuthering Heights* in the trunk and flipped through it. She was just twelve years old when her mother died in a car crash on a visit to England. The afternoon the news had come, Eleanor had just closed the book, which her mother had loaned her, when her father knocked on the door. Happy to think he'd learned to respect her privacy, she called for him to come in.

His face was gray, the muscles limp, but the hall phone rang again, that day, and he turned to answer it before he had a chance to say anything. Still, she knew the worst possible thing had happened. She looked at the small book, whose spine she'd broken as she listened to her father's conversation.

She hadn't wanted to be there. It was the kind of gray day that wells with rain but never yields release. She had offered good reasons for not going to the memorial—her mother's body was still far away in England, where she'd died—but her father insisted that Eleanor go and Miles had stood beside her all day until the moment she slipped away, tucked herself behind a nearby tree, and wished she were little again, wished she were small at the park with her mother on the swings, wished she were quiet at the edge of a battered picnic blanket as her mother unpacked chicken, then potato salad, then fresh corn on the cob. She wished she were small again and would be prepared to make any pact with God. And then the sky opened up and the sun shone through so that suddenly everything had color and contrast and shape. Eleanor had looked up through the branches above her and hoped that when she looked down again, everyone would be gone and she'd be alone there leaning against the tree with her mother waiting at home for her, as always.

IT STILL FELT LIKE RAIN OUTSIDE, BUT IT WAS JUST THE damned pressure of rain about to explode and clouds as dark as the steel wool under the kitchen counter. Long after midnight, Eleanor's mind was still restless and she called Miles again. She wanted to lie down next to him, but he didn't answer his phone.

There were no more bear claws in the fridge, there was no coffee in the canister, there were no apples in the bowl or blueberries in the freezer. Eleanor grabbed her purse and made her way down six flights of stairs to the ground and up the street to First Avenue to catch a cab.

"Eighty-third and Columbus." Her head rattled with the windowpane. Her eyes closed, she recollected images of their weekend at the lake: the first time she popped up on one ski, the fresh fruit jam they made and spread on biscuits he'd bought in the little town. They'd kissed each other, that day, with sticky faces, licked jam off each other's lips, tasted the crumbs of oats and berries. She remembered how her body ached in the morning after skiing. She remembered the feeling of gliding on water, breaking through the wake, Miles' face turned toward her, perched on the top of the seat as he took her around the full perimeter of the lake.

Eleanor had said yes to Ms. Angle on the phone, but she wasn't at all sure she should have, not at all certain she had the courage to go. She hoped Miles might come with her to Yorkshire, as she'd never really been anywhere without him.

"Thanks," she said as she paid the cabdriver. She looked up at the brownstone's black front door and brass lion knocker. It had once been his parents' pied-à-terre. She'd been here so rarely.

The street was silent and all the houses were ready for Halloween, just days away. There were fallen leaves on the ground. The air smelled of earth and worms and damp. She took the steps one at a time. Stopped at the top and looked east down the long, quiet street. Perspective drew her eye to as far as she could see and then she turned to the heavy lion's head. As she reached for the bell she noticed the ring on her right hand, the band of jet and the lovely carved cameo. It had arrived in a pink box tied with a black satin ribbon, and inside the box was a handwritten note: *A Victorian ring of Whitby jet, sent with love, passed down for generations and meant to be yours. Aunt Alice.*

Eleanor pulled the lion's head just to feel the weight of it, dropped it against the plate, and heard the hollow sound resonate in the inside hall. She leaned her back against the door and wondered if she should use her key. Miles often used his key to her place, but she spent so little time here, hardly any at all.

Still, she longed to feel the flannel sheets on her skin. She pictured him with three pillows around him all in pale-blue-and-white-striped flannel. She would take off her clothes and slip silently into his warm, high, king-size bed.

The key was lost in her capacious bag. She fumbled past lipsticks, pens, wallet, coin pouch, bills she meant to mail, then felt the satin ribbon. She opened the main door and then the bright red door to his apartment. Through the dark living room, she saw a low light from his bedroom glowing into the hall.

The tangle of skin was confusing at first. The breathing was vivid; they hadn't heard her come in. She regretted using the key as she stood there. When she came to a dead stop on the carpet in the hallway, she hoped she'd got spun about and was in the wrong apartment.

If she hadn't used the key in her bag, she'd have rung the bell. If it hadn't rained, she might not be here. If Ms. Angle hadn't called, she'd be asleep in bed now. Time might unwind. There would be a different tomorrow.

Eleanor stood in the hallway and watched, without Miles hearing her heartbeat or catching her shadow or feeling her.

There must be presences that linger all around us, she thought, which we simply ignore. We must get used to shadows nearby.

The light was so perfect it may as well have been on film.

The light from his bathroom shone on their bodies. He'd left the light on and the door slightly open, so he could see the naked body that lay beneath his naked body, which Eleanor could see was tangled in cotton sheets. Not striped and not flannel.

He'd left the light on so he could watch as the pixie tipped her head back, the bony rise of her throat, had left it on so Eleanor could see the urgent way he sucked the unfamiliar mocha skin and the fervency of his kisses. She did this and he did that, and their bodies glistened as if they'd sprayed themselves with oil for maximum effect. Miles was moving as if he couldn't manage enough parts at once, had left the girl's neck and was holding her tight to flip her on top of him when he saw Eleanor's face, just as she decided she was leaving and had begun to back her way down the hall. Too close to coming to stop, Miles finished before he pushed the girl aside and scrambled naked down the hall after her. The front door and the street door were open. The key was on the table in the front hall.

ELEANOR WENT STRAIGHT TO SOHO HOUSE, WHERE Miles had a membership, to get drunk and take a wild dip in the pool on the roof, but after a quick drink at the bar she hadn't the heart. Instead, she went home to her apartment where she broke dishes, wreaked a little havoc, and realized she had to get out of there, too. She sat in an all-night café till the sun came up and then, in the early hours of the morning, headed toward the sliver of a workshop she rented in SoHo. At Balthazar she stopped and bought two hot chocolates and a bag of buns to share with her assistant who would be there, as she always was, in the quiet of a Sunday morning.

Gladys was about to cut into a swath of wool when she saw Eleanor looking tired and lost as she struggled to open the door. Gladys hurried to open it for her. "Hey," she chimed.

Eleanor lifted the Balthazar bag.

"Are you okay?" Gladys asked.

Eleanor shrugged, strained a smile. "I knew I'd find you here." She made an effort to sound strong and cheery.

"It's true. I like the quiet," Gladys said. "I sneak out early, before breakfast, leave the paper and the kids' waffles to Harry." Gladys took the cups and bag and placed a gentle hand on Eleanor's back. "You don't look so good."

"I'm all right. I've kind of been up all night."

"I can see that."

Eleanor picked up a pile of sweaters to sort. "I had a call from England, from a friend of my aunt. My aunt's not well and they want me to come for a visit." Eleanor dropped the sweaters and sat down.

Gladys pulled up a chair beside her. "I didn't know you had an aunt in England."

"She's my mother's sister. She's fifteen years older than my mom, and it sounds like I should go. Did I already say it was her friend who called?"

Gladys nodded.

"I wasn't sure at first if I'd go, but now I think I will."

"This was last night?"

"Yep. I think I should. Her friend was pretty insistent. She said it was important, so . . ." Eleanor shrugged, and as she shrugged her eyes filled with a thin line of tears.

"Well, it's a good time to go," Gladys said tentatively. "The collection's sold, production's under way, it goes on pretty well without you, and I'm here in case of anything." She spoke softly. "Hey, you've done it, El." She quoted a yoga teacher they shared, with a lovely singsong voice, "In doing, in doing, it is done."

This made Eleanor smile.

"You've made it happen," Gladys said and gazed at her. "You deserve to celebrate."

Eleanor took a breath as if it were her first in quite a while. Tears flowed silently.

Gladys' voice grew even softer. "Eleanor, tell me what's up . . ."

Eleanor closed her eyes. "I'm just tired." She'd been working day and night since she was in high school, hadn't gone to college with her friends because she'd already started making clothes and had made a small name for herself—reviewers called her the Wool Wunderkind for the clothes she made from recycled woolens accented with fabulous buttons. For more than ten years, she'd worked without a rest.

"I get that." Gladys hesitated before she returned to her cutting.

The quiet rhythm of scissors slicing soothed Eleanor and she lay back on the flokati rug. She felt spent from inside out, wracked from her bones to her skin. "You must be great with your kids," she said.

"Why's that?" asked Gladys.

"You're just so gentle. You don't ever press. What's your favorite thing with them, the thing you like to do best?"

The scissors made their silvery sound. "When we curl up with books and Lily keeps up with the words and Jonah just listens to the song of it all. That's my favorite time."

In the silence, Eleanor said, "If I didn't make clothes, I think I'd make books."

"Me, too." The cloth fell away as Gladys cut, and a piece fell to the floor as the scissors turned a corner. "One day they'll be reading on their own and I'll miss it," she said.

"We used to have this photograph—my dad framed it but I don't know where it went—of my mother reading to me in a hammock. I was probably three or four then." Eleanor couldn't remember herself that small but she had cherished the picture, could almost feel the hammock swaying, hear the rustle of the low wind in the Chinese elm, loved the moment captured, her mother just kissing the back of her head, her hair probably warm from playing in the summer sun all day and her innocent eyes intent on the picture book's page.

Gladys came back to the table and sat down, took a sip of the chocolate.

"You're going to have an adventure in England, I can feel it. Whatever happens, it's going to be good over there."

Eleanor's eyes welled again.

"Do you want to tell me? Do you want to talk about it?"

Eleanor shook her head no. "Thanks, though."

"For how long will you go?"

Eleanor shrugged. "I hadn't even thought of it." She looked up at Gladys, her eyes blank with incomprehension.

"Well, you know I've got things covered here," Gladys said.

Eleanor reached across the table to touch her hand. "You're sure it's not too much? I guess that's what I needed to know."

"I'm positive," Gladys said.

❦

MILES TRIED TO CONTACT HER EVERY WAY HE COULD that day, and in the late afternoon he knocked at the door, even tried his key when she didn't answer, but the chain stopped him, and though it was hard to hear him stand silent on the other side of the door, hard not to go after him as she heard his feet move slowly toward the stairs, she had nothing to say. On Monday morning, the sun rose over the Williamsburg Bridge as she headed for JFK.

PART
TWO

SHE ONLY TOOK HER EYES OFF THE VIEW OUTSIDE HER window to take the blanket and a pillow, then a glass of wine and lunch. Eleanor watched day turn to night in a few short hours. The full moon rising in the sky. The coast of England visible. And when the plane arrived at Heathrow, the landing was easy and smooth, and when there was no one to meet her as she exited through Customs, no one with a sign, no one with a smile of recognition, she pulled the bag behind her, found her way to the London Underground, then through King's Cross Station, and boarded a train for Yorkshire. All in a long day.

"THERE SHE IS," THE CABDRIVER SAID AND POINTED TO an enormous stone house on the crest of a steep green slope. "That's her, Trent Hall."

Eleanor got a glimpse of lights before the building disappeared behind some trees and a wall of stones chiseled to fit one against the other and hold without mortar. It was midnight when they passed through a break in the wall and climbed the mile-long driveway to the flat top of a hill, where the house stood wrapped inside another wall, this one covered with red-leafed ivy. Through the wall, under a thick stone archway, they drove into a large courtyard flagged with pavers and grass. There was an evocative crunch of gravel as the car slowed to a stop and the driver jumped out. The building, in the shape of an L around the yard, looked like a church with two towers and mullioned windows. Eleanor stepped out of the cab and stared around to take it in: a three-storied entrance in a wall of light gray stone extended to the right and to the left with stables and a carriage house behind her.

"My God, look at this place."

The hinges on the trunk of the car creaked for oil and the driver shrugged a cute apology before he pulled out her bags. When she tipped him, he gave half of it back. "That's too much, lass," he said. He doffed his hat and wished her a good evening.

She watched as his hand rose out the window to wave good-bye. As he drove away she imagined he'd be on his way to a warm house for a good night of sleep. Her red leather bag sat on the damp gravel, her satchel hung from her shoulder, and the wind was so strong she had to take a stand against it.

Alone in the courtyard she was seized by fear: a choked feeling in her throat and a chill, as if she'd been brushed up against. One hand squeezed the soft leather of her suitcase handle and the other hand held tight to the strap over her shoulder, as if these would anchor her, so she startled when she heard a crunch behind her and turned to see a man.

"I'm Granley," he said and reached to take the burden of her suitcase. "Don't be concerned, you're in the right place. You're Alice's niece, Miss Eleanor Sutton, eh?"

"I am. I'm Eleanor Abbott. Eleanor Sutton Abbott." She smiled. She rarely used her full name. Reluctantly, she let go of the suitcase, then shifted her bag and reached to shake his hand, but he didn't take it.

"You were worried," he said.

She wrapped a strand of hair behind her ear. "I was a bit." He picked up her suitcase and reached for her satchel. She followed him. "Is it always this windy?"

"'Tis more or less this way always. 'Tis wutherin' weather." There were leaves hanging in midair. "The dull roarin' sound of the wind, that's it." He threw his head in the direction of the moor where the land rolled away from the house.

An echoed crunch of gravel as they walked across the drive, Granley led her inside the shadow of an arch into a well-lit entrance hall whose walls were paneled in aged dark wood. With the bags set down, he reached to take her coat. Again, she startled.

"Steady," he said. She felt his gaze unwavering on her face. "Are ye timid?"

A girl in lace leggings and a short skirt. "I'm not. I'm really not." She laughed at herself. Took a deep breath to calm down. Tucked her hair behind her ear again.

"I help Alice with most everything needs doing 'round here. Well, not everything . . ." He cocked his head for her to follow and led her into the kitchen. She smelled fresh-baked bread. "The women take care of some things," he said. He stooped as he stepped through the doorway because he was too tall for the passage. Inside the spacious kitchen, with well-worn yellow-stone floors and ancient fixtures, were two women busy as if it were the middle of the day.

The older of the two, handsome and somehow elegant despite the white apron tied around her middle, turned and gasped, "Eleanor, you're here!" She wiped her hands and took off her apron, then opened her arms and gave Eleanor a warm hug.

"I'm sorry it's so late."

"No, we were expecting you."

The kind stranger stepped back and looked into Eleanor's face. "You're much like your mother, do you know that? Alice is going to be so pleased." She held Eleanor's face in her hands and saw her confusion. "I'm Gwen Angle, dear. We spoke on the telephone."

Eleanor nodded and smiled. She noticed that under the apron was a well-cut wool dress. Ms. Angle's face was long, lean, with a broad jaw and high cheekbones. Her eyes were intelligent and deep blue. Her cheeks were flushed from the heat of the oven.

"This is Tilda," she said briskly, introducing the woman who'd just pulled fresh loaves from the wood-burning stove. Tilda nodded her head with a confident smile.

"Will you sit down and have a bite? There's dinner warm in the stove and it's good."

"It smells incredible, but I'm not at all hungry right now. Later maybe?"

While Ms. Angle kicked off her slippers and stepped into a pair of heels, Eleanor had a chance to take in the room, pristine and intact from another century: the refectory table and a mismatched collection of tatty Windsor chairs, dishes draining on a rack, stone walls, and a brick fireplace deep and almost tall enough to stand inside.

"The kitchen could use an update," Ms. Angle said as she led Eleanor out, under the front stairs, into a large sitting room with high, coffered ceilings. It was gracious, with deep upholstered furniture and a lush Oriental rug that was pretty, feminine, with an abstract design in ivory, pale apricot, and celadon.

"Alice is sleeping, of course," she said. "I'm sure you're eager to see her. You must be exhausted. Will you have a glass of sherry?"

Granley interrupted, "Ms. Angle, she's all set. In the best room."

"Thank you, Granley, good night." Ms. Angle rolled her eyes. "Alice's idea of the best room is an odd, small room at the corner of the house with a lovely view. If it's not all right . . ."

"She'll like it," Granley broke in abruptly and left the room.

"I'm sure I will," said Eleanor.

"There's another one across the hall from it, if you don't. Sit down, darling," Ms. Angle said.

There was a log fire blazing in the fireplace and Eleanor picked a large chair close to the warmth of it. She was out of sorts, felt a buzz at the edge of her skin, was confused by the stately home and by Ms. Angle's warm and familiar welcome at such a late hour.

"It's such a pleasure to *see* you," Ms. Angle said. She seemed in good spirits.

"It's good to meet you, too."

"I hope you don't mind not seeing Alice tonight, but I'm worried she won't sleep again if we wake her now. Do you mind terribly? Waiting till the morning?"

"Not at all, it's fine. Of course. Is she any better?"

"She will be when she sees you, dear. It means the world to her, your coming. Since she fell ill, it's been a steep slope down, and she's been working so hard since then. It seems like her soul is urgently taking care of things, packing for a very long journey, you'd think." She poured dark sherry into a small, tulip-shaped crystal glass and handed it to Eleanor.

"How long has she been ill?"

"Not very long." Ms. Angle was firmly cheerful. She stood and walked to the window to close a gap in the drapes. Then she took the poker and stirred the fire, careful not to tumble a log. She turned back to Eleanor. "I sometimes wonder if she'd have felt it at all had no one told her, had the doctors not given it one of their names."

Ms. Angle adjusted some long-stemmed cut flowers in a vase, getting them to stand against each other in a different way, and Eleanor said, "This is an unbelievable place."

The furniture was pulled close to the fire, the windows were draped in rose velvet against woodwork painted a pale olive green. The design was spare and lived-in, but everything was large and very old: gilt-framed oil paintings, Chinese porcelain, piles of books, and antiques from many centuries. The stone walls, the massive Oriental rug that warmed the floor, there was nothing fussy about it, but it was grand.

"I've never seen anything like it. These thick stone walls . . ."

Ms. Angle joined her. "It's a good old house," she said. "But it's a bear to keep warm." She smiled. "It's been in your family forever, you know."

"My family." Eleanor shook her head. She made herself more comfortable in the low upholstered chair. "It's not at all what I expected."

Ms. Angle sipped. "What did you expect?"

"I wouldn't even know how to say—just less." She laughed

an embarrassed small laugh that barely left her chest and throat. "You said I'm much like my mother. No one's ever said that to me before, you must have known her . . ."

With a warm smile, she leaned forward. "I knew your mother since the day she was born. I was Alice's friend way back then. We were girls, still, and excited about a baby coming." Ms. Angle offered Eleanor some spiced nuts in a bowl and she took a handful.

"Did you grow up here?" Eleanor's eyes were on the furniture and the high ceilings and the cold stone walls.

"Not I, no. My family lived nearby, but Alice did, of course, and your mum until she left. They left here when she was just a girl, and she wasn't at all happy about it, but that's how it was." Ms. Angle changed the subject, gestured to the room itself. "Alice has put a lot into the place over the years, though there's still a lot to be done. It was a tatty place when we were girls racing about and tracking mud, breaking windows, the house itself ripping at the seams. And that yard out there full of chickens and even goats at one time. Quite a bit 'less,' as you said, than it is now."

Eleanor laughed with Ms. Angle. They laughed easily together. "Yes, that's much more what Mom described." The fire crackled and the logs shifted in the fireplace. "Really, she never said a thing about a house like this."

"Alice loves this place." She seemed to see the bewilderment Eleanor was feeling and took her hand in hers. She shook it gently with encouragement. "It will come to seem smaller, in time." Her voice was more intimate. "It's not as big as it looks."

They sat for a quiet moment. Eleanor was taking in the tired majesty of the place: the faded but still lush velvet drapes, the deep seat in the bay window, the thick stone walls.

Ms. Angle lifted her glass. "Finish up your sherry," she said in a kind tone, then drank hers down in a swallow. "You must be hungry."

"I'm bleary with exhaustion."

"Of course you are." She stood. "Let's go up."

"Thank you for staying up so late to wait for me."

Eleanor was reluctant to leave the room with the warm light from the blazing fire casting its glow and so much still unknown. She stood and looked around. "All this will still be here in the morning?"

Ms. Angle smiled. "The fire will have died by then." She took Eleanor's hand to lead her into the hall and up the front stairs. "But the sun might be out, if we pray hard enough."

THE DOORS ALONG THE UPSTAIRS HALL WERE CLOSED tight. There were portraits on the walls. They passed one door after another till Ms. Angle stopped and opened one into a room with a yellow and cream silk Persian rug. There were empty bookshelves on the walls and nothing more in the room except what looked like a large three-sided box, paneled and carved in oak. It took up a third of the room and had its own door.

"I know it looks odd, but there's a fine view from inside," Ms. Angle said. She opened the door and beckoned for Eleanor to pass through into this room-inside-a-room with its high four-poster bed, crisp white linens and drapes. Leaded-glass windows ran behind the bed and along the wall from the wainscot to the ceiling. Ms. Angle pushed the drapes aside till they framed the full moon high in the sky.

"If you'd rather have the other room . . ."

"No, it's great." Eleanor gazed around, enchanted.

"You must feel entirely upside down."

"I do." Eleanor took off her cardigan.

"I'll bring up a tray, just in case you change your mind and find you're hungry."

Then she was gone. Eleanor lifted herself up onto the mattress and lay back on the bed. The room shifted and spun, so she closed her eyes for a while. When she opened them again, she was still dizzy. Feeling thirsty, she went into the hall and tried a few doors, looking for a bathroom till she found one, and a glass, and ice-cold water from the tap. She sat on the edge of the claw-foot tub and drank two glasses down.

Above the bed in the room was a chandelier with flame-shaped bulbs and marble-sized crystal pendants in five different colors. The bed was in front of the windows and she could feel the wind outside right through the glass and two layers of the drapes' fabric. The branches of a tree blew against the glass, scratched against the window, and Eleanor wondered if she'd be able to sleep.

First she would unpack. There was no dresser but a low empty bookshelf where she stacked her jeans, some shirts, and sweaters. She looked for a hanger, then hung the dress and the suit she'd brought on hooks on the back of the door and put the box of her mother's letters on a low shelf. In her haste, she hadn't remembered to bring pajamas or a robe, and with the bathroom down the hall, she regretted it. She took off her clothes and crawled in naked under the thick down comforter on top of at least one layer of feather bed.

She lay without moving, listened for something beyond the sound of the wind: for dinner plates downstairs, the sounds of the kitchen. Her laptop had no charge, and there were no plugs in the small room. She was restless. She was tired and stirred up. She wanted it to be morning.

Then she noticed a bundle of ivory fabric hanging from a hook partially hidden behind the far end of the curtains. She slipped from the bed, went to the fabric, and took it in her fingers. It was warm. She held it to her nose and the linen had a sweet perfume. She thought it would be all right if she slipped it on, and did so. It was a nightgown, a long-sleeved poet's gown with full arms and ruffles at the wrists, small buttons that buttoned up the front. Out the window, the wind had suddenly died down.

Her long hair tumbled out of its bun when she unfastened it. Eleanor felt old-fashioned and fanciful in the nightgown, felt her figure under the thickness of the fabric, felt the cut of her waist and her hip bones. At the sudden knock, she almost jumped out of her skin. She opened the door.

"I startled you, I'm sorry." Ms. Angle had a silver tray with sausage rolls and a large glass of beer. She set it down.

"They smell delicious." Eleanor smoothed the gown. "I hope it's all right," she said, "I borrowed this." She was blushing. She felt caught and she was blushing.

"Of course you can wear that. It suits you, doesn't it? Let me show you where the toilet is, and a bath if you'd like one."

"I wandered around already. I peeked in a couple of doors and I found it." Eleanor was still flushed.

"By all means, you make yourself at home, dear."

Embarrassed that she'd already presumed to do just that.

Ms. Angle took in Eleanor from head to toe. "It is good on you. Where did you find it?"

"On a hook." Eleanor pointed toward the end of the curtain. "Ms. Angle, are you sure I can't see her tonight?" She was surprised by the depth of her childlike desire.

"I promise, the morning will be better."

"Would you wake me up? Make sure I'm awake?"

"Of course I will, if you'll call me Gwen." She winked, stepped close, and kissed Eleanor on the forehead. "Sleep well, dear."

The pastry around the sausage was a crunch of juicy,

sweet, and salty. The meat was perfect. It was about the best thing she'd ever tasted.

She couldn't picture her aunt's face. She could hardly recall her mother's face anymore.

The dark beer was cold and refreshing. She finished the one large glass and wished she had another. She thought of tiptoeing down to the kitchen, once everything was quiet, but decided she'd better stay still and get into bed again, stay there through the night, hope the morning would come quickly.

Eleanor tucked herself in: she turned on her side and pulled pillows behind her, pulled one against her chest, and tucked one between her knees. She missed the feeling of Miles curled in behind her. Drowsy, dizzy with travel, she allowed herself to think about what Miles would offer as an explanation. Maybe in a full life, these things just happened. Maybe she would see the house and find out about her family here, then head home and forgive him. Her eyes drooped, then dropped, then melted closed. She thought she heard whinnying horses and the sound of carriage wheels.

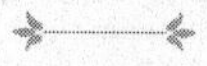

THE TREE BRANCH CRASHED AGAINST THE WINDOW-pane without stopping, crashed as if it were insisting, and Eleanor tossed through the night. She clutched the pillow to her stomach as she slept and dreamed.

She dreamed of stars in a clear sky over the moors and the moon growing as big as the sun with enough light that she could see a fox and his family curled up in a corner of earth like a cave, and she walked on the moors in her dream and felt the peat moss settling under her feet.

When suddenly she wakened, there was a very young woman on the far side of the bed, just sitting there and watching her. The young woman sat as far from Eleanor as she possibly could, perched so lightly she seemed weightless, making no indentation on the bedcovers. Then she spoke to Eleanor in a calm, quiet voice. She was young, but her face looked drawn and tired and was wet from rain and her hair was tangled. She said, "It's my nightgown you're wearing," and she ran her thin white fingers through her damp hair.

Eleanor felt foolish wearing a gown that didn't belong to her.

The young woman straightened the blanket at the foot of the bed before she got up and gingerly walked across the threshold into the other room. Eleanor called out, then climbed from the bed and followed her, but there was no one. Not in the anteroom, not in the hall. Not on the dark back stairs into the kitchen, where copper pots hung from hooks, and dishes dried on the counter. There was no woman sitting by the kitchen's fireplace, reading a book on a small low chair, as Eleanor had half expected.

If she *had* seen her there, Eleanor would have been more

surprised. It was a dream—that edge of a dream that lingers even after you're awake. It was a waking dream she couldn't quite shake, because everything was strange but familiar, old and new at the same time. Still, the feeling of the young woman somewhere persisted, so Eleanor searched the downstairs rooms.

Anxious with every step she took, Eleanor kept thinking she was crazy to go forward, but she didn't turn back. Through a hall past a series of rooms along the front of the house where the moonlight shone bright through French doors and windows, she was afraid to find the young woman but too curious not to try.

Through dozens of rooms, the young woman was nowhere. In her life Eleanor had never seen nor imagined a person who wasn't there. Her pace slowed. Maybe the woman had turned the other way in the upstairs hall and slipped into one of the rooms behind a door. Eleanor thought she'd followed close behind her, but maybe she hadn't at all. Maybe it had been part of a dream, maybe she was still dreaming.

A set of French doors opened into a courtyard with a dry fountain and two bicycles against a wall. The full moon made the courtyard as light as a cloudy day. She sat on the edge of the fountain and longed for Miles. She imagined him on this trip with her, holding her hand while she talked to Gwen Angle, standing in the doorway while she met her aunt Alice again, holding her heart through all of it, and then taking her home at the end of it, back to New York City and everything as it was.

⁂

SHE DIDN'T SLEEP FURTHER, BUT AS SOON AS IT WAS daylight Eleanor walked through the upstairs halls hoping to find Alice's room. Past a landing and down a small flight of stairs, she saw Gwen tying the belt of her silk robe and closing the bedroom door behind her.

Gwen pressed one finger to her silent lips. "She was in some pain in the middle of the night, so she'll be sleeping now for a while. Come down and get some breakfast with me, will you?"

Still in her nightgown, she followed Gwen down the front stairs past a mullioned picture window. It was a cloudy dawn with blue skies coming, and she saw the bright green rolling hills of the moors for the first time.

They passed a large empty room and went into the kitchen, where they drank coffee, ate biscuits with butter. It was early and the house was quiet.

"Why did they leave here, my grandparents?" Eleanor asked her. "I've never really understood what made them leave. Leave Alice behind and take my mother away . . . And now seeing it . . ."

"Your mother was just a girl. Your grandfather decided to try it in the New World."

"Just like that? Leave all this?"

"Alice can tell you more, but it had to do with the inheritance of the estate and the way things are here. We have some quirky old systems for property, and this one has its own particularities."

Eleanor was quiet and clearly curious.

"There's an entail that defines the way the property moves and this one is unusual because it requires the estate be passed to the first daughter in each generation."

Eleanor considered what that would mean. "And what if there isn't one, a daughter?"

"Quite. Exactly right. When it came to it, when your great-grandmother died, it jumped right over your granddad and went to Alice. Your mum was still young, and your grandfather felt a bit strange living here, in Alice's house, once it passed over his head. He knew it was coming, of course, but hadn't anticipated how he might feel about it, I suspect." She shook her head and tossed one shoulder. "He found a good placement in a law firm there in New York, so they crossed the pond and made a good life of it. That's the long and the short of it."

"They just left Alice? Here on her own?"

Gwen pursed her lips and nodded solemnly. "She was ready for it. She was grown and good at it. She did just fine, but she missed your mum."

Eleanor sipped the last drop of her coffee. "I think I'll go out for a bit and walk, if that's all right with you."

"I'm sorry you're having to wait again . . ."

"No, actually it will be good to get some air, see what's out there."

Eleanor went to her room and dressed for the cold, wrapped her scarf tight around her neck, pulled on her gloves and her boots, and braced herself for a walk in the countryside. In the front hall, her coat hung from a hook. The front door was neither bolted nor locked, so she opened it and started out.

Out through a wood gate in the wall, she walked down the hill where sheep were already grazing. She didn't remember seeing them when she'd arrived, thought maybe a boy brought them in at night and out in the morning, so she looked about for him: a shepherd or something. The hill sloped up and over a crest and on the other side was moorland: thick coarse vegetation and irregular ground. It wasn't easy walking, but by the time she had made it down one hillside, she felt she wanted to lose herself in the middle of this wild, wonderful place.

Now she found herself on flat land, a stretch of flat meadow that extended far into the distance—meadow and rolling gray-green hills all the way to where the sky met the earth—and there she saw what she was sure was the same young woman running. Eleanor headed toward her as quickly as she could, but the ground in this part was covered with heavy white stones. Yet the young woman seemed to stride across them without concern.

Eleanor wanted to reach her, to meet her and speak to her,

so she hurried, but as she hurried she stumbled a bit and tripped, and it was almost impossible to keep her eye fixed on the woman running. Eleanor gained a better footing on the flat white rocks, but there were crevices between them, so Eleanor had to keep looking down at the rocks, while the woman ran effortlessly; she appeared then disappeared only to reappear in a slightly different place, much farther along and running, running from boulder to boulder and turning her head about as if she were talking to someone; and then a deep laugh resonated from somewhere else on the hill, and Eleanor turned and slipped. Her ankle twisted, her foot caught between two rocks. Bruised, she felt tired and lay back on her jacket, rested there, and watched the fast clouds move by. She laughed at her sweet sorry self.

"Can't lie down and let yourself die out here . . ."

Between her face and the sky was the face of a man. He had dark curly hair and before her eyes could focus on him, he'd squatted beside her, taken hold of her foot, slipped off her boot, and simply released it from where it was caught between the boulders. "There," he said. "That's better." He reached for her hand and helped her sit up. "Are you lost?"

She shook her head back and forth with three fast jerks.

"Well, you're about as far as you can go without falling off the edge."

"There was a woman out here. I was trying to catch up with her."

"A friend of yours?"

She shook her head again.

"Don't you know you shouldn't be following strange women on the moors? May I?" He turned her bare ankle in gentle circles.

"Ouch."

From his pocket he removed a small blue jar, opened it, and rubbed some balm into the sprain. "This will be better." He rubbed and looked toward the crest of the hill. His hands moved firmly and his palms were soft despite calluses. He had tanned skin and strong muscles in his forearms. When he was done, he slipped her boot back on and offered his hand to help her onto her feet.

She dusted off her backside and tucked her pants into her boots again.

"Thank you. I'll walk more carefully," she said politely.

"Ought not be following them about, without considering. She might be a ghost, you know." His eyes smiled but not his mouth. "Good day to you." He wandered off and Eleanor looked around trying to orient herself. She had goose bumps and a chill ran through her. She kept her eyes on him for a while before moving on, to make sure he wasn't a ghost himself, that he didn't disappear in midair. She smiled and headed away from him down the hill toward a tree she was sure she'd passed on her way from the house. It was a memorable tree with writhed branches and orange bark on the crest of the hill.

⁂

THERE WERE THOUSANDS OF ROCKS CARPETING THIS edge of the heath and the trees that rose up through the ground between the rocks were gnarled and bent by the strength of the wind. One rock she came upon was as large as her own body and had a perfect hole in the center of it, like a modern sculpture by Arp, shaped by a constant current over centuries.

Everything smelled fresh of decay and damp with a perfume of heather and gorse and grasses at the top. There were spots, as Eleanor trod along, where something sweet rose up and hit her in the back of the throat, something so sweet she didn't want to swallow.

The landscape changed as she walked. The sun cut through the clouds and made a pattern that looked like the fingers of God. Like a companion, the force of the wind pressed against her and the grass stirred around her. She felt not at all alone, was stronger with every step, and liked the way her heart pounded against the boisterous wind that seemed determined to knock her down. She trudged her way along through the grays and greens.

She heard laughter and saw that tied to the branch of a tree was a wooden swing. The branch reached sideways and looked like the arm of a crooked old woman stooped to let the kids play, there with the ropes tied to her bony elbow and wrist.

A dark-haired little boy of eight or nine pushed a little girl from behind until she got so high he couldn't reach her. She giggled as she leaned back, looked like she might slide backward off the seat.

❧

"CANNOT CATCH ME." A PURE SOUND, A RESONANT CHANT of sound carried on the wind.

Eleanor kept the kids in her sight and walked toward them. Now she had ghosts on her mind. Now she remembered the moors and stories of ghosts and was relieved when faraway and down in a valley she saw a village, a line of trees that suggested a river, a church steeple, and smoke from chimneys. Maybe the children lived there, and not only the children but the young woman as well.

The girl propelled herself off the swing, bent in half with her hands on her knees, and dodged back and forth. She shrieked a girl's giggling fear while the little boy darted this way, then that, to catch her, called out a threat to throw her to the ground when he caught up with her. "Wicked thing," he said as he tackled her and they tumbled down, over and down the other side of the hill.

Eleanor hurried to find them. The hill was steep and on the other side there was no sign of the children. A deer darted into a copse and she followed it through the trees, where there was a waterfall and the deer was drinking from a pond.

The trees kept out the wind, so it was quiet. In the air were the scents of fir, wet stone, moss, and something like floral honey. The deer lifted its head every time Eleanor moved, watched her as she settled on a ledge of stone above the waterfall. Eleanor pulled her feet beneath her, wrapped her arms around her knees, and made herself into a snug, warm ball.

What a world, she thought, that can hold this soft falling water, this crazy wind, and birds that screech more piercingly than Manhattan's ambulance sirens. She stretched her sweater over her knees.

She saw the young boy first, then heard a happy scream in the middle of thuds and leaves crunched as the little girl tumbled through shrubs and rolled down a hill. The boy had seen Eleanor. Their eyes made contact, but he didn't say anything or draw the girl's attention to her. He loaded and flung a wad of moss that hit a tree and sent the little girl running. At the waterfall, they stripped down to underclothes and leapt in.

Amused by their courage, but worried about the cold, Eleanor leaned forward to make sure they would come up.

They tried to drown each other. He pushed her head. She pushed his head. He was the stronger. The little girl's lips turned blue then almost purple before she scrambled along the banks of the pond to get out, shivering and fumbling to get back into her clothes. Her chest heaved and as she straightened to standing, she saw Eleanor and held her gaze for a long moment. She didn't shift her eyes away, even as she stepped into her woolen stockings and pulled them up, stepped into her dress, and reached around to try to button up the back.

"We've got to go, Annie," the boy said and gestured with a sweep of his arm.

Eleanor looked at the little girl who had the same name as her mother. She looked carefully at the little girl's face, then shook her head at the ridiculousness of imagining ghosts everywhere.

It was like twilight inside the lush gathering of trees around the pond.

"A merlin!" the girl screeched. She pointed to the sky and moved slowly, gestured to the boy to come closer. She put her finger to her lips to say, "Quiet," and Eleanor saw the white belly of a falcon in the sky. "Look, Gare," the girl whispered to the boy, "it's the same one." They watched the blue-gray raptor land at the top of a tree nearby.

"It is the same one," he said. "He's walking with us."

Even after the children disappeared in the brush, Eleanor could still hear the little girl chattering about the lives of red squirrels and swallows, dippers and foxes.

Eleanor headed back in a direction she hoped would bring her to the house, through a field scattered with small flowers.

AS ELEANOR CROSSED THE COURTYARD, GWEN CAME through the gate of the kitchen garden, her hair bound up in a scarf, a bloody apron protecting her dress.

She put her hand on Eleanor's back and ushered her into the kitchen. "I was starting to fret about you, but you've found your way home. Tilda's making Alice's favorite pudding."

"It smells great," said Eleanor.

"Molasses and burnt sugar," said Tilda.

"As you see, I've been laying waste to chickens." Gwen untied her apron, balled it up, and tossed it on a chair. "Fresh from a local farmer. Let's go on up."

They came to the landing halfway up the stairs, and there was a hall to the right. At the end of the hall was a pair of carved wood doors left slightly ajar. There was a pool of light in the hall and Eleanor realized Alice was inside the room. "I'm scared," she said without thinking.

Gwen put a warm arm around her, pressed her head against Eleanor's head, and whispered, "There's no reason to be scared. She's the most lovely woman."

"I'm scared of myself, honestly. I'm scared of how I'll feel."

"Don't worry. You're quite safe here."

It was a kind thing to say. Eleanor untied the jacket from around her waist and dropped it in the hallway, pulled her sweater over her head and tossed it on top of the jacket, so she wore just a heathered oatmeal crew-neck T-shirt tucked into her jeans with a simple brown leather belt. She wrapped her hair in a bun and knotted it there, tucked stray hairs behind her ears. She might have been a girl from the '70s. Gwen's eyes approved and she led her to the open doors.

Alice's pretty, gray hair was in a smooth French knot that

sat low on the back of her head. It was all Eleanor could see of her when she came into the room, because Alice was sitting in a bay window with her back to her, but as soon as Alice heard them come in, she turned her wheelchair. She took hold of the right wheel and spun the chair to its left. She wore a pale blue sheer blouse with full sleeves rolled up, exposing lean forearms with creamy skin. The collar sat open and the blouse was unbuttoned to just above her breasts. Eleanor noticed the youth in her chest and neck as she walked toward her. She was striking not because her features were simple or even, but because her eyes sparkled and she radiated appreciation.

Alice smiled and instantly Eleanor recognized the smile. Though her mother's face had been less luminous, less hopeful, as she recalled, Eleanor remembered this smile, as if it were part of her everyday life, it was so familiar.

It was only when Alice lifted her two arms, to extend her open hands to Eleanor, that she saw the weakness in Alice's body. It seemed an effort just to lift those near-weightless arms.

Eleanor crossed the room to her, knelt beside the chair. Alice put her hands on either side of Eleanor's face and said, "My God, you're so pretty. Isn't she pretty, Gwen? I bet you're happy. I can see you've taken good care of yourself. Are you happy?"

Eleanor inhaled a huge breath and tried to find words, the

right thing to say, but instead she laughed nervously and her laughter made Alice and Gwen laugh as well.

"She's been out walking all morning," Gwen said.

"Really!" said Alice.

Eleanor's cheek was still held, in her aunt's thin hand, and her eyes closed for a moment, then opened, and looked at her aunt looking so deeply into her. "It's incredible here," Eleanor said. She stood up and looked for somewhere to sit, pulled a chair close to her aunt's chair. "You look so well."

"I'm not," Alice confided chummily. "I feel well, but they have me on oxygen at night, so I guess that explains it. Should have started a long time ago, eh?" Alice drew a shawl up over her shoulders. "I could sit here all day and just look at you. Would you let me do that?"

Eleanor scooted back in the chair to get comfortable, smiled to let Alice know she'd be staying for as long as she liked.

"You were a scrappy kid last time I saw you, and not at all a happy one, but look at you now. I want you to tell me everything."

"I was hoping you'd tell *me* everything."

"Elevenses?" Alice said to Gwen. "Let's have some tea, whatever time it is. No time like the present." Her eyes sparkled. "Let's have Christmas and Easter, too," she said to Eleanor with the eager delight of a child.

Gwen left the room and Alice spoke more quietly, "Do

you think you might help me back into bed? I look stronger than I really am." Her smile was weak, her eyes someplace deep. "The smallest thing takes it out of me."

The pale blue blouse proved to be a floor-length nightgown and beneath it Eleanor saw Alice's lean body as she helped her under the covers and tucked her in. Just the move across the room had left Alice breathless. The room was not large but the floor was carpeted and the walls were paneled rather than stone, so this room was warmer than the others. Eleanor pulled the chair up beside the bed and sat down.

"It's true there are things I want to tell you, before I go. Answers to give, if you have questions," Alice said. "I'm so glad you could come. I can hardly believe you managed to come, and I want to hear everything you have to tell me. Tell me about your life there, about love in your life—tell me everything."

Eleanor glanced out the window at the view from the bedroom. This room looked over another part of the landscape: a small lake with wild grasses and flowers surrounding it and hills that swelled beyond the lake.

"Aunt Alice, I'm a little numb, to tell the truth. There's so much I can't make sense of." She turned her upper body to look out the window and she could see everything from the chair. "Walking around out there . . . after the city all my life, it's unbelievable. I mean, living here you would probably think this is what the whole world is like, but I thought the whole world was like New York City. I know I sound ridiculous. But I mean it, sort of. I mean I've been places, lots of places, obviously, but this place is completely different from anywhere I've been. I suppose I've just been from one city to another city. I guess you could travel the whole world and never leave the city."

Alice's face was compassionate and calm. "I'm not surprised you're numb. It took a lot of courage for you to come." Gwen came through the doors with a silver tray, and Alice shifted in the bed, as much as she could, to make room for it. "Let's start in telling stories, shall we?" Alice said to Eleanor. "I might look fine, but I'm not here for long."

"She's a forthright woman," Gwen said. The tray had a porcelain pot and cups, buns, and boiled eggs. "Here's a picnic for you two. Be gentle with her, will you?" she said to Alice. On her way out the door she turned. "By the way, Mead stopped in the kitchen and asked if he might come up now, or should he wait till the afternoon?"

"Oh, not as long as the afternoon, but perhaps not right now. Would you ask him to give us just a while?"

She turned to Eleanor and asked, "Do you remember Mead?"

"I don't think so . . ."

Alice's face brightened. "Ah, Mead. You should know him. I'll tell you his story, if you like, but it's a long one. Do you want to hear about him?"

"I do." Eleanor leaned back and draped her arms on the arms of the velvet-covered chair.

"He was one of the miracle babies of Juarez Hospital in 1985."

"The year I was born."

"Yes, exactly the year you were born." She touched her bony finger to the side of her nose. "It was 1985, September nineteenth. There was a terrifying earthquake in Mexico City that morning, the morning after Mead was born. I was there visiting my dear friend Duncan Macleod and his beautiful wife, Fermina Meardi.

"We'd been to dinner and were still at the restaurant when Fermina went into early labor. Her water broke and the baby was coming, so we rushed her to the closest hospital.

"But Mead came easily. The birth was beautiful and uneventful and Duncan spent most of the night in a chair by Fermina's bed." Alice spoke as if she were seeing it again. "Fermina and the baby were sleeping soundly, so Duncan left early in the morning, just to rest a bit, to get things for Fermina and the baby, to change his clothing.

"He came back to the apartment about three in the morning. I was already asleep. I'd left soon after the baby arrived. He was a beautiful baby, with a full head of hair and deep-set eyes.

"Anyway, Duncan and I were both still sleeping when the earthquake hit at quarter past seven.

"We hurried through the streets to the hospital. It took forever. Through so many frightened people and so much destruction, it was odd, the city was so quiet. After the horrid noise of the earth rolling and shaking, the city was hauntingly quiet.

"We came up the steps from the tunnel to where the hospital building was, where it should have been, but there was nothing but empty sky. The building Fermina and Mead were supposed to be inside was just a flat waste of rubble in front of our eyes. You can't imagine. I'll never forget all that clear empty sky."

Alice took a strained, deep breath.

"You know his full name is Meadowscarp Macleod." Alice smiled. "It's a beautiful name Duncan gave him. You know a meadow is a heath and a scarp is a cliff. Do you see?"

Eleanor shook her head no. "Not exactly."

"I expect Duncan meant it for me."

"But Mead's alive, isn't he?"

"Oh, yes, darling. Very." Her eyes seemed to have come back from somewhere vivid and far away though her voice was weak. "They were miracle babies.

"Mead was with Fermina all night. They surmised a nurse had thrown him out the window when the shaking began and the walls were coming down. He was found in the rubble with a tag on his wrist. Other babies, in the nursery, survived in their cribs. Maybe they were used to being in small spaces, with no expectations from life, their nervous systems strong and ready for survival—no one knows why they survived, really, but they did."

Alice tried to reach for a glass of water on the bedside table and Eleanor stood and helped her take a sip.

"Duncan was too broken from it, losing Fermina and the shock. He couldn't manage. For a long time, Duncan couldn't manage at all, and Mead became my son, my ward."

They hadn't poured the tea or touched the buns. Eleanor cleared the tray from the end of the bed and set it on a low cabinet.

"That's an incredible tale."

Alice nodded. "Look how fit and strong you are," she said. "Already out on the moors all morning. They will keep you hardy."

Eleanor pulled the covers up on Alice's chest, and Alice took her hand. "How about if I tell you about that beautiful ring you're wearing, then?"

"Aren't you tired?"

Alice nestled under the covers a little more deeply. "Perhaps it will be a short story." She was drawn and her voice was weak as she began, "This lovely ring was made in Whitby sometime in the century before last. A young woman named Victoria Enswell, an ancestor of ours generations ago, put in her will that it should go to the first daughter of each generation when she turns twenty-seven."

"The first daughter, like the house."

"Just like that." Alice put her cool thin hand on the side of Eleanor's face and gazed at her. "Do you know you have a lot of Annie in you?"

"I do?"

"You do."

"Why at twenty-seven?"

"I don't know for certain, but I think it's meant to protect against a certain bad habit of heartache." Alice's eyes fluttered and almost shut. "Sweetheart, there's so much I want to tell you and I can't sort out what goes where." Eleanor wanted to hear more. "It's something that's said, a story that's trickled down, that women in our line, women torn between two loves, choose the wrong one. Take the wrong turn for the wrong reason. It used to preoccupy me, but not much anymore." There was a worn smile on Alice's face as her eyelids closed then opened again. "It doesn't happen to all the women," she reassured Eleanor, "and this ring is meant to protect against it."

Alice spun the ring on Eleanor's finger. "It's beautifully carved, isn't it? Have you ever seen anything like it?" Alice's eyes fell closed and it was minutes before she opened them again. "You're happy, aren't you, dear? You look wholesome and happy."

Trying her best, Eleanor said, "I am."

ELEANOR STRIPPED OFF HER CLOTHES AND LAY DOWN for a minute in the late afternoon. Naked under the duvet with the window slightly open in the small room, she closed her eyes and soon was half dreaming. She saw the tree with orange bark on the moor and now its shape looked like a woman screaming. She tried to picture another tree, but instead her mind moved closer to this one and she sat down beneath it. She looked up at the orange female tree and realized she was not screaming but running her fingers through her hair, stretching and yawning in the evening. The tree shivered and the leaves fell like snowflakes onto the bed.

Against the window above the bed where Eleanor slept and dreamed, the tree scratched against the pane. She was damp with sweat and moaning when she felt someone come in and cover her bare shoulders with the comforter, then push the branch away from the glass and close the window.

By the time she wakened, it was dark outside.

Disoriented, she wondered if she'd missed a day or just dinner. She was hungry but dank with sweat and when she climbed out of bed she was shocked by the cold, her nipples so hard they hurt. With fresh clothes in her arms, she went down the hall and waited for the bath to fill for a hot, steamy soak.

In the cupboard beside the sink she found some fragrant oil and poured it in, then slipped under the oily water. Her arms by her sides, palms just above the waterline, she felt herself inside Millais' great painting of Ophelia: the dead shock in the eyes, the jaw loose, and the mouth ready to speak. She slipped under the water and held her breath. Touched the softness along the backs of her thighs. Gazed through the water at the coved ceiling ten feet above her.

In their talk, Alice had asked after Miles. She remembered him from when she'd visited New York for the funeral. She mentioned how attentive to Eleanor he'd been, how unusual it was for a boy so young to be so overtly concerned, asked if she still knew him.

Eleanor wanted to protect him. She wondered what had taken him so far from what he'd always been. His face, in that split moment when he saw her and before she turned away: he hadn't wanted to ruin everything.

She came up out of the water for a mouthful of air. Her mother had grown up inside these stone walls. She might have bathed in this very same bathtub, deep and made of heavy iron to hold the heat for a long time. Eleanor grabbed the large, fragrant bar of soap and rubbed it into a lather. She extended her legs and washed her feet, her knees. First she hummed, "Lavender's blue, dilly-dilly," and then she sang, as she soaped herself. She remembered when she couldn't sleep at night her mother, and when she was very young her grandmother, would whisper with a song. "Dreams for sale, fine dreams for sale . . . hush, my wee bairnie, an' sleep wi'oot fear." Now she knew where it came from: the strange accent they sometimes fell into together, her mother and her grandmother.

In her short time here, Eleanor had come to accept the child her mother had been in this house. Now it dawned on her that this was the world her mother had come back to just before she died. As a grown woman she'd walked the halls.

Why hadn't she brought Eleanor with her? Why hadn't she asked her mother if she could come along? Maybe there were questions she'd known not to ask, all those years ago.

The towel was thick and dried her quickly. She pulled on white tights and a cream cashmere dress and her big cream sweater, because it was cold in the house. She wrapped a black satin ribbon around her bun and headed downstairs.

Her dress had a flirty flare at the hem and she swung her hips side to side to feel it swing around her knees. Her hand on the rail, she had her eyes on the chandelier in front of her and over her head. The house was Tara after the war, a bit worse for wear, but still dignified, and she was heartbroken and the loneliest girl in the world.

"That's a fine sashay," a man said from where he stood at the bottom of the stairs, just behind the bend in the banister.

Embarrassed, she said, "Um, thank you?"

"I take it you're the lady of the manor." He bowed and Eleanor wasn't sure if he was mocking her or being kind or what he was doing.

"Are you Mead?"

He bobbed his head forward and back, his top lip buried in his bottom lip. Solemn. "I am." He waved to her and went into the front hall and out the front door.

In the kitchen, Gwen had just made a thick sandwich and was about to make another.

"Tilda's making some chicken and potatoes for Alice, but I'm having a sandwich. Which would you rather?"

"I'd love a sandwich."

"It's not a proper dinner," she said as she set her sandwich on the table for Eleanor, "but we're all turned about in terms of schedule. Did you rest well?" Gwen went back to start a sandwich for herself.

"I slept for a bit and took a wonderful bath."

"Did you and Alice have a good talk?"

"We did."

A bowl of fresh brown and green eggs sat beside bottles of wine on the counter, next to the flour bin, the sugar bin, and the saltcellar. There were crystal glasses and stacks of dishware on one of the counters, a few open cardboard boxes on the floor. Tilda hummed as she stirred butter into a bowl with boiled potatoes and basil. The mood in the house was cheerful. It wasn't at all the same feeling she'd had when Gwen had called, sounding desperate and urging her to come.

Eleanor hadn't dealt with a house full of family in a long time. After her mother died, her father withdrew from her and five years later died of what they called a massive coronary, but she knew it was a broken heart. For so long, she'd only dealt with herself, with some friends, with small choices and never anything extended.

Sitting with Gwen in the warm kitchen, Eleanor confided, "Aunt Alice started to tell me something about a bad habit the women in the family have, a habit of picking between two loves and choosing the wrong one. She was tired before she started and got more tired as she spoke and then fell asleep midsentence, so I didn't really get it. Do you know what she was talking about?"

"Ah, the bad habit, where to begin?" Gwen rolled her eyes. "This house is rumored to have been the house of Heathcliff and Catherine. The real Heathcliff and Catherine, somehow . . ."

"I didn't know the book was based on something real."

"It isn't. That's just the rumor here, and Alice has picked up a tale about something in the bloodline, a tendency—she calls it a habit. The idea is that it runs in the blood and inclines the daughters of the family to choose the wrong man, between two men. Of course, it's never been clear at all to me that Heathcliff would have been the right choice for Catherine."

"Heathcliff was the great romance, wasn't he?"

"Not by me, but the trouble with all this is that if one tries to choose the right way in anything, one will get all turned about and confuse oneself entirely. I'm not sure why Alice brought it up, really. It's nothing you need to be thinking about."

Eleanor responded, "Well, I guess one of those bloodline daughters would be me."

A different young woman, someone Eleanor hadn't seen before, passed through the kitchen with a bundle of wood in her arms. She didn't look up, didn't say a word. Eleanor didn't have time to offer to help her before she disappeared.

"Let's go on in," Gwen said, with her own sandwich on a plate. "Come on." Gwen led the way under the stairs to a much smaller room not nearly as fine in its decor, but with another stone fireplace. The walls were lined with half-empty bookcases. There were two deep armchairs, so Eleanor took one and Gwen sat in the other with the plate on her lap.

"Did Alice make a wrong choice?"

Gwen flushed red and said, "I certainly hope not."

They shared a smile and Eleanor considered what Gwen implied.

"There have to be two choices and for Alice and me there's always been just the one."

"That's good, that's so nice," Eleanor said. She realized they were a couple. "I'm confused, though. Then who made the wrong choice?"

"All I know is what I've heard, and what I've heard has a good deal of fancy wrapped about it, but it had to do with a couple who took in their friend's orphaned daughter, more than a hundred years ago. The child was named Victoria, and she grew up in this house, married the family's son, inherited Trent Hall, and set the entail to pass the estate the way it does."

Eleanor was fixed on a thought she couldn't shake, but she wasn't sure why as she spun the ring on her finger. Her skin was cold and her head was filled with ancestors she'd never known. "And did *she* choose the wrong man?"

"What an interesting question," Gwen said. She looked at

Eleanor intently. "Goodness, you're worried about this. Are you facing a romantic crossroads?"

"No, not really. No." Eleanor pulled herself up taller in the chair and realized she was preoccupied about the beautiful black ring failing to protect her from heartache.

"You're from the New World, dear. Old Yorkshire tales can't touch you."

Tilda dropped a glass and it shattered. Worried, she looked about and apologized.

"They're old glasses, it's all right, Tilda," Gwen said. "That's a good sandwich, isn't it?" she said to Eleanor.

"Very." Eleanor took her last bite. "I met Mead in the hall."

"Ah, that's good. I've been meaning to find him for you."

Gwen put her plate aside and knelt by the fireplace. "You know, dear, Alice's mind is fairly muddled. She's just recently been put on morphine. It really is the end, and sometimes she seems to be working very hard on something. I see it in her face, like she's puzzling through decades, maybe more than that, putting things in order. She wanted you to come so she could see you and touch you and I don't think she imagined it would really come to pass. I know she's overwhelmed with wanting to catch up and tell you everything she's ever known, make an impact." Gwen's eyes were awash with tears that didn't fall. "But she's made things simple for you. This place takes rather good care of itself so it won't be any burden when it all comes to you."

"To me?" Eleanor was taken aback.

"Good God, I've put my foot in it, haven't I?"

Eleanor was stunned. She thought back through what Alice had said to her. "It all coming to me, what does that mean?"

"You're the first daughter in this generation. Clearly, Alice didn't say anything."

"No. Not in so many words. She told me about Mead, and about this ring, and I guess she said the ring and the house went together, but I didn't put it together. The house is coming to me?" She stood up and then sat down again. "I guess that's what she meant." On the sideboard there were crystal decanters with whisky and some cocktail glasses. "I'm going to pour myself some of that." Eleanor stood up and walked to get herself a glass. "Can I pour you one, Gwen?"

"Absolutely. This is altogether too much coming at you."

"A bit." Eleanor threw back two fingers of whisky then poured another and one for Gwen. She handed Gwen her glass and sat down. "Upside down and inside out is what I feel. I can't live here, you know. I can't stay."

"You don't have to. Most estates can't keep themselves, can't make it without opening up to the public in one way or another, but this one takes care of itself, produces quite a lot of income."

"Income from what?"

"The livestock, rapeseed oil, heather and lavender, rentals

from properties in the village. Alice has been vigorous about making the most of this place."

With whisky warming her, Eleanor gazed at the jet ring on her hand and said, "Why didn't I come here sooner? I wonder why I didn't come right after my father died, or even with my mother sometime."

"You had your own life, dear. You were a young woman with a big life. Alice always kept track of you."

Gwen took her glass and sat down beside Eleanor close to the fire.

"What about Mead? What about all this going to him?" Eleanor asked.

"Dear, there's nothing to worry about." Gwen was shaking her head but hadn't yet answered when Mead came in. He went straight to the fireplace and stirred the logs with the poker, then got himself a whisky before he sat down, before he said a word to them or they'd said a word to him.

His hair was longish and unruly, dark brown to the nape of his neck. He had a square jaw, tanned skin, full eyebrows, and a prominent nose. There was nothing delicately handsome about him, but he wore smart navy trousers that draped beautifully and a thick gray wool cardigan. Eleanor took in his clothing, clear down to his shoes, dark suede desert boots, scuffed and tumbled with wear, and just as she was putting together where she'd seen the shoes before, he said,

"How's the ankle, then?"

She exhaled a laugh. "I hadn't put two and two together till just now, when I saw your shoes. My mind's not working very well today, but my ankle's fine, thank you." She said to Gwen, "I tripped on some rocks and Mead happened to be out there, and he put something on my ankle, and it's all better." She turned to him. "Just as you said it would be."

She was glad to see a young person, to have someone else her own age in the house with her. She was curious about him, but didn't ask him any questions. She felt nervous and flustered and looked about the room. Her eyes landed on some boxes stacked high in two corners. "Are those books in the boxes?" she asked Gwen.

"Boxed-up books, yes," Mead said.

"Are they going somewhere?"

"I've been building a library here." His head tipped in the direction of the courtyard. "Out there."

"Wow." Eleanor wrapped her arms around her knees. No one spoke for a while.

"Perhaps you could explain, Mead," Gwen said.

"Let's see, about a year ago, I decided to go through the house and check the collections for mold, and silverfish, and book lice, see what shape things were in, and I saw what we needed was a proper library. There are random bookshelves in every room, you see, and Alice has loads of books stored all over the country, so the barn was the most likely place, the biggest building"—Mead took a breath in midspeech and

Eleanor saw he was weary—"and though it took a lot of sealing up to make it right, a new roof and insulation, glass doors for the shelves, it's coming along."

Eleanor looked to Gwen, then back to Mead. "Will it be for the public, the library?"

"God, no." He spoke harshly.

"Ouch," she said in a playful way.

"I mean that's not the plan," he said, his tone chastened. "I suppose anything could happen."

Eleanor stood and crossed the room to look at the bindings of some of the books that remained on the shelf.

"I'm going up to Alice." Gwen kissed Mead tenderly on the top of his head. "Did you get a chance to see her today?"

"I've just come down. We had some chicken and delicious potatoes."

"Perfect." Gwen left them alone.

After a long silence, with Mead drinking whisky and Eleanor looking through the books that were still on the lower shelves, she said, "You've a lot of Brontë material."

"Alice was a Brontë scholar in her early academic life."

"Huh." Eleanor pulled out an edition of Brontë poems. "My mother had a copy of *Wuthering Heights* in this trunk I have, and I found it just before I left." She turned to him and held out her palm. "It's as big as my hand. Fits right there in the palm. I started reading it again. I know I read it before, when I was younger, but I don't remember much of it."

"Did you like it then?"

"Mm-hm."

"Are you liking it now?"

She shook her head. "I just started it the other night and it was, I don't know, kind of irritating."

"Irritating how?"

"Irritating like too many questions."

She dropped onto the couch. Relenting a little, she said, "The guy who tells the story sounds so pressed and urgent."

"It's gothic. He's creating suspense," he said in a tone that suggested anyone would know that.

"You've read it."

"I have, many times. What did you like about it before?"

She considered for a moment. "I was a kid. I guess I liked the romance. I don't remember it that well, but I remember some vivid scenes. Not what the book was about, so much. I remember that my mother was worried when I borrowed it from her. She told me to put it down if it made me uneasy. It made her uneasy. I remember that." She rocked back and forth. "Do you want to tell me what it's about?"

"You're not going to read it?"

"I will. I'm sure I will, but tell me anyway."

Mead studied Eleanor's face. "You're not going to read it. I'll tell you what I can. Get yourself comfortable." He started in. "*Wuthering Heights* is a story of love, but also of siblings and rivalry and revenge. The house itself was a wild, dark, and motherless place, the home of the Earnshaw family."

He paused and she nodded for him to continue.

"Mr. Earnshaw brought home from his travels a dark gypsy boy he named Heathcliff. The older brother, Hindley, resented Heathcliff, but little Catherine adored him from the start. They grew up together, rode horses and ran wild on the moors. Mr. Earnshaw treated Heathcliff as his son, and some think he might have been.

"Hindley's jealousy—first of their father's affection, then of Catherine's, then, too, of Heathcliff's affinity with the moors—grew vicious once Mr. Earnshaw died. Hindley exiled Heathcliff to the stables and treated him like a servant from that moment on. He was brutal and cruel to Heathcliff, and this drove Catherine and Heathcliff even closer together, till they developed a sense that they were alone together against the world.

"They were wild as the moors are wild, Catherine and Heathcliff. As they grew, their love grew romantic and they shared an unspoken promise to be together forever. One evening, mischievous as ever, they climbed into the garden of the Lintons at Thrushcross Grange. Watching through the window, they made some noise and dogs came running. Catherine was bit and Heathcliff was chased away—"

Eleanor broke in. "Didn't they die together in the book? I'm embarrassed how little I remember."

"No, no, not exactly. No, they didn't." More thoughtful now. "But you see"—he cleared his throat—"there's the book that was written, and then there's the book that's remembered, and all the movies in between. It's hard to get at what people really know about the love story. Which love story they mean." This last bit he spoke into his drink, his eyes fixed on the bottom of the glass, and then he drank it down. "From all the things that happened to him, Heathcliff was a pretty nasty character in the end."

"I remember Catherine saying, 'Nelly, I am Heathcliff!' and Heathcliff cursing her, somehow, never to rest. Is that right?"

"It is. I gather from the look on your face, you're not a fan of that sort of love."

She looked into the flames. "I hardly remember any of it."

Gwen strode back in. "She's soundly sleeping. Did I hear something about Heathcliff?"

"You did." Mead stood. The crystal decanters were each filled with a different whisky and he poured Gwen a glass from one and Eleanor a glass from another.

"I suppose I started that." Gwen settled into an easy chair and Eleanor got up to sit down at the end of the couch closest to the fire.

It was turning into a sweet lazy evening.

"Tell us more," Eleanor said to Mead.

Mead perched on the edge of a chair and started, "We know they loved each other since they were small, but as they got older it got more complex till they were all tangled up in each other, as you noted, and couldn't tell themselves apart."

He walked across the room. "Cathy spent five weeks with the Lintons, healing from the bite, and came home elegant with airs and manners and Heathcliff was crazed to see Cathy so changed. She teased and provoked him, taunted him with Edgar Linton's courtship." Mead opened his throat and swallowed the glassful in one gulp. He noticed Eleanor's sleepy eyes.

"The story's longer than this night allows for," Mead said.

"No, go on."

"The rest is all mistakes and betrayals and running away. Heathcliff disappears and Catherine marries Edgar Linton. Heathcliff returns a rich gentleman. He's won Wuthering Heights, from Hindley, in a debauched game of cards, but he wants more. He fights and connives and won't give up, even after Catherine dies. Heathcliff becomes a monster, from all the bad done to him . . ."

"A monster?"

"He's not a bloke I'd want for a mate." He poured one more whisky and knocked it back. "There's more to it—all the slamming stuff is at the end. You should read it again."

Eleanor laughed. "Okay, I will."

"I believe I'm done in." He smiled a broad smile, the first smile Eleanor had seen on him. "Good night, ladies."

"You have him in a fine mood," Gwen said after he was gone.

Eleanor put her sweater on and said she thought she'd return to her room. "Will it be okay if I pop my head in just to kiss her good night? I won't wake her."

"Of course. It will ensure her dreams. Good night, Eleanor. Have your own sweet dreams."

In the hall, Tilda was drawing the curtains closed on every window. "There's to be a wicked wind tonight, so bundle up."

"I will. See you in the morning."

There were only a few lights lit on the stairway and in the upstairs hall. She crept into Aunt Alice's room and saw her sleeping, propped up against a few pillows, her face calm. She wanted to take Alice's small hand in hers, but feared she'd wake her. Still, she bent down and kissed her cool forehead.

ALICE HAD A HARD NIGHT, GWEN SAID IN THE MORNING. She said the wind kept her up, but Eleanor could see it was more than that. Despite the veil of morphine, there was pain in Alice Eleanor hadn't seen the day before. Eleanor asked if it would be all right to spend the day with her, and so she held Alice's thin hand and watched her sleep till the early afternoon when Alice wakened and stirred and pulled herself upright. Alice rested against the large square pillows and, still groggy, asked Eleanor if she'd go into the closet and find the tall jewelry box set somewhere inside.

Beyond a pair of doors, the dressing room had a chaise longue made up as a bed with pillows and a comforter. There was a table beside the chaise and a book splayed flat on the table with Gwen's reading glasses. There was an easy chair, two sinks, a freestanding claw-foot tub, a vanity, and a long wall of closets. On a chest of drawers inside one of the closets Eleanor found the cream leather jewelry case.

The box was heavy, so Eleanor placed it on the floor as she cleared the bedside table, then brought the box up and, with a nod from Alice, opened the top of it. It was deep with jewels: strands of pearls, carved carnelian, garnets, sapphires, as well as more precious things for which Eleanor had no name.

Alice tried to turn onto her side. "They're fine, are they not?"

"They are." Eleanor beamed. "Do you want to see one? A particular one?"

"No, goodness no," said Alice. "They're yours now, but I can tell you stories about almost every one."

Eleanor handed her a necklace.

"Carved sapphire," Alice said. "Mead brought this home from Italy when he was studying architecture there for a time. The tiny black beads are jet, like your ring. Jet, you know," Alice explained, clearly excited to share what she knew, "was originally for mourning, but not that ring. By the time whoever he was had that face carved into this fine mineral, it was a most fashionable thing: jet in all kinds of jewelry. You know it's from millions of years ago, the stuff of which that ring is made. It's wood, originally, compressed for hundreds of millions of years. Imagine . . ." Alice's eyes sparkled, then she returned to the necklace Mead had brought home less than a decade before. "And these are Moravian crystals." She pointed to each small part of it. "I think it's an eighteenth-century piece. He never finished his studies, but he brought home some beautiful things, for Gwen and for me."

Eleanor handed her another necklace.

"This one has family history." Her eyes seemed to wobble in their sockets as she tried to remember. "Just a moment, it's to do with great-grandparents, many times great. These are chips of fine rubies, nonetheless fine for being chips, and these white beads are Russian crystal, but I can't recall whose this was." She seemed frustrated, worn and hazy as she was from the morphine she'd been given. "These are old-fashioned, aren't they?" She dropped the necklace and turned her upper body toward the jewelry box.

"Eleanor dear, would you open the bottom drawer of it? There's something more interesting than jewels I want to show you."

Eleanor's fingers were moving gently about in among the necklaces—they felt like her buttons, made the same sort of sound—but she withdrew her fingers now and opened the long drawer at the bottom of eight other drawers. Inside there was a folded piece of paper. Eleanor was careful as she maneuvered the paper out of the drawer, where it was squeezed in tightly. Alice's fine white hands trembled as she reached toward it.

"Could you open it for me?" Alice spoke in a whisper from lack of strength. "Years ago, I was moving that old armoire there"—she cocked her head toward a piece of yellow pine on the wall opposite the windows—"from downstairs where it sat in the kitchen up here to this bedroom, where Gwen and I started to stay whenever we came up from Cambridge. It's from the seventeenth century. If you look at its details you can see it's held together without one nail, and inside it there are secret drawers. And in one of them, I found this strange dry parchment paper."

Alice held the paper. "Granley's father took the piece apart to move it upstairs. I was still a young woman. He took the top off, then the drawers out, and I don't know what made me look to the back of it." The inside of her lips stuck together as she spoke. Eleanor brought a glass close to Alice's mouth and placed the straw between her lips. Her eyes closed in quiet pleasure as she took a slow, long sip. "I suppose I was bending down to slide the bottom drawer in when I saw the little knobs hidden inside. And I got a thrill." The strength of Alice's voice came and went. "When I opened it. Well, pumpkin, you should open it."

Eleanor did so, slowly. The paper was dry and fragile, so she was careful not to break it at the folds. It was a finely drawn family tree with some small portraits, mostly at the top, but Eleanor's eyes were drawn to her mother's name and Alice's name and above that her grandmother's and grandfather's names. She saw that her grandfather had had a younger brother and a sister who died in childhood. Eleanor's eyes climbed the tree trunk up the branches, taking in the names of her ancestors all the way to the top, where was written *Emily* and no name for her partner, a couple who bore a child named Victoria, who married Bertram Enswell and began this family tree's long line.

Alice's eyes were almost lifeless today, but the corners of her lips lifted in a small smile. A smile on the other side of a dark morphine haze. She said, "I was in my twenties when I found it. Gwen had her own thoughts about it."

The end of Alice's forefinger was crooked with arthritis, but she pointed to her parents' names, her own, and her sister Anne's name. "That's my hand. I wrote those in. Once I realized I wasn't going to do anything with the tree."

Exhausted, her head now fell back on the pillow, so light it hardly left an imprint.

"It's a gorgeous thing," Eleanor said. The tree was drawn in pencil and colored with watercolor wash.

Alice's eyes had fallen closed and her breathing rattled and was shallow.

Eleanor sat on the side of the bed. "Aunt Alice?" she whispered.

"It's a good family to be part of, all in all," Alice said as she was drifting off. "It's a good family you belong to."

Alice's beautiful face lifted and there was a mischievous twinkle in her eyes. "Gwen says it's nonsense, but I know it's not. Nothing I care to make a fuss about anymore, but you, dear . . ." She suddenly faded. "Dear Eleanor, I'm afraid I need to sleep again." Her eyes were already closed and her tongue was fairly thick in her mouth when she spoke. "For just a while. Would you mind if I drifted off for a bit and we'll talk in the morning?"

Eleanor traced along the branch that ran from her mother to her grandparents and then to their parents, then set the family tree aside and watched Alice sleep. In the quiet she heard the whinny of horses and went to the bay window. On a hill in the distance she saw Mead on a chestnut horse with a white colt on a lead. The white colt was shaking his head and pulling against Mead, who sat tall in the saddle, yanked the rope sharply downward, and seemed to encourage the colt to cooperate, because soon the two horses and rider were cantering down the side of the hill.

Gwen had come in quietly. "Oh, my, she's been telling you stories," she said. She'd brought a simple ham sandwich and some lemonade for Eleanor. As she laid them on the table, she noticed the drawing on one side of the bed. "Did she say much about it?" Gwen lifted the edge and gazed at the delicate drawing.

"She said you had your own ideas."

Gwen dismissed this with a shake of her head. "Well, we were young when we found it. Alice was studying English literature at Cambridge, teaching a bit already, working on her doctorate and very curious about history, so when we chanced upon this odd document, well, you can imagine how excited she would have been."

"She's a little excited about it still," Eleanor said. She thanked Gwen, and took a big bite of the sandwich.

"I haven't seen it in decades." Gwen looked at Alice's face, the face of her one great love. "I haven't seen it since then." She shrugged. "Anyone could draw a family history saying anything, I suppose." Gwen pulled the covers up on Alice's chest. "It might be a story worth considering, but there are some things people just don't want to know."

"Alice wanted me to know."

"Apparently so." Gwen smiled warmly, looking at the drawing. "Certainly a good deal of it's accurate. It is your family tree."

She folded it and slid it back into its tight place in the drawer. Alice stirred.

Eleanor sensed the sadness in Gwen. The lemonade was fresh and sweet and delicious. She finished her sandwich as Gwen carried the jewelry box back into the closet and Eleanor called to her, "I'm going to go for another walk, if that's okay."

"More than okay." Gwen came back in the room. "It's healthy."

Eleanor kissed Gwen's cheek and then her aunt Alice's thin hand before leaving the room. Downstairs, she borrowed some Wellington boots from the mudroom and headed straight for the hill with the orange-barked leaning lady.

THE SWING FELT SOLID AND THE SEAT WAS WARM. IT hung from heavy twined ropes wrapped in velvet that had once been some color that had faded to brown. Eleanor had only been on swings at the city parks, swings that were lined up three or four seats side by side and suspended by short chains with a meager motion compared to this one. These ropes were long and the arc was wild. It made her queasy to swing so high.

For a moment Eleanor thought she saw the same children, but they disappeared in a dell, and when she saw them again they both had their heads down and were climbing a faraway hill.

She bent her legs tight beneath her to miss hitting the ground when she swung back across it. What an odd world, she thought to herself as she swung. A family tree that reached back for what looked like seven or eight generations. She hadn't been on a swing since she was small. She remembered her mother telling her to reach her toes for the sky. Her mother would have told her to reach for the leaves on the top branches of this tree, if she'd been here. Had her mother swung from this tree when she was small, she would have leaned back so far that her hair would have brushed the ground.

What an odd place, Eleanor thought. She had been in England for only two full days and already she couldn't remember what it felt like to be in New York City. Unbidden, the scene in Miles' bedroom came to her and she tried to push it away by leaning as far back on the swing as she could manage. She came close to touching the leaves on the branch with her toes. Her hair fell out of the bun and it did brush the ground. She felt it to the roots, and at the same time could hear the sound of Miles making love to the woman in his bed, heard him in that awful confusion she was there to witness as he was caught between ecstasy and dread, as he saw her seeing him through the doorway.

Working the swing to its greatest height, she brought her arms forward and leapt to the ground. Her sweater kept her warm as she walked, preoccupied, with her jacket tied around her waist. When she came upon two crosses in the ground, she stopped. They stood about as high as a ten-year-old child, thick, chunky crosses so close together that whomever was buried beneath might be holding hands.

Nausea overtook her and she wanted to sit down, but here the ground was muddy. Through a haze of feeling, she recalled an open grave. It was the wind, the swing, the exhaustion, she thought. Choked-down sobs turned her stomach sour as she remembered the day when her father stood beside her, not crying, the day of her mother's funeral, when they placed the headstone on an empty grave. She had listened to recollected stories of her mother's life, and prayers, but all she had in her head that morning was the passage she'd read in a book just days before of Heathcliff as he climbed into Catherine's grave and cried out her name.

Eleanor hurried away, back toward her room at Trent

Hall, and when she looked back at the crosses, they seemed to turn toward her, with their arms spread wide and their chests lifted high.

IN THE BACKGROUND OF THE DAYS BUT PARTICULARLY alone at night, Eleanor felt a certain anxiety: an urge to pick up her e-mail, text on her phone, read Twitter, find news from home.

She'd lost track of time since she'd left New York, since she'd seen Miles on that day that was mixed up with bear claws in the morning and a pixie tangled in his sheets at night, but here she was lying in a bed on the other side of the world, in the middle of nowhere.

Eleanor looked for a phone. There was no Internet connection in the house, and her cell phone had no signal, but she found a phone in the hall. She dialed Miles' number and when he answered, she hung up.

It was late at night and the small library was empty, but the fire was going. The chair was large enough for her to curl up in, and it was warmer by the fire than in her room, so she nestled there.

Her breath rose and fell. The house was silent. Wind and rain and crashes of thunder outside with flashes of lightning she could see right through the thick curtains. She'd brought her mother's letters downstairs, to read them for a while.

The first one she pulled out of the pile, she'd read years

before and remembered. Her mother had written to her from a trip she was on in North Carolina. She wrote about the shoreline and the low gray skies. How cold it was at night on the beach, but when she wrapped up in sweaters and a slicker, it was fine. Her handwriting was even and curvy, elegant and refined.

Eleanor picked another letter at random, pulled it from the middle of the pile. It was a letter she hadn't seen before. A letter to her father from her mother, written in Yorkshire, while they were engaged. Anne spoke of the imminent wedding, suggested a quiet elopement and beside this had drawn a smiling face. She'd been in London and had seen *A Midsummer Night's Dream*, was on her way to Stonehenge in the morning. She wrote John that she missed him terribly, that at night she sat on the edge of the fountain in the courtyard and imagined he might be looking up at the same moon. She made him promise to come, promise never to let her come back to Yorkshire without him. It was all love and purple prose: they would take their honeymoon in Jamaica and find the waterfall they'd seen in a brochure. Eleanor put the letter back into its envelope.

Relaxed by the sounds and the flames of the fire, Eleanor was finally growing tired. She pulled a pink envelope from the bottom of the pile. It was addressed to Martin Garrens in Scarborough, England, but there was no stamp, no postmark, and the envelope was empty. She unfolded the back flap and caught the scent of her mother's perfume. She had expected to cry when she sat next to Alice, but she hadn't. Now, the scent of her mother was strong and tears came. She closed the envelope and opened it again, brought it to her face and inhaled.

Eleanor reached for another envelope and saw the return address from Martin Garrens in North Carolina. The letter was simple. It started, *Dear Anne, I'm still on the beach watching the sun come up, because that's where my memory keeps you . . .* The body never bartered with the truth. Eleanor's heart clenched at the intimation of an affair.

But she read on and found the rest was a common letter to a friend in which he asked mostly about her, about Eleanor, about the play she'd been in and the basketball games her team had won, about the weather he heard they were having in New York. Tucked in the envelope was a note in her mother's hand that read, *There's a storm outside, so El and I are going to make Thunder Cake from the Polacco book you sent her. There's a recipe for wonderful chocolate cake at the back. A chocolate wonder with strawberries inside and one on top. We'll eat a piece for you. Always, sincerely, your Annie.* He seemed to have received the note and sent it back because below her signature, in another hand, was written, *I can picture the cozy scene and can just taste the strawberry.*

Eleanor gathered the letters together, pulled her sweater close, and closed her eyes. Her heart let go and now it fluttered. Her eyes beat like butterfly wings under the lids and the sky was bright white inside the dream she fell into, where there was a snowy white owl, close up, turning its head all around and batting its wide eyes slowly. A knowing owl who watched Eleanor as she folded letters into airplanes and made them fly, letters that disappeared against the white sky and then the snow on the ground, when they landed. The owl's tree oozed sap that dripped onto the ground where Eleanor lay and Mead arrived on a horse, covered her with a blanket, then stepped away into the fireplace and burned in the flames.

She startled awake, wiped drool from the corner of her mouth, oriented her eyes.

"I was set to stir the fire a bit. I wakened you," he said.

She rubbed her eyes. Her body stretched, writhed like a waking cat, an involuntary shiver, and she ran her fingers through her hair.

"I've been considering carrying you upstairs over an hour now."

Eleanor moaned. "I've been sleeping that long? God, I'm glad you didn't. I would have been scared."

He sat down.

"What time is it?" she asked.

"Three or four, I'd say, the fire will burn awhile more."

"What are you doing up so early, or didn't you go to bed?" she asked him.

"No, I did. I slept." He gazed beyond her face, into the fire. "I woke up at two or so and went in to check on Alice," he said. "And what about you? Your clock still boggled by travel, eh?"

"You know, it's not just that. I hadn't realized how much tension I held in my body till it started to unwind. That first day walking on the moors I could feel it, and now I'm this strange new mix of vivified and ready to sleep at the drop of a hat."

He sat down with his legs wide and his fists dropped between his thighs, his shoulders collapsed. "I must say I'm glad you're here. Maybe I was hoping to wake you." He looked despondent.

"What's wrong?" She sat up.

"I just happened to wake and come in the house, which I don't often do. Alice was barely breathing. Of course Gwen was there already. Should we have come to get you? I didn't think of it . . ."

Her hair was all mussed and her eyes were unfocused.

"The doctor's here. Gwen's up there, and if you want to see her, you might . . ." He bobbed his head from side to side.

"Will you come with me?"

His eyes held her eyes and saw she hadn't understood. "She's gone," he said. "She went just a while ago."

"Mead?" Empty and dry, she felt a stiff familiar feeling, the edge of going lifeless.

"Yes, I'll go with you. But we don't have to go up, right now. We can stay here awhile, if you need to."

But she stood. She waited for him and they walked together to the stairs, where she stopped because she felt herself moving like bones without flesh and blood attached to them, a skeleton swinging its limbs making its way through space on to the next thing that had to be done. She thought she was going to faint from the emptiness.

"Would you take my arm?"

He took her arm as they mounted the stairs.

The bedroom doors were open. Eleanor saw the doctor was there. Gwen was lying on the bed beside Alice's body.

"I can't believe she's dead," Eleanor whispered. "I don't know if I should go in."

"You should go in," he said. "You can't do wrong here. You belong here." His accent seemed strong with a Yorkshire lilt now.

She hesitated a long time.

"You don't need me to give you a hug, do you?" he said. Rough and sweet and young and sad.

Alice's face was already blue-gray. Gwen climbed off the bed when she saw Mead and Eleanor come in. She hooked an arm into each of theirs and said, "I can't cry unless I lie down beside her."

It all seemed so strange, so warm and convivial. Tilda brought tea and small sandwiches into the room and set them on a table. When Eleanor's mother had died, her body remained in England. When her father had died, they took him away before she had a chance to see him. The housekeeper found his body and they had him in a big black bag coming down the front stairs when she burst into the house, unaware. The boy who, just then, let his end of the gurney fall looked mortified. In weeks or months, a wood box came in the mail with her father's dusty remains inside.

She'd never seen a dead body, but here was Alice, whom she'd kissed just hours before. Time and change were overwhelming her.

Gwen joined Eleanor where she sat in the bay window. She drew up the wheelchair and sat in it to drink her tea, saying to Eleanor in a hushed tone, "I lay beside her and prayed she might hear me say a few last words of love. I'm not a believer, but I was praying that God might be able to tell her I was lying there waiting for her to smile at me, when suddenly she turned her head and gave me a wink. A saucy old Alice wink." Tears streamed down the fine woman's lovely old face. "Wherever she's going, she'll be altogether well there." Gwen nodded. "She was my only love. I can't believe she's on her way without me."

Mead sat on the lounge chair on the far side of the room, sitting still for the longest time and not speaking to anyone.

"Is he going to be okay?" Eleanor spoke softly.

"He is. They've had a good life together with no regrets, nothing left unsaid."

With a sharp pain behind her left eye and a headache in her temple, Eleanor felt a churning in her stomach. A feeling surged inside and she thought, I'm not a part of this, I shouldn't be here. She felt cold, thought she might be sick, and stood up, asked if there was a bathroom nearby, and was shown to it by Granley, who seemed to come from nowhere and moved quickly with her on his arm.

AFTER THE STRONG RAIN IN THE NIGHT, THE BARK OF the trees was dense with saturated color and everything sparkled as if dappled with diamonds. The sun cut right across the moors as Eleanor walked away from the house in the early afternoon.

She hadn't gone to bed after Alice was gone. The coroner came in the early morning and the doctor signed papers releasing Alice's body. Mead whispered things to Alice before she was taken down the stairs and out the front door on a stretcher, covered with a linen blanket, her face open to the air.

Gwen called a friend, Mr. Wilcock, who would arrive at the house by early afternoon. The plans for cremation were already set, and Gwen sat with Mead in the library, both of them quiet, his arm around her on the couch by the fire. Tilda filled vases with flowers that had already begun to come from locals and friends from Cambridge.

Outside, the snap of cold air on her skin felt good as Eleanor crossed the moors. The orange bark of the tree at the top of the hill was now the color of a persimmon after the rain, or deeper still. Eleanor sat on the swing and moved gently back and forth, her cheek against the damp worn velvet. Dreamily, she turned the swing around and around as she tried to recall her mother's face, the way she moved, the things she'd taught her.

The swing was a comfort. On it, she felt like a little girl. Feelings she'd put aside since her mother died came back to her, abiding and ineffable. Eleanor lifted her feet off the ground and the swing spun in mad circles unwinding itself, then winding back in on itself, then back again until it stopped. It seemed the wind on the open moors never stopped. "Mother," she whispered and listened for an answer.

She remembered a picture her mother had had on the wall of her sewing room. It was a large, bright watercolor of a woman serene on the back of a churning crocodile. The Never Not Broken Goddess, she was called, her mother had said. A creature unafraid of heartache, of pain, of being broken in two, who stands on the back of a crocodile that doesn't snap at its prey but whips and spins her into a state of perfect confusion.

ELEANOR TOOK THE LONG WAY HOME TO AVOID SEEING the crosses again and ran into Granley.

"They'll heal most anything, the moors will," Granley said as she came in through the gate.

"The air's been good for me."

"You're a bonnie walker for a city lass. You've got a good bit of Alice in ye, and it'll serve you well." He started away then stopped. "Aye, you'll not 'ave seen the abbey, 'ave ye? She's right beyond that hillock there, 'round the other side of the house. Take you no time at all to get there and the sun's still high. Head straight that way over th' hill and you'll recognize her."

"Recognize who?"

He saw the fear in her eyes and assuaged it with a wink. "The abbey. She's a girl."

"I'm sorry." She lifted her long neck into the wind. "I'm on a scavenger hunt and I don't know what I'm looking for."

"Scavengers don't."

"Well, I'm going to find this abbey to start."

The mist was waist high at the far side of the house and she stepped gingerly through the dense foliage there, found the strength to climb the steep side of the hill, and descended into a valley where she saw the abbey in the distance. Gray stone against the blue sky, its bare bones still standing. It was an emptied ruin flooded with light and ivy that climbed inside the broken walls.

Through a Gothic arch in the thick outside wall, she stepped into a long arcade with a low, rib-vaulted ceiling so strong it had withstood wind and time altogether intact. She smelled the damp earth, the cold stone, her own body, and the clothes she'd spent the night in. She proceeded through the darkness, through the bones of the abbey, the walls so close she could touch them both with her hands, a splash of sun in a circle of light and then darkness again. At the far end of the long arcade, there was a rounded archway that drew her. Now she smelled fresh green moss and faint lavender.

Through the archway she stepped into a courtyard, a cloister with broken-down stone columns, and on the other side of these the land fell away down a steep face. Close to the edge of the hill, Eleanor bent forward to see what lay below, and on a smooth flat stone she saw the young woman.

Eleanor's heart beat so hard her hands trembled, but she went to the edge of the cliff. Though she felt herself rushing, she was careful as she held tight to the edge of a rock and reached with steadiness to the next ledge and so to the next one as she climbed down.

The only place her feet could stand on the flat stone, once she arrived, was inches away from the young woman's hand. She was more beautiful than Eleanor remembered. She seemed more mature, and her skin was so light it appeared pale blue.

"I come to watch the sun set," the young woman said.

Eleanor felt awkward, perched there with nowhere to stand but almost on the woman's hand.

"I was hoping you would come down," the woman said. "Do sit. Standing there could be a risk to you, if a gust should blow by."

As impossible as it was that she was here, waiting for her on the side of a hill, Eleanor accepted it as if it were normal.

"Shall I tell you why?" the woman asked.

Eleanor nodded, but was not hearing her words. She was

sure the woman had been younger when she first saw her sitting at the end of the bed, but now she seemed like someone about her own age. The deliberate way she moved was unusual, something contained and formal with a different sense of timing. Her body lacked tone, her head moved slowly, when she talked, as if she were underwater or in a dream. She wore a dress that was distinctly unmodern, in a deep blue fabric made of wool thicker than any wool Eleanor had ever seen. The seams were hand-sewn.

Eleanor believed that if she reached to touch her, her hand might pass right through the dress and the body, but she didn't feel frightened. Eleanor was sad and tired, and somehow the woman's presence soothed her.

"From here we could walk to the house and I'll show you," the woman said.

Eleanor hadn't been listening, but responded, "The house I'm in? I know the way. Once I get back to the top, I know the way."

"You'd rather I didn't come with you?" the woman asked.

"No, no. I would rather you did." Eleanor was confused and didn't want to ask what it was she had missed in what had been said. She started to her feet.

"Even if you found your way home, you wouldn't know the bookshelf the letters are in. It's gone quiet and dusty in there. The children all grown and gone." She turned and waved for Eleanor to follow. Her tiny hand flicked at the wrist.

"You know this way well," Eleanor called out, catching up to her.

"I do."

The woman's skirt didn't touch the ground but grazed her ankles, and she gathered the full fabric in her hand and lifted it as they walked side by side through the heather. It was not hard for Eleanor to keep up even though the woman walked very fast on the uneven ground.

"I should by now," she said matter-of-factly. "Let's run!" And she took off. Like a child in her body now, she skipped and swirled, and as she ran her hair tumbled out of her bun. She called back to Eleanor not to lose her, to hurry and keep up.

Eleanor ran, but her boots were clumsy and she tripped and fell into a clump of bright yellow gorse and got thorns stuck in her hands. Exhausted and on the verge of a temper tantrum, she plucked out a couple of them and got herself up only to find the woman gone.

If she knew her name, she'd call it out. Now she was lost. She had known the way home from on top of the hill, but down in this valley she had no idea. From here, she couldn't see the abbey. She couldn't see the tree that held the swing. She couldn't see the house and had probably taken herself a mile or so in the wrong direction. Because everything was the same color, the landscape was mesmerizing. To be in the center of so much that is some shade of sameness: rolling, climbing, falling away. The land rose up a hill to the right on ahead. That was where the house had to be. She kept her eyes on the ground and her mind carefully fixed on every thought that flitted by.

A fox moved on the hill and when Eleanor looked up, there was the young woman. She was doubled in half with her hands on her thighs, catching her breath and smiling. "I would have headed back for you, now I've caught my breath."

Eleanor was bothered.

"For a lass not accustomed, you're not at all bad."

Eleanor walked without speaking up the hill toward what she hoped would be the house.

"Come on, I was teasing running away from you like that. Don't you like teasing?"

For Eleanor, it had been an impossibly long day.

The woman's wrap slipped off her shoulders and she pulled it back up. "Out here on the moors there's lots left behind. You can see it, can't you? Sometimes broken hearts, some broken children left with the task of pulling together what's gone amiss. Out here, there's lots left behind. You can see it."

The woman's shawl slipped again and Eleanor stepped close to wrap it tight around her. "This really is beautiful wool." Eleanor spoke softly.

"You need to mind my words. The letters are where I left them tucked inside a box hidden inside a cupboard. It was a sitting room when I hid them there, where the children played."

Eleanor heard a whistle and, turning away from the

woman, saw Granley at the top of the hill waving his arms broadly to let her know she was on her way home.

When Eleanor turned back the woman was gone. She looked all around and as far as she could see. There were trees she might have hurried through, but the sun was setting.

❧

AS ELEANOR STARTED UP THE HILL, SHE SAW GRANLEY heading back inside the cottage where he and Tilda lived.

Eleanor went in the house through the mudroom and up the back stairs. She had barely closed the door to her room inside a room, when she heard her name and saw Mead below. She cranked open the window.

"I'm going in to the village to pick up some rents. Want to come?"

It had been an exhausting day, but she wanted to be with him, to get away from Trent Hall and escape her confusion. It was late in the evening and almost dark. "Can you wait? I'll be right down."

He nodded, put his hands in his pockets, and leaned against the car.

Eleanor hurried down the back stairs through the vegetable garden and onto the gravel driveway, where Mead waited inside a handsome old Aston Martin.

"You ready to go, then?" he said.

"I am, I guess." She felt out of sorts from the recent encounter, but was determined to shake it off. As she slid into the car she noticed the burled wood dash, the cream leather seats, soft with wear and care. She looked around for her seat belt, but there was no shoulder strap.

Mead reached across her lap to find the belt and his hand, as it brushed against her leg, sent a surprising shiver up her spine. "She was my father's once. She's quite an old thing now."

"It's beautiful."

"Came out the same year I did," he said.

She cinched the seat belt around her waist. "Thanks for asking me," she said. "I'm tired, but I've no interest in going to bed."

"Well, that's fine, I don't fancy you, either." His voice feigned umbrage, but she was distracted and the tease went right over her head. "We're off, then." Mead drove down the long drive onto the wide road for a stretch till he turned onto a dirt road that bounced through the moorland.

Shaggy wool sheep with black faces grazed. They bent to chomp and chew on grasses and heather, on their way home. A ram lifted its head and broke into a clumsy sheep's sprint. Mead downshifted and let the ram run beside them.

"The thwaite's just beyond the bending tree on that hill," Mead said. "You know they grow that way against the wind."

"I wondered about that." Eleanor pulled her feet up onto the seat and looked closely at his face. She saw the pain there: eyes that had been crying, skin gray from nights without sleep. She felt drawn to stroke his cheek and comfort him, but couldn't. Instead, her voice a good deal warmer, she continued, “You’d think the wind would kill them, but they just bend.”

“It’ll happen to you, if you stick around long enough.”

“How long does it take?” She smiled at him, but his eyes were on the road and he didn’t see it. “Well, I won’t be sticking around, so no chance of that.”

The wind was growing strong and the clouds looked like a storm might be coming. It was quiet in the car until, with a jolt, Mead turned onto another dirt road and they bumped to a stop in front of a pub called Fiddleheads that popped up out of nowhere in the shadow of some shade trees.

“Up for some Yorkshire brew?” he asked Eleanor.

“Sure.”

In a dark corner, she settled in and looked around. Nervous, she twirled her hair and let her eyes adjust. There was a young couple tangled up in each other in the opposite corner and two old men at the bar so drunk their eyes were closing.

“Tim Taylors, Danny,” she heard Mead say to the barkeep, then watched as he managed two large mugs and a bowl of nuts to the table.

The jukebox blasted U2.

The lager was bitter, earthy, chocolate brown, tart, and cold.

Dark wood in the tables and paneling, red leather, and a red and green plaid. The customers were familiar with each other.

"What do people do here?" Eleanor asked. "I mean, I'm sure there are lots of things to do, but what *do* people do?"

"Work hard and end the day at a pub. That's the truth."

"Do you live here all the time?"

"I am for now. For most of my life I've come and gone. I was at university, got a degree in literature, studied architecture."

"Architecture."

"Drawing some things and building others, really."

"What do you build?"

"Dreams, castles, bookshelves, whatever one needs."

Her face propped on the flat of her hand, she leaned on the table with her body turned toward him, her half-drunk lager behind her elbow. She felt golden from the fire. "I need a castle," she said fancifully.

"Wait till they read the will, milady."

"Oh, that. Sorry. I was kidding, actually . . ."

Mead gestured to Danny, who brought them another round and dropped an envelope on the table.

"Danny, this is Eleanor Sutton."

"Goodness, it's an honor to meet you, miss." He bowed a bit.

"You, too," she said.

He cuffed Mead on the shoulder and shuffled away.

"What's that?" Eleanor asked, indicating the envelope.

"It's the rents we came for. Lately, I've been taking care of things." He stopped and sipped and held her eyes for a moment. "You were a bit of a pleasant surprise."

"A pleasant surprise? That's nice."

"It meant the world to her that you came, it really did. What made you decide to come, after all?" he said.

Inside the warm leather of the booth where they drank the strong lager together, Eleanor could have drifted into telling every part of the story that led to her coming. Sorting through her thoughts, she said nothing.

"I suppose Gwen wouldn't have taken no for an answer," he said. "But I know Alice wanted you to visit all along . . ."

"I should have come sooner. I don't know why I didn't."

"Don't be worrying, you've done nothing wrong. Far from it. She was so pleased that you came."

"I might have come sooner."

One of the two drunk old men was asleep on his forearms and his friend shuffled out of the pub. Danny polished his wood bar. A middle-aged woman in sensible shoes and a skirt to her knees came in and waved to Mead.

It was dark outside and the strings of tiny white lights around the windows flickered in the wind.

"Is that snow out there?" Eleanor asked.

The wind was rising and a hard snow had begun to fall. Eleanor and Mead watched it blow sideways in the halo of lights outside the small leaded-glass window. "That's a good sign, snow falling tonight," he said. Mead was pensive and

Eleanor noticed the handsomeness of his features, something indomitable and appealing through the sadness in his eyes.

Two loud young men burst into the pub. Cool with spiky hair, beaten leather jackets, and jeans as tight as skin, they groused about the coming storm as they shook the snow from their coats. Mead smiled at the sight of them and they hailed him, sauntered over, and started to bump their way into the booth with Mead and Eleanor.

"Who's the smashin' bird you've got this time?"

One young man elbowed the other hard.

"Gosh, sorry, Mead, we heard, we did. We were right sorry to hear."

"Thanks." Mead moved to the other side of the booth, next to Eleanor.

The young men slid in, across the table.

"You're a right fine lass. We mistook you for one of his."

Mead smiled uncomfortably.

"This is Eleanor Sutton Abbott."

They sat up, straightened their hair. One adjusted a tie that wasn't there.

"Alice's! Right. Good to meet you," they said.

"Eleanor, this would be Charlie MacKenzie and Len Perkins."

"Bubble and squeak," Danny said as he placed before them four plates of sausages cooked up in beds of shiny potatoes, cabbage, and onions all stewed together.

"Thanks, Danny." Mead and the young men talked about Alice, but, famished, Eleanor dug in. There were four more large mugs of beer on the table. The sausage was rich, fatty, thick. She devoured it while the three men talked fast in a strong Yorkshire tongue and with words between words she couldn't understand, till she wiped her mouth with a napkin.

"Sorry, I don't know when I've been so hungry," she said.

"You haven't eaten all day," said Mead. His thigh touched hers and moved away.

"You knew Aunt Alice?" she said to the men.

"Aye, knew 'er well," Charlie said. They nodded, the two young men. "Loved her, we did. She was a great one and ye'd not forget her if ye'd been near her for even a moment in yer life."

"She taught us loads o' things," said Len. "Pointed in the right direction, 'at's what she did, eh, Mead?"

"She were fine," said Charlie, "weren't she? She were keen. We'll miss her. You're from America, eh?"

Danny brought over some whisky. They toasted to Alice, and Eleanor savored the taste of peat, welcomed the warmth in her belly, and drank down the whole thing.

"Would you guys excuse me?" Eleanor said. Mead got up and let her out.

"You all right?" he said.

"I am."

He looked dubious.

"Maybe just a little tipsy." She smiled.

Danny pointed the way through the curtain to the water closet, and she glanced at herself in the mirror as she passed by. It was a round mirror and looking at herself she saw photographs on the wall behind her. She pulled the sweater off over her head, looked at her unhappy face and mussed-up hair, the sweat under her armpits, the stained cotton turtleneck. She lifted her arm and smelled the sweat, fingered her hair into an organized tousle, pinched her cheeks pink, and tried to smile. As the strained smile moved, another wallop of emotion seized her.

Mead knocked, then opened the door a crack. "All right, in there?" He stepped back into the hall. "Listen, it's become a bad storm, so we can get a couple of rooms here for the night. It's easy enough, and we'll go back at the first sign of daylight."

She splashed her face and wiped her eyes. "Really?" Still in the clothes she'd walked in all day, she longed for a bath and a change of clothing.

"Those chaps, they said their good-byes. A nice bit ruined, they were, but they're good kids. The last of Alice's crew, kids she helped this way and that. Pissed on a Saturday night, that's pretty much all that happens around here."

She came into the hall. "Did you say we'd get a room?"

"It might be safer than driving now. Sleep and we'll be off in the morning."

"All right, then." It seemed a good idea to spend a night away from Trent Hall, after all. "I could use a drink of water."

Mead came back with fresh water that was ice-cold in the glass, and she lifted her eyes—gladdened, gratified.

The photographs on the wall behind her were of local people. She turned to them and recognized parts of the landscape. There were pictures inside the pub, soccer victories and prom pictures, weddings and such, but there was one of a boy and a girl fishing in a pond and another of the same kids: the girl with muddied boots over her knees displayed a frog in the palm of her hand and the boy had a fish he held upside down. They looked like the girl and boy Eleanor had seen on the swings and at the waterfall. There was a black-and-white picture of a pretty woman in a wide-brimmed hat and khaki clothing holding a baby. These caught Eleanor's attention.

"Who are they?" Eleanor asked.

"I don't know all of them, but this woman is Alice, I'm sure of that . . ."

She stepped up close.

"The wee one is me."

Eleanor noticed the pained look on the woman's face and the ruins of a building in the background.

"Over here, this one is you." He walked her to a small, framed picture on the lower half of the long wall. It was a picture of her mother with Alice and a tiny girl, all dressed up in greens and blues, standing between them, holding one finger of each woman's hand, at the Central Park Zoo.

"This *is* me," Eleanor exclaimed. "What's it doing here?"

"Danny puts pictures up, so people give them to him. Alice started it."

He led her away from the picture, down the hall, and opened the door into a small quaint bedroom wallpapered many times, with some of the layers torn and other layers exposed, so it looked like a patchwork of pretty florals.

The bed looked inviting.

Eleanor was sleepy from the day, from rich food, beer, and whisky, and also from a bizarre quantity of change and strangeness, upsets and bolts from out of the blue. She sat on the edge of the twin bed. On the wall around her, layers of wallpaper peeled into animal shapes. She lay back on the bed.

When Mead came back, she'd slipped off her shoes, socks, and turtleneck and was lying down in her T-shirt and jeans with her arm across her forehead. Mead sat down beside her.

"Why's my picture on the wall here?" she asked.

"Because you belong here," Mead said.

"I do?" She was willing to believe him.

"Are you sleeping right here, like this?"

"I am," she said.

He would sleep in the room down the hall, but right now his body was warm and felt good, so close to hers. Mead unfolded the quilt and laid it on top of her, made sure to cover her bare shoulders.

Eleanor breathed in the scent of the man beside her who rested his face on his own hand and traced the shape of her face with his eyes. He smelled of burning wood and green herbs.

"Would you mind," she whispered, "telling me another story?"

"A story?"

"Mm-hmm." She nodded yes.

And he started in like a man who knew how.

"Then it was, in the years before you were born, that two young girls lived in a vast stone house on the top of a graceful hill . . ."

Eleanor curled up warm and happy against him. "No, tell me *your* story," she mumbled. It was good to feel him close and she stretched out.

"Ahh." Steady like the shifting of gears, he adjusted.

"Now, far away beyond and above the highest reach of man or beast"—he rolled his words in a Scotsman's brogue as he began the story of his father, Duncan Macleod—"there grew a child from boy to man in the Outer Hebrides. And he walked with a very large stick in his hand, from the time he was small." Mead placed another light blanket over her. "When he was wee, the stick was taller than his da—so tall it reached halfway to God—and helped the boy up sides of scarps, to poke about in caves, and down into cracks in the crags on the mountains." Mead looked to see if she was sleeping. "For fear of impossible wolves. The boy warred with hedgehogs, toppled anthills in a blow, and waited. He waited"—Mead's voice became a whisper—"till the boy was taller than the stick he held, and confident as a hawk in the sky, he met a woman and so he fell. Fell inside my mam's fair green Spanish eyes. Where neither stick, nor God, nor any man could help him."

IN THE NIGHT, SHE WAKENED THIRSTY WITH A HEADACHE and took a sip from the glass of water. She rummaged through her purse for some Advil and looked at her phone, saw that it had a connection. There was a split second when she regretted the reality of New York City intruding on her, but there were texts from Tabitha, Gladys, and Charlotte. Her friend Violet's texts were earnest and Miles' even more so.

Sitting with the pillows behind her against the wall, she read them all again and then listened to her voice mails. Miles was contrite and worried. He'd heard from Gladys where she was, but was confused about her disappearance. In the last message his voice was tender and he sounded like he was sitting right beside her. He said he was on his way to England, wasn't sure how he'd get the address but was on his way. On his way to bring her home, he said, and then in a whispered voice, "Sleep tight, sweet girl."

She had a craving for hot chocolate in the morning, and she tramped down to the kitchen, where a kind-faced woman made her a perfect pitcher of it. It felt good to be in a small place and to find Mead in a dark corner of the empty pub reading the *Financial Times*. Absorbed by something he read, he saw her and cocked his head for her to join him if she liked. The paper rustled when he turned the pages, and then he peered at her.

"I don't read the paper, but if I did it would be that one . . . ," she said.

"Because?"

"Because it's pink."

Mead pulled the paper far enough away from his face as if to see whether or not it was pink. He shook his head and scrunched his face to tell her she couldn't be more wrong, he'd been reading it most of his life and it was quite clearly some vague sort of beige.

In a worn Windsor chair, she sipped her chocolate. "I've seen almost no pictures of my mother. My father kept a wedding picture and I've seen a couple of their honeymoon, but nothing from when she was young."

"Makes sense. I suppose they'd be here, the pictures from when she was small," he said.

"I guess they would." Her mind was miles away and befuddled. She ran her fingers through her hair. "I'm a mess. I want to take a bath at the house. Can we go back soon? Do I seem a prima donna?"

"Not in the least." He folded the paper and got out of his chair, touched her arm. "You've been through the worst of it."

"Mead, you've been so kind to me, but how are you?"

"I'm fine. It was coming and we knew it, and I'm fine. Thanks, though. We best get on home."

As he said the word *home* she realized it was at least partly her home and she shared it with Mead, in some way. As peculiar as it was in Yorkshire, different from any place she'd ever been, she was beginning to feel something at ease in her soul here, something hard to pin down.

With a faint trill, the cell phone rang inside her purse. It took her a moment to realize what it was. On her phone was a picture of Miles' most seductive face, the one where he lowered his chin and looked up from under his brow with a bare, faint smile.

She said, "Hi, Miles," in a voice that was soft and weaker than she expected it to be. The relief she heard in his voice as he spoke her name was almost heartrending.

"Just a second." She put down the phone and put on her coat and stepped outside.

Miles repeated her name, because she didn't say a word for a while. Again he said, "Eleanor."

"I've been in this place without any connection most of the time," she said. "It's kind of a fluke that you caught me." They weren't the words she wanted to say. Her tone was not the one she would have chosen.

The snow was already melting, and the sun felt warm.

"I'm glad I caught you."

"You caught me?" she said and immediately regretted it. She hadn't meant to address it, not now, not on the phone, not in the middle of nowhere. She hadn't meant to say anything. She wished she hadn't answered the phone.

"Oh, God." He'd heard exactly what she meant. "I'm going to get this wrong, but I want to get it right, because I love you. I've never loved anyone but you. I know you don't have to listen to any explanation, but I do have one, a lame one . . . Shit. I'm meant to make you happy and instead I hurt you. I'd never— I didn't mean to hurt you." He waited. "El?"

"I'm here."

"It's not enough—nothing will be enough—but I want to have a chance to explain, to hold you and explain. God, it's awful not to be able to . . ."

Though there were tears in her eyes, she ignored what he was saying and interrupted him. "I got to see Alice and talk to her. Do you remember Alice? She sure remembered you."

His breath changed. She imagined him shifting his posture. "Of course I remember her. From ages ago. How is she?"

"She died." Eleanor remembered. "My God, I forgot, you don't even know why I came. That night, it was that night, you know? Anyway, Alice's partner called me to say she was sick and wanted to see me. That night. Anyway, I guess it was yesterday, or the night before last night. I'd been with her just before, and I'd kissed her good night. She was sleeping when I kissed her and then, just a few hours later, she was gone, just like that."

He was silent. He waited a while for her to say something else, but she didn't and he said, "It must have been great to get to be with her. I can't imagine, El. God, I wish I were there with you. Should I come? Are you all right?"

"I am. I'm tired and a mess today. This house here, it's called Trent Hall and it's huge and right in the middle of the moors." Her body responded to the sound of his voice and fell into friendship. "And it's kind of just the way you'd think it would be. On the moors." She wished she had a cigarette and an hour or more to sit with him. Despite herself, she unfolded like a sunrise. "Except it's like another world, another planet. I mean another century, for sure." She knew he would be sitting at his desk in lower Manhattan. His legs would be up on his desk, his chair tipped back, and there'd be that appreciative smile he always had when she rambled on. "Anyway, Miles, I should go. I'm dizzy, I'm so tired right now. I'm not thinking straight." She saw Mead coming out of the pub. She should be mad at Miles, she knew, but she couldn't find it. It was so good to hear his voice again.

"Before you go, El, I just want to say I want to come over there, I really do."

"You said something about that on the message."

Mead leaned against the hood of the car.

"It's probably not a good idea," she said. "Miles, I'll be home. I don't know when, but I'll be home. We'll talk about things then.

"It's good to hear your voice. It feels good that you remember Alice." She started to cry a bit.

"El . . . I'm coming over there."

She heard Mead start the car. "I'm gonna go now," she said.

She clicked off, pushed a button, and he was gone.

MORE THAN A WEEK HAD PASSED SINCE ALICE'S quiet funeral. Eleanor was sleeping through most nights and always waking hungry. Her long walks on the moors had her soul feeling strong and her muscles almost sinewy. She was beginning to grasp the idea that this house and the land, for as far as she could see, were hers.

There was a stable of horses, there were crops, pigs, poultry, and sheep on the land, with complicated grazing rights. The entailment could not be changed without an appeal to Parliament, Gwen had said, so the land was hers and would continue to pass through her children as long as she had daughters, but without daughters it would skip a generation and go on regardless. It was a lot to take in.

She resolved not to worry about it, as she sat on the edge of the bed.

She'd been invited for lunch the next day at the house of Alice's old friend and lawyer Mr. Wilcock, who happened to live in Haworth, the famed Brontë town. She'd met him briefly at the house the day Alice died, but couldn't remember him. He was handling the details of the transfer of the estate, and she had to go see him.

Mead had offered to drive her, but Eleanor wanted to go

on her own, to stay the night at an inn and wake in the morning. Though it might be nice to take another long drive through Yorkshire with Mead, many of the questions she wanted to ask Mr. Wilcock pertained to him. It felt wrong to take away the only house he'd ever known. Now that she knew him, it felt even worse.

Still, she had to borrow his car to get there, so she would stop by the old barn for the keys. Something felt different, she was nervous about seeing him. She walked through the kitchen and grabbed a brown roll from a basket of rolls on the kitchen table. She went through the vegetable garden into the courtyard and heard a shout.

"Christ almighty!" she heard Mead yell, then the crunch of gravel as he ran. "What the hell . . ." His voice faded.

Granley was on the gravel with a box on top of him and books spilled all around.

"Are you hurt, old man?"

"'Course I am." Grumbling, he sat up. ". . . blasted boggy books. Help me up, lad, damn it." He swept the books off his body like barnacles that clung.

"Not on the wet ground, man!" said Mead. The box was split in two and books were splayed open. "Can you get that wheelbarrow over there?" he called to Eleanor.

"Where?"

"That one against the barn—can't you see it?—it's right there." She'd never heard his sharp, angry tongue, but she got the wheelbarrow and maneuvered it up the rocky hill.

"They can bear worse than mud, where they already been," the old man said. Mead bore the weight of Granley and held him steady. "A book's just a book, after all's said and done," Granley muttered, embarrassed to have fallen and making light of the mess around him.

Eleanor picked up one book at a time and placed them gingerly into the wheelbarrow. It started to drizzle and then to snow a bit while she and Granley moved the books into a small shed, where he laid the wet ones out to dry under a heat lamp used for sprouting seeds.

In the old barn there were bookshelves on the floor and a sky-high ladder against the wall. Cracks and holes had been sealed, so there were no owls or mice or windy corners. The walls were dry and sturdy and though the work wasn't finished there was a living area with a large desk, an oak cupboard, and two armchairs.

Mead held the weight of one tower of shelves and tipped it up straight, then shimmied it across the room till it found its place between two other shelves—a corner piece, stained but not polished, that slid in with a snap. He chewed his lower lip and picked up the ladder, leaned it where he needed it to be, then climbed to the top, where he secured the corner piece with some screws and a drill, then smoothed what was rough and blew off the dust. He climbed down and started in again.

The bookshelves were unwieldy, but he knew to pivot their weight and swing them upright, then tip them, wiggle them, swerve out of the way to accommodate them. Eleanor watched without making a sound from the doorway. She stood still and took in his bare torso, the muscles on his belly from hard physical work, his thick hair tied back and his body brown and damp with sweat, an arc of sinew on the side of his hips. As he danced each shelf across the room, he ground his teeth and heaved it into place. Eleanor recognized the grim aggression in his jaw, the sharp angle of his cheekbones, the wide lip he seemed almost to bite through. She was used to a more refined figure of a man.

Eleanor cleared her throat. With a grunt to punctuate the heave, Mead tossed the shelf back against the wall with a slam, bang, and it wobbled. For an endearing moment, his face showed doubt, as together they watched. He stood ready to catch it, should it fall, but it settled where it belonged and he smiled at her.

She picked up his shirt and held it out to him, the woolen button-down. She watched as his body disappeared inside the fabric.

"Give me a hand with the books, will you? It'll take your mind off things."

Many more boxes had arrived in the morning. As she started to unpack the books, Mead continued working on the far wall of shelves.

"Is there an order to this? Don't you want to put them in categories or something? Dewey decimal system?"

"I thought we'd just get them out of all these boxes."

"Where are the boxes from?" She started in again. She

grabbed a chunk of books and slid them in, then another chunk beside the first chunk until a box was empty and a shelf was full of faded colors. "The bindings are beautiful."

"Well, some have been in Haworth for a while, and some have come up from Hay-on-Wye. I think that's mostly where they've been. But the oldest ones, over there, they come from Scarborough."

Eleanor grabbed a handful of books and arranged them. The colors worked no matter how she placed them: the bindings were soft and lovely, and it was better that they didn't move from tallest to shortest, she had decided. A wall of pale red, blue, green—all dull and dusty colors—she stepped back to look at her work once three lengths of shelf were filled.

He came down from the ladder. "You've arranged them by color," he said, deadpan.

"Looks pretty," she said. "And they stack way better than sweaters."

The wind blew the door open.

"Would you mind kicking that closed?"

She closed it but it swung back open.

"Slam it."

She slammed it.

"Now would you slip that bolt into place, if you don't mind."

"Sure." She did. She slid the bolt into its slot and turned it to lock it in.

"What is it you've got on?" he said, suddenly taking notice.

She wore wool trousers, full in the leg like trousers in the 1940s, a fitted cashmere sweater tucked in, and a strong leather belt. Lace-up shoes with smooth leather soles. "You look smart," he said, having taken her in from foot to head.

"Thanks," she said. She took in the bookshelves, the capacity of them, and he watched her.

"They're your books now," he said. "They've belonged to your family for a long time. Alice collected a deal of them herself, stepped in when your granddad wanted to get rid of them, and it's a good thing she did, 'cause there's a fortune in them."

"If someone sold them."

"Well, yes, that, too, I suppose, but I mean a fortune of history. They're gems, some of them. Originals, first editions hardly even touched, some of them."

She remembered the first edition Miles had given her of *Alice in Wonderland*, on her last birthday. She was puzzled by the book, having expected a ring. Now the thought amused her.

"Whisky?"

She flopped down into one of the large upholstered armchairs. "Sure, but I can't stay long, I've got to get on the road. You know, Mead, these are your books, not mine. I live in New York City. I don't know anything about this place and the value of first editions and"—she looked around the barn—"sheep."

Mead drew a bottle and two chunky glasses from the cupboard.

"You know, I must have been twelve, or maybe thirteen, the last time I saw Alice, before coming here."

"I know. I remember."

"You remember?"

"I was there."

"You were there?"

"Shite, I've yet to get the echo out of this barn . . ." Mead checked to make sure he hadn't offended her. "Yep, I was there, but I don't expect you'd remember. I remember watching you. You had a lot going on, down here, up there." He pointed to his heart and then his head.

"I shouldn't really drink this—I'm driving." She took a sip. "I don't remember your being there. I only remember bits and pieces anyway." Another sip. "But I can't help imagining what it would have been like to have known Alice sooner, when I was younger, to have had a chance to know a little more about myself."

"To know about yourself?"

"I feel like that. Yes. Somehow. I don't know if it's been getting a chance to know Alice, just this tiny amount of time, or just being here, but I feel more . . ."

She stopped herself. She had no idea how to put into words what it was she was feeling. "Like I've taken hold of a string and it's pulling me toward something." She looked up to where there was one large window, high on the far wall where the hayloft might have been. The window was framed and filled with stained glass, but without sunshine coming through, Eleanor couldn't make out the design. "There were things Alice started to tell me and didn't have the time."

"Listen, I've got some bread and cheese," Mead said. "Should we have some?"

"I'd love some. I'm always hungry out here." A natural and pretty laugh rumbled in her chest. "But I should get on the road . . ."

"You sure I can't drive you?"

She wanted to stay. The chair was the most comfortable deep chair she'd ever been in. The whisky was warm and she felt safe. Different from the way she'd always felt safe with Miles. Miles' safe had to do with moving on, moving forward and not stopping. Knowing someone, growing with someone, like growing in an environment without thinking about where the sun comes from, what the ground is made of.

She didn't want to leave, but she said, "Thanks, no. You sure it's all right to take that fine car?"

He nodded.

She got up to go. "Thank you. I'll take good care of it on the road."

IT WAS AN EASY TWO-HOUR DRIVE ACROSS THE PENnines, from Trent Hall in the North York Moors to Haworth in the Yorkshire Dales. When Eleanor arrived, the woman at the Old White Lion Inn urged her to rush to the Brontë Parsonage before it closed, and it was less than a few minutes' walk down a cobblestoned lane through a charming village.

At the parsonage there was an exhibit called the Infernal World of Branwell Brontë and from what Eleanor read in the show's brochure, the dark imaginings in Emily's novel were no surprise: Emily alone had borne the care of her brother in the last years of both their lives, when he'd been murderously mad and wild from unrequited love and an addiction to alcohol and laudanum.

Eleanor hadn't known the children had lost their mother, early in their lives. She hadn't realized they lived this close, one room right next to another in a small home in a very small town. She pictured the family, their complicated relationships. Each small room with a desk, a hard wood chair, paper and pen set out for writing. Everything plain and spare.

Almost closing time, the parsonage had emptied of visitors and Eleanor ventured to the far end of the house to see Emily's bedroom, with an undraped window that reached to the ceiling over a twin bed squeezed between two walls. Eleanor imagined Emily sitting up in bed, looking out the window with a pen in her hand and a small book to write in, but the house felt closed and tight and suddenly Eleanor wanted to get outside.

It was twilight and if she hadn't seen the tiniest pale blue bird on a branch in the parsonage graveyard, Eleanor might have been sorry she'd come, but the bird was as round and small as a Ping-Pong ball. She watched it hop up the branch, the way little plastic windup toys hop and flip, and at the end of the branch it spread its tiny wings and fluttered away. Like a cotton ball floating upward into the sky, it flew till she couldn't see it anymore.

She sat at the base of a gravestone. In the end, Yorkshire was a place where it was all right to feel grief. If nothing else, she'd begun to feel things differently. While she walked on the moors, with the wind as a friend, the mist above the ground and the boggy peat below, she was more alone than she'd ever been, but felt less alone. The Yorkshire moors were alive with something, and it matched the way it felt to be Eleanor.

A steep cobbled street sloped out of town, away from the graveyard, but she took the road up to the Old White Lion where she would be staying the night. She stepped inside the Rose & Co. Apothecary, which was quiet and dimly lit and seemed like it hadn't changed since the nineteenth century. Eleanor bought a pair of blue frilly knickers meant for naughty Victorian girls and a box of bath patisseries from a vintage apothecary recipe. She ordered haddock, chips, and mushy peas for dinner, then took a bath and went to bed early.

J. M. WILCOCK, ESQ., AND HIS WIFE LIVED ON TIM LANE just minutes from the Old White Lion. Eleanor took a tiny wrong turn and wound up on Mytholmes Lane, where the town went untidy, with wires everywhere and straight lines of attached row houses. When she reached Victoria Avenue, she turned the car around, headed back to town, and tried another way out Lord Lane and over a bridge.

The Wilcocks lived on a hill with a long drive and horses in a gated field. A pink bicycle and a blue bicycle rested against the stone wall by the orangey-red front door. Mr. Wilcock opened the door as she was walking up the path. His square face and round belly smiled. "It's a damn good thing to see you, good to have you here. Come in, come in." He led her into the hallway and then the front room. "I'm so glad you made the drive. On the wrong side of the road, too."

"Oh, it was fine, except for the roundabouts, but here I am."

"Let's have a drink, shall we?" he said. "Drinks first."

"Always," Eleanor said.

"What will you have?" The doorbell rang. "That will be Jane . . . ," Mr. Wilcock said.

Mrs. Wilcock came in with a tray of bottles and glasses. "Our daughter insisted on joining. I hope you don't mind . . ." Her limpid blue eyes looked directly into Eleanor's. "Still a bit bewildered?"

"I'm much better. I've been doing a lot of walking and it's helped to clear my mind."

Mrs. Wilcock dropped ice cubes in four glasses and poured a generous amount of gin, vermouth, and a splash of Campari in each one. She handed Eleanor a drink.

Jane Wilcock came into the room, tall and elegantly dressed in this year's Burberry soft black leather pants and a mahogany-red fitted sweater, with sensible walking shoes. As Jane shook Eleanor's hand she said, "You're a brave girl coming all this way to this quiet place. It must seem terribly dull after a life in Manhattan," and then took her drink from the cocktail table and sat down.

"It's not the end of the earth," Mr. Wilcock rumbled.

Mrs. Wilcock smiled at her husband. "It's true," she said to Eleanor, "it was brave of you to come."

"I wish you'd had more time with Alice," Mr. Wilcock said. "She outlived what the doctor said she'd do, but still, she was so happy to have you come."

Through lunch, the couple bickered a bit and Jane seemed accustomed to smoothing their differences. Mead had warned her, when he'd offered to drive, "Whatever you think of me, I'd be the best part of the journey, I'm pretty sure," but Eleanor was enjoying the change of scene, the more modern home with large windows, linen curtains, bright lights, and white furniture. For the most part, the conversation was light and lively: a little American politics, a bit of fashion with Jane.

"There was something you didn't want to discuss on the phone," she reminded Mr. Wilcock as he scooped the last bit of cream and cobbler from his bowl.

"Oh, that. Sorry, no. I suppose that was just a ruse to get you out here." He dabbed around his mouth with the linen napkin.

"Ah . . ."

Jane interjected, "Father wanted to know you better and we knew you wouldn't be staying long."

"I want to make sure," Mr. Wilcock began, "that you understand we are all your family. You shouldn't be the least bit anxious about Trent Hall and all that goes with it. It won't be a burden you're inheriting, I promise you that. I'm here, I'm always here to help you in any regard."

"Gwen said it takes care of itself, but it's not that . . . ," Eleanor said.

"I knew your mother, when we were young. I think she'd be pleased." His eyes moistened. "It's a long time ago, but I thought the world of her, and I think the world of you. Whatever you decide to do with Trent Hall"—he reached and took her hand now—"it's something you want to be proud of. It's a fine estate, Trent Hall."

"Yes, well, Papa." Jane rolled her eyes at Eleanor in a friendly way. "Are you up for a walk, Eleanor? We hear from Mead you're a noble walker. I imagine it's in your blood! I think we should take you to Top Withens."

"Do you know it?" Mrs. Wilcock asked.

"I saw something about it last night, at the parsonage."

"It's our little Disneyland," Jane said. "Haworth and the Brontës. The parsonage, the ghosts. Top Withens is thought to be Emily's inspiration for Wuthering Heights, the house itself, that is. Do you want to go? It's not a difficult trek." Jane's accent was particularly British, with musical lilting intonation, sharp consonants, and swallowed syllables. Eleanor nodded and without delay everyone was up and gathering scarves and coats.

ALONG THE WAY THE MOOR GREW BARREN AND DRY, BUT the walk was easy. Mr. Wilcock reviewed with Eleanor some of the details of the estate, what it meant for Eleanor, whether she stayed in England or not. The house could not be sold under any condition, he reiterated, but she needn't live there all the time—Alice and Gwen hadn't. There were people to care for it, if she found she couldn't stay. Still, he encouraged her to find a way to stay and she began to feel obligated.

"What about Mead? Can't I give it to him?"

"You can't. No. One has nothing to do with the other . . . ," Mr. Wilcock said, somewhat breathless as they passed a low bridge and the climb grew more steep.

"But he lives there and he should stay there. I mean, of course, he'll live there as long as he wants. It's his house." She looked at Jane.

"Mead makes do," Jane said, and there was something about the way she'd spoken his name. Eleanor supposed that Jane had been a girlfriend of Mead's at one time. And this made Eleanor a little more curious. Everything she'd encountered on this journey seemed to have another side: a shadow, a shimmer, an underbelly.

Jane hooked her arm through Eleanor's and walked with

her more quickly so they'd pull ahead of her parents. In a conspiratorial tone she said, "Don't be overly bothered. Father wants you here. He's sentimental that way. You must do what's right for you." She slowed down to light a cigarette, cupped her hand around the flame, her arm still hooked with Eleanor's arm.

"Mead won't be turned out—of course he can stay at Trent, but he has a mysterious place he'll inherit one day." She pulled in a deep draft of smoke. "An estate on an island in the Outer Hebrides."

"Really? Does everyone have an estate here?" Eleanor said.

"Hardly. He doesn't go there, but it is his ancestral home and he's never been under any illusions about Trent Hall." Jane unhooked their arms and they mounted the last part of the hill to see Top Withens for the first time.

"You don't have to worry about Mead," she said.

Eleanor had pictured a grand house, dark, with bent and twisted trees, cliffs, and ditches dug out by rain and wind, all in a forbidding landscape, but Top Withens was a disappointment. Most of the building was gone, there was no roof, and there were woolly sheep with black faces and piercing pale eyes mulling about inside the broken walls.

Eleanor walked down the slope to the front of the house and stood next to one of the two remaining trees on the hill. It was unromantic and the whole place seemed an unlikely site for the place in the book.

"This can't be it. It doesn't feel like the house in the book at all," Eleanor said to Jane, who'd just made it down the side of the hill to join her.

"Not convinced?"

"This can't be it."

"Starting a revolution?" Only half of Jane's face lifted when she smiled. "What do you think the ghosts must make of it?"

"If I were a ghost I'd stay pretty far from here, wouldn't you?" Eleanor said with as much levity as she could muster. It was wearing her down, all the glib talk of ghosts.

"I can't imagine they're fond of tourists," said Jane, smiling.

Jane was kind and irreverent and it was good to have her around. Her deep brown hair was tied with a scarf. She was more handsome than pretty, with a strong square jaw, full crimson lips, and almond eyes.

"You know I can't stay," Eleanor said. "I don't understand why no one said anything about this to me years ago, so I could have planned something, but how in the world can I stay?" She shook her head with small rapid shakes. "It makes no sense to me."

"Father can't imagine anyone *but* you in that house," said Jane. She lit another cigarette with the one she'd just finished. "Trent Hall's an old estate and it's meant to be yours. Over here, these things mean something."

"I just think Mead should stay."

"Mead *will* stay," said Jane. She nodded her head toward the other tree and they climbed the slope to stand under its shade. Jane leaned against the trunk and Eleanor sat in its crook.

"The thing about Mead is, he's got an idea in his head that there's a Catherine for him, out there somewhere, and he's doing all he can to prepare himself for her."

"A Catherine?"

"Heathcliff's Catherine. Alice was a Brontë scholar and those books were his bedtime lullabies. A great love requires a sturdiness of self, he says." Eleanor thought she heard an ache in Jane's voice. "A hardiness developed in accord with these Wuthering Heights moors." Jane shook her head as if shaking away a pesky bee.

"This place doesn't look anything like Wuthering Heights," Eleanor said, "but Trent Hall, on the other hand . . ."

"You're absolutely right." Jane brushed off her pants and sweater.

"I sleep in the room within a room."

"I've seen the room. It's true," Jane exclaimed. "Must have been a fashion at the time. Let's be off, shall we? We can have tea at the Rochester before you get on the road. How's that?" She called out, "Mum, Papa," with the accent on the last syllable.

THE INSISTENT TREE WOKE ELEANOR IN THE NIGHT and she cranked the window open to push the branch away, but it found its way back and continued to scrape and scratch the pane. Eleanor woke and slept and woke again and each time wiped tears from her face. She'd brought up a Goethe book she'd found on one of the half-empty shelves in the study downstairs, so she read for some hours, then slept again.

Like sap from a tree, her eyes wept all through the night. She might have dreamed, but she couldn't remember the dreams. Even in the morning, with the curtains open and the sun in her eyes, she turned over in bed and pulled the comforter up to cover her shoulder, pulled a pillow against her belly, read with the book perched on a pillow, and soon fell asleep again.

Gwen had been up to check on her late in the morning, but hadn't wakened her. Tilda came up at noon and left a tray with tea and warm biscuits that went cold. In the early evening, Mead knocked on her door.

Eleanor woke and wiped her cheeks dry. "Come in," she called, trying to make her voice light and bright. She wriggled up in bed, kept the comforter close to her chest.

"Hey, you," he said. He came in and sat tentatively on the edge of the bed. "You all right?"

The wall of leaded windows let in lots of light. She'd drawn the curtains wide.

"It's not that I'm so tired."

His smile was encouraging.

"I've just not figured out a reason to get out of bed today."

"Just thought you'd be thirsty or hungry."

"No, I'm not, but I was thinking . . ." She leaned against the pillows, the scratched window ledge behind her. "Would you be willing to take me out on a ride sometime, maybe tomorrow?"

"If you mean horseback, I would."

"I do."

"Are you as masterful on a horse as you are on foot?"

"It can't be that hard," she said.

"You've never been riding?"

She shook her head no. "I saw you wrangling the horses one day. I'm not here for much longer."

"Is that a fact?"

He touched her foot under the covers and Eleanor's heart jumped in her chest. She wondered if Mead and Jane had taken rides. Jane seemed the kind who'd be a natural on horseback.

"Hard to say, I guess," she said. "Maybe not a fact. But I'll be ready to ride in the morning, if you are."

Mead stood.

"Can we ride without running into anybody?" she asked.

"I should think so. You'll need a good jacket as it's cold in the clearings. We'll do our best to make the ride utterly uneventful, how's that?"

"Perfect. Thanks, Mead. I'll see you early in the morning."

"You don't want anything at all now?"

She shook her head again.

"I'll wake you," he said.

"I'll hear you in the courtyard."

"COME ON, THEN." HIS HEAD COCKED AWAY FROM THE house the next morning. Mead untied the horses and she realized she had imagined herself on the back of his horse with her arms wrapped around his middle.

At the edge of the field, he gave her a boost up onto the saddle then slipped her foot into the stirrup, went to the other side, and slipped the other foot in. "Keep your heels down and away from her body." He placed a rein in each of Eleanor's hands, then climbed on his mare.

"We're so high off the ground," she said.

Mead introduced her to Kindred and she leaned forward to touch the smooth auburn hair.

"Now, keep your hips nestled into the deep part of that seat, keep your face pointed in the direction you want to go and your hips square." Eleanor wriggled in deep and pressed her heels down against the stirrups, sat up tall.

"Good. Now imagine you're part of that beautiful horse. Your arms are relaxed, the reins loose and easy." He urged his horse forward without moving anything. "Ready?"

Eleanor's heart beat hard, her knees were loose, her calves were pressed against Kindred's belly, and they rode away from the house. They rode straight on for over an hour. First they walked, then Mead encouraged a trot and a canter, till Eleanor was confident enough to let Kindred gallop the way she wanted to.

The mare all fresh and wild in the morning, it didn't matter so much what Eleanor knew about riding, she had only to relax enough to let Kindred soar. Eleanor laughed with joy when she cantered, then whooped when she galloped, all the sound swallowed by the wildness of the wind. Kindred's ride was muscular and smooth, and as the hour became two hours, Eleanor felt the possibility of staying forever on the moors.

What had been unnerving those first days—unbroken landscape, unmeasured time—now seemed wholesome and very fine. Mead's solid body moved in rhythm with his mare as he bounded over low hedges. Unruffled, he turned his face to her and smiled, all satisfied. She wished they could keep riding, wished they would never turn back, wished there were nothing for her to decide.

When there was a river to cross, Kindred headed in without hesitation; she pushed through the water as high as her shoulders, soaked Eleanor's legs in the cold. Eleanor clung; she was scared and then she was stunned by the strength it took for the mare to climb up and out onto the river's edge. The ripple of muscles under the blanket, Kindred's legs rose high as she climbed out of the mud onto the bank.

Awed by the power of the horse beneath her and the river

and the wild, Eleanor kicked Kindred lightly, as she'd learned to do, and caught up with Mead on the river path.

The horses paced themselves to each other, side by side. They panted, the sound of their heavy breath and the creaking of leather, wind in grass, and in all the silence Eleanor said, "I've been wondering. Where *are* the Outer Hebrides?"

He tipped his head, curious. "Where do you imagine they are?"

"Somewhere near Antarctica, I think. Or off the tip of Africa, but not near here."

"Not very near."

She reached across the space between them and touched his arm. "Do you know how to play cold, colder, warm, warmer, hot?"

He held one eye half-closed, peering at her with lighthearted suspicion. "Start in, then." He kicked open a gate in a wall in the middle of a field, and they passed through it.

"Antarctica is too cold, I think, so how about off the southern tip of Africa?"

"Very cold."

"The coast of Africa?"

"Which coast?"

"Umm. West coast."

"Moving in the right direction."

"Say *warm* or *cold*," she said.

"Right. Cold."

"The Baltic Sea."

"Closer."

Eleanor liked him. "Ireland?" she said.

"I'd have to say very warm, almost hot."

"Scotland?"

"Right you are. The lady wins the cigar!"

She smiled and he smiled, as if they'd accomplished something.

It was another hour back, this time over a bridge, this time with the wind blowing against her. Mead had lifted her up to the horse and down from the horse and had kept his promise: the most serious thing he'd said all day was that being with her was as good as being alone. She'd looked at him with a quizzical, screwed-up face, but she knew just what he meant.

When they finally stopped, Eleanor's hair was tangled and knotted. She tried to run her fingers through but couldn't and didn't have anything with which to pin it up. Drenched from her knees down and mangled by the weather, she was out of breath, without a thought in her head.

He was kicking the mud off his boots at the kitchen door, when he told her, "I was seven the first time Alice took me to Manhattan. There was snow on the ground and it was quiet. I remember Alice stepping to the curb and raising her arm high, and it seemed like a miracle, every time a yellow car pulled up and invited us inside where it was all smoky and warm. Like we were kings and queens. And in we climbed."

Mead crouched before her where she sat on the bench and he pulled one boot from the heel and then the other. For a moment he gave a tender rub to what had been her swollen ankle and her warm blood rushed to her heart and back again. In something of a swoon she realized what was happening and it was something different from anything that had ever been.

When she walked into the kitchen, her face bright from fresh air, her hair a mess of wind tangle, she was sore and felt bowlegged, cold through and through.

From the back of his head, she knew him. Miles. He stood and Eleanor swallowed her gasp, then hurried to hug him, because she should, but stopped short of it. "I'm a mess and I smell of horse . . ." She padded across the kitchen in thick socks to wash her hands at the sink and gather her wits.

Gwen kept light conversation bouncing around the room so Eleanor could collect herself, slow things down. They'd been discussing the fate of British estates, Gwen said. Miles introduced himself to Mead and they shook hands. Then Mead stepped behind Eleanor and suggested he take her coat. His fingers touched her collarbones as he reached around to slip it off her shoulders.

Eleanor looked around for a towel. All the time she'd been there, she'd never washed her hands in the kitchen sink. It seemed such a homely thing to do. In her sweaty jeans with just socks on her feet, she felt like she lived there. With Miles waiting just behind her, she turned.

Now, she greeted him warmly and hugged him close.

This was not the time for her to take a stand. This was not the moment for a confrontation. She wasn't sure what she would have felt, had she known that this moment was waiting around the bend.

"This is Miles," she announced awkwardly. "I guess you've introduced yourselves, and you already know Gwen . . ."

They stood together, the two men seeing what was there to be seen, what each saw in the other.

"You've come up from London." Mead attempted a casual air.

"I have." Miles' eyes fixed on Eleanor. "I was at the Stafford Hotel for a few days trying to get through. El, I left messages for you."

Eleanor said, "Let's sit down." The chairs scraped in and out on the stone floor.

"I knew the name Alice Sutton, but I didn't know anything else," Miles said. "Then I remembered you said Trent Hall, so I put it to Google and there it was, a little triangle on a satellite picture and then I got a sense of where you were, and I couldn't not come, after I saw it."

"You saw it on Google?" The number of times they'd sat together finding this place or that, but to imagine he could see this house from up in the sky, catch her walking on the moors perhaps. Anyway, it was just a little bit fun watching Miles explain himself. "That's great," she said.

"I rented a car and drove. My God, it's a gorgeous country."

Eleanor was pleased and stunned and miffed, all at once, but she was also relieved to have him close again. There was nothing but the familiar. That was all she felt. Just the familiar face and the hands she loved on her skin. She had all but forgotten the kindness in his eyes, the steady sameness of his mood and his manner. He put her at ease, felt like family. Not at all the way she'd felt with Mead, a short while before and all day long, a mix of steady warmth and edgy unpredictability.

As they drank tea and cut into Tilda's scones—light and airy and nothing like the dense scones chock-full of grains, currants, figs, or ginger that were sold with lattes in New York City—Miles engaged Mead effortlessly. Mead was vexed, shifted into bravado when Miles asked about the construction of the wall along the driveway, and then the renovation of the stable he'd noticed under way. His accent became more lofty than she'd heard from him, all the tenderness gone. She'd seen this part of him in slivers, just fleeting moments of testiness and pride: when he walked in on the first night she met him in front of the fire, when she helped to load the books in the shelves, his temper with Granley.

Eleanor was about to suggest they move into one of the sitting rooms and make a fire when Gwen suggested Eleanor go up to freshen herself and change her clothing.

Eleanor said, "I should. You're sure?" to Gwen, to Miles.

"Yes. Take your time."

"Okay, then, I will." As well as she could, she threw Mead a gentle look of apology. As she climbed the stairs, she heard him say he'd build a fire.

Neither Mead nor Gwen had heard anything about Miles, knew anything about the story between them, but Miles' face—as he watched her mount the front staircase—said everything they might have wondered.

Eleanor ran up the stairs. She could take her time. It had been weeks since she'd seen him, but he'd betrayed her and deserved to sit about a bit waiting until she was ready for him. Though there was no denying the lift of pleasure she felt seeing him. Tall and lean, lithe and patrician, with his thick blond hair as it fell in his eyes and the way he stood casually inside his clothes, without any sense of his own beauty. She'd forgotten how utterly beautiful he was, a crystal beauty.

THE HOT WATER IN THE TUB. THE JASMINE OIL. WHEN she closed her eyes the perfume carried her to the tropical island she wished she'd traveled to. She wished a hundred things but three were these: that Miles hadn't cheated on her, that nothing had changed, that she'd stayed in New York City and had drunk more champagne. She'd almost completely forgotten the sale to Barneys and everything her life had been. Seeing Miles made this seem important again.

Her hair fell down her back and she climbed into the tub before it was half-full. Hot as she could take it. The way she liked it. In the steamed-up mirror over the sink, she thought she saw a face and turned her whole body in a snap, so fast that her back cracked. An adjustment. But there was no one there, and she slid under the water with her eyes closed tight. Felt her hair all around her face like seaweed. Her skin was slick in the oily water and felt soft, smooth, and with her eyes closed she explored the contours of her body. Surprised by the round firmness of her bottom, she recalled Miles' hands supporting her there as he pressed into her. She held her breath a little longer.

It was early afternoon, and Mead would by now be offering his best example of Scotch whisky to Miles. Gwen would be doing her best to entertain them without overstepping any unseen boundaries.

Eleanor held her breath until she had to come up for air. When she surfaced, there on the side of the tub sat the young woman, in her blue wool dress. Thinner than she'd seen her. Maybe older but certainly drawn and scrawny, looking feverish. Eleanor was naked and in the middle of a gasp for air. She hadn't sensed her sitting there. When a tiny scream emitted, the woman didn't startle or try to stop her. There was time to call for help. Eleanor might have called for Mead or for Miles, and they would have come, but as she considered it, the woman started speaking.

"You haven't found the letters yet, I know." She looked the

same but she also looked different. The bloom in her cheeks was gone and she wasn't breathing right as she spoke.

This time, Eleanor was afraid and felt the choked feeling she'd felt the first time she'd seen her at the end of the bed. But she'd been too worried about looking crazy to ask anyone a straight question about the likelihood of a ghost at Trent Hall. Now she wished she had. Now she wished she'd enlisted some help in this strangeness.

"Who are you?" Eleanor demanded in a meeker voice than she intended.

"Emily." The woman waited before proceeding. "I'm here . . . as it's to do with you. And any child that will come to you." The woman spoke with such conviction, Eleanor was speechless. "Forgive me for what I've done," Emily went on, "I'm certain you can't understand all of it, but if you'll listen . . . take my hand."

Eleanor took it and felt the cold in her bones. "You're freezing."

"That's what it's like." Even tired and worn, Emily's face was youthful and some of the anxiety that had been in her face was gone now. "This part is awfully cold, in the days before I go."

Though most of Eleanor believed this was a ghost, she struggled against it. It was possible this was a woman lost in delirium. She was rambling, but she was clearly ill. Eleanor should listen, try to help her, find a way to bring her downstairs to the others.

"What do you mean, the days before you go?" she asked.

Emily didn't answer but looked up—through the closed door and down the hall—as if she could see someone.

Out of the tub in the warm room, Eleanor wrapped herself in the biggest towel. There was no one in the hall, when she opened the door. Emily stood and silently followed her. Once inside her room, Eleanor turned on the chandelier and watched mutely as Emily fingered the heavy cloth of the nightgown, then lay down on the bed, as if Eleanor were not there.

"Can I help you?" Eleanor said. "I don't know what to do. Could you tell me how it is I might help you?" She felt restless and impatient now.

Effortful, Emily's chest rose and fell. Her cheeks were hollow. Her fingers clutched the comforter, fists full of fabric squeezed so tight the knuckles were white. The hands already bone thin.

"You're ill," Eleanor said.

"I am, it's true." Her voice was unconcerned. "I'm dying, but I need you to know this." She lifted her upper body off the bed with alarming strength of will. "I don't know why Robert came, but he did." She looked into Eleanor's face as if for absolution, but Eleanor had no idea of this man Robert. "I was out walking—I was always on the moors, God knew that—but one day there he was, and it seemed a most natural thing.

"I shouldn't have written 'bout such a fierce love, but it

was how it was. I was torn between Branwell and Robert—it set a curse in the blood. Give me your hand." Emily brought Eleanor's jet ring up to her cheek and tears streamed. Bewildered, Eleanor heard Emily whisper, "It was in Whitby he gave this to me."

Emily wiped away tears, urged Eleanor, "Listen to me, I burned most of what I wrote in those last years, but I hid the letters and they are there for you, in the house where you can find them."

Eleanor sat on the edge of the bed now, stunned and frozen with what she couldn't fathom. She took Emily's hand between her own two hands and Emily closed her eyes and continued, "I pray you, be brave enough." She had barely breath enough to speak and her forehead was cold with sweat. "I chose to stay and take care of my brother when I should have gone with the man I loved. It's too late now. But, my darling, you can set your heart upon changing it. I pray you."

It was impossible, but Emily pulled in her last ghostly breath and she seemed to die on the bed. She disappeared and didn't leave a vapor, not an imprint, not a stain or a scent.

There was nothing Eleanor could do—she couldn't think, felt if she tried she wouldn't be able to move—but she got up and threw open the drapes and all the windows in the room. She brushed off the comforter. It seemed like a crazy thing to do, but she brushed until it was smooth.

Out the window, the day was so clear she was sure she could see farther than she'd seen before, to a perfectly rounded hill deep in the distance, rounded like a breast or a pregnant woman's belly, without a tree on it, or a river passing through it, and the grass on it was smooth. A scream welled up from inside her, but she swallowed it whole. Frantic and panicked, she wanted to call down to Mead, to tell him the story from beginning to end, but Miles was waiting.

It was madness, she thought, and she hurried into her navy tights, stepped into her cherry-colored narrow skirt and then the matching fitted jacket. Chanel perfume behind her ears. A torrent of feeling surged and she took a breath so deep it strained the tight wool jacket. She had the keenest sense it was Emily Brontë she'd witnessed dying, but it was absurd. Though Mead, and then Jane, had spoken casually of ghosts. As she straightened her stockings and grabbed a scarf, she thought of them now, the words they'd spoken.

It was almost irrepressible, the urge to turn the house upside down and find whatever letters were hidden in some library, in some part of the rambling house, half emptied. But downstairs Miles was waiting. She was dressed for the city, so she'd take him somewhere, into the closest big city.

WHEN ELEANOR CAME DOWN THE STAIRS, SHE MADE AS little sound as she could. She carried her boots with her. Black leather boots with a heel she liked the sound of on wood. She loved the smell of the leather as she sat down at the bottom of the stairs and pulled them on. She could hear the hum of conversation in the other room, where Gwen seemed to be telling a story that Miles punctuated with questions. She half hoped Mead would have found a reason to go to the library, would not be there when she came in to say she was ready to go.

"Look at you," Mead crooned from the corner where he was sunk into a deep chair, whisky in hand. The chair swallowed half of him, but the part that stuck out was brooding. He'd given Miles a whisky with one cube of ice, not a drink Miles loved but one he could drink when company required it. Miles sat up at the edge of the couch and was entertaining Gwen with harmless stories about Eleanor's life.

"Your friend is delightful," Gwen said.

Eleanor took a seat at the edge of one of the chairs.

"Oh, you should go to see York with Miles, Eleanor. You could drive there . . ." Gwen turned to Miles. "You have a car." He nodded. "Then you could come home on the train, Eleanor, when you've seen the town. Or come back here together. York's wonderful." She looked back and forth between them. "With a rather famous train station. You'll work it out."

"We should," Miles agreed with satisfaction.

Eleanor looked over at Mead. "So, let's go," she said to Miles and hooked her arm in his proffered arm.

ELEANOR GUIDED MILES OUT OF THE DRIVEWAY AND past the small villages she knew. "Thorpe, thwaite," she told him, "that's what they call villages around here," she said. "No, really they do!"

He'd already mentioned how good she looked, how impertinent it was to come without reaching her first, but he'd tried as long as he could, he'd insisted, and she was happy to watch the countryside go by, with Miles driving and the window rolled halfway down.

They'd been driving quietly for miles when he asked, "What's the story with Mead?"

"Mead's part of the family," Eleanor answered.

"He seemed upset." Miles was fishing.

"He was."

"About Alice . . . ? Or was it me?"

"It's not you."

"You looked pretty happy coming in off that ride."

"I was." She glared at the side of his face. "You really want to talk about looking happy?"

He downshifted the gear stick to pick up some traction.

In time they'd talk about that night, but she was distracted. It wasn't just a bad habit that ran in the blood; Emily had called it a curse.

"Do you remember snipe hunts?" she asked Miles after a long road of silence.

"What brought that up?"

"Do you remember them?"

"I don't think I ever went on one. Did you?"

"Yep." She nodded. "Once at camp. I mean, I wasn't the

worst fool. I knew it was fake, but everyone kind of went along and there were a couple of kids who took it seriously and they were the ones who wound up crying when it was obvious—you know, eventually it gets kind of obvious there's no such thing as a snipe, after the sun's gone down and you've these bags in your hands with marshmallows on a hook to catch them."

"What are you saying, exactly?"

The woolly sheep sometimes seemed to smile when they watched the cars go by. Eleanor wondered if they knew what a rarity they were, in the big world.

"The older kids are in the trees making snipe sounds and telling you to run this way then that way. It's sometimes what it's been like, being here. Starting with that night I walked in on you, really. A rite of passage, more like a hazing . . ." Her voice trailed off.

Miles pulled over to the side of the road and parked, stretched his arm across the back of her seat, rested his hand on her shoulder, and she flinched.

"You're not comfortable, I know," he said. "It was wrong to just show up."

She glanced at him, then out the window. "I don't want to talk about serious things yet."

Having him next to her, she began to see the tapestry of things take shape. Threads hanging that hadn't been woven in. The man in her mother's letters, Martin Garrens, might still be in Scarborough, for one thing. She could hunt for

Emily's letters in the house, see if they were there somewhere after all, see what was in them. She wanted to find out what it meant that Mead had his own land somewhere, what he made of what had happened with his father, and why he didn't live there. Not that she wanted him to live there.

Here was Miles sitting beside her with his long legs under the dashboard, his body relaxed. Her hand on the gear shift knob so that when he wanted to, he could touch her. A major thread in the warp and weave was the sense of betrayal she felt when she left New York, when she landed in England. They needed to talk about that. But right now, she just felt this wave of weariness. She reached for his hand and said, "You know, Miles, in time I'm going to want to know how that happened. Why it happened. How planned it was. I'm hoping it was more like spontaneous and less like planned, but in either case I want you to tell me the truth. I don't want to talk about it now, but sometime before you leave, I guess, we have to talk about why you went there."

"Eleanor, it was . . ."

"But not now." She raised the window. "You know, when I got home that night, I broke all those dishes. It was probably the morning by then, 'cause I'd stopped at Soho House and gone up to the pool."

His head turned to look at her face. "You did?"

She nodded. She knew where he was going in his head. "I thought about stripping down to my bra and pants and swimming in that pool up there. On the way up, in the elevator, I saw it all exactly as it should have been. Some hot late-night drunk swim. But the reality was I had a sad solo drink at the bar and went back downstairs and got a cab home alone. Anyway, that's when I broke all those dishes."

"You mean the Italian ones?" She'd piggybacked onto a business trip he'd taken to Milan, and they'd chanced upon a little shop with lovely, quirky, hand-painted pottery.

"Yep."

"Tell me it's not so . . ."

"It hurts, eh?" she said.

Miles put his hand on the back of her neck.

❧

THE COUNTRYSIDE ROLLED BY AND MILES COMMENTED on it, mile after mile. Smooth, sweet green on the side of the road, green that rose, green that rolled, green that sometimes rolled so high they lost sight of the sky. There were times that trees closed in on either side of the road, as through Stoney Haggs Rise, and then cleared to another endless stretch of green, dabbed with white sheep from Uncleby Hill, past and through some unappealing and modern-patched towns, till they pulled into York and found a car park.

Whip ma Whop ma Gate—they passed a broad street sign that marked where the local whipping post had once been placed and walked down that narrow street to the church nearby and then down the shadowed street called the Shambles and into the Juicy Moosey, where she ordered a large Well Being and he a Green Peace.

The buildings bent into each other and kept the lanes in shadow for most of the day. Narrow streets and passageways built for little people—half the size of Eleanor and Miles—a thousand years ago. Down the Shambles to Little Shambles, around a bend, then back again. The store windows were low to the ground and the doorways so low that Eleanor and Miles had to stoop to pass through them. Through a break in the wall they followed a sign to Newgate Market, a dank passage of stones and bricks on the other side of which lay an open square, a bustling market. It was nice to wander in a city neither of them knew. York was a quaint town and strange enough, to each of them, that they held hands moving through it.

The bistro, which had a very good chef according to Miles' phone, wasn't warm in its decor but had a mix of aromas that were appealing. Miles held her elbow in his hand as the host escorted them to the table. He slipped her coat off her shoulders and said how pretty she looked in the skirt to her knees, the tailored Chanel and printed scarf. He pulled out her chair and touched the back of her neck where it was bare between the scarf and her hair in a full French twist held with a clip and not her glasses. Eleanor crossed her legs at the knees as Miles ordered red wine.

With a gesture that was very Miles, he ran his fingers

through the front swath of his thick hair. He'd done it the first time she saw him as she approached him on the playground when they were in the sixth grade. When he'd seen her coming toward him that day, he'd dropped the basketball he was dribbling and had run his hand through the thick hair to pull it off his forehead where it always fell. He always kept it long enough that it would fall there.

"El," he said.

"Don't be nervous," she said.

"I am nervous. Are you not nervous?"

"I am, but it would be better if *you* weren't."

"I'd no business just coming up, without calling, but I did leave messages."

"I know."

"I came to see you."

"I know."

"I was just at the hotel and . . ."

"Pacing," she said. He paced when a big deal was pending, and he paced when he watched the news.

"Thanks for making it easy when I got there. I know I interrupted something."

Eleanor looked down at her hands and they sat quietly.

"You seem different, you know?"

"I'm sure I am."

The sommelier arrived with the wine and uncorked the bottle. Not a fan of silencing conversation for the performance of serving a meal, she asked how she seemed different.

"More mature, I think."

"More mature." She took her first swallow, invited him to elaborate.

"More steady?"

"I'm probably more confused."

"I was going to say more full. In French they'd say 'good in your skin.' "

"Ah." A wave of tiredness overcame her and her eyelids actually weakened, drooped. A shot of a headache right above her left ear. "Well, I can tell you one thing. I can tell you one thing for sure. Without you, I've kind of had to pull things together, and I didn't know how much you were doing for me before."

"Before when?"

"Before now, before always. Since forever. It's true. I think I realized it when I was flying here. Halfway across the ocean, what it was like to not have you there. Not just not next to me in a seat, but anywhere."

She could feel how he wanted to assure her that he was there, that he was right here, that he was always there, would always be there, and she appreciated that he didn't say it. She appreciated that he said, "Go on, I want to hear."

The headache was like a bolt in her temple. She forced herself to take a deep breath. "I don't know if I have the energy for it."

"That's okay." Miles was still in a straightforward sense of time and place. She had been there, or somewhere near to that, all of her life. But she wasn't there any longer. She wasn't sure she ever would be again. Having seen what she'd seen and felt what she'd felt, even just the strength it took to stand against the wind on the moors, to feel the wildness of nature pushing against her, she had doubts about what mattered and what was real. She'd been invited to be brave enough to know things, to discover things about ancestry, to know herself sincerely.

"Grazing menu," he said. "How about if we order a few things to share?"

"That always works." She spoke softly.

"Smoked eel, Whitby crab." He looked to her for approval. "Rabbit pie and mash, fish and chips, 'unusual carrots.' "

"We have to have 'unusual carrots,' right? Taste these. They're good." She split and buttered a roll for him.

"Jeez, it almost hurts more that you're being so good to me, El. Can you tell me how awful it was? Can you kick me under the table right in my shin, even by accident?"

"Wow, that's extreme." They had a brief laugh and then she got serious. "Yeah, I'm sure I can tell you. I went to Soho House hoping to do something awful that night. Our friend at the door assumed you were there and let me in. I was . . . I don't even know what I was feeling. If you'd come by that night, I could have shown you. It was awful, what I felt. I'd never felt anything like it." She took a long sip of wine. "Actually, it's not true I hadn't felt it before. Do you remember how cut off my dad was after Mom died?"

This was the harshest thing she could say, though she hadn't exactly intended it that way. It fell out. Onto the table and there it sat.

"It was like that?" he said. "It was worse than that. I hurt you worse than that."

"As you know I've got a mind that's good at not thinking about what's just awful. Right?"

"I didn't mean to. It wasn't about you . . ."

"I know. I really do know that." Her voice sounded high and young. She felt how vulnerable she would be if she bothered to ask more. "I mean, I sort of know, but that last day we were together, did you know you were seeing her? Miles, it's not just what you did, it's what I saw."

"Oh, God, I know." He exhaled. His body cringed he was so uncomfortable.

"Did you lie to me about where you were going that night?"

"I didn't."

She made an effort to avoid hysteria, to pull her feelings down low in her belly.

"That's kind of hard to believe, given the scene at the coffee shop the day before."

"I know."

"That was coincidence."

"Not coincidence. It was pure accident."

She wasn't sure what he meant, what was the distinction. Was she going to tumble into the details of it?

"You met the pixie when, then?"

"We met her at a party. She flirted with me. You didn't notice it, but that's where we met her."

"I didn't meet her," she said.

He dropped his head, rightly ashamed.

He went on. "She was at the coffee shop that day and then she was at the bar we were at that night. The guys, lots of them left early, and I stuck around."

"By accident," she said.

They looked at each other for a long time. Finally she looked away and said, "Anyway, I'm here now," she started. The conversation was over. There was nothing new to learn. "You've been my best friend forever. It's something that happens, right? Stuff that happens to people."

"There you are being kind."

There was a large empty silence.

"You know, El, I see it. You seem settled in yourself like I've never seen you."

It was impossible not to think of riding on the scarp that morning, at the top with the broken cliffs below. Both their heads of hair a tangle and the chestnut horses in a sticky sweat underneath them. Just that morning.

"It was awful seeing you that way that night," she said, "and it might have changed things for us in a way we can't get back from." She held his eyes and this was all the punishment she would give him. She didn't blink. Though her eyelids felt weak, she didn't blink. Her eyes bore into his, and his held steady. He was capable. He withstood the universe of understanding that bears no explanation, ineffable like love and death, truth and betrayal.

The server announced the crab from Whitby and Eleanor remembered that Vikings once came into Whitby on wild-looking ships from the North Sea.

"I'm glad you're here," she said.

He divided the grazing plates. Taking and giving some.

"Tell me something, would you?" Human, he needed to hear it in black and white. "Was it unforgivable?"

She thought for a moment. "No, not unforgivable."

She had no appetite for eel or crab or macaroni and cheese with ham hocks. "Could I have some water, please?" she asked the waiter and picked at the unusual carrots.

The water came in a cleaned-out milk bottle, fresh and cold. He poured the water for them and they each drank a glass or two, because the food was rich with butter and also salty.

Then she said, "We'll stay here, right?"

"Here in York?" His mood brightened.

"Just the night, okay?"

Facing him, she knew nothing was simple.

As they ambled about in the narrow streets of the oldest part of town, she spoke in a low voice. "My mother lived here in that big house, when she was little, and back and forth all her life, and she came here for visits, and in all that time she never brought us here, Dad and me, and I've never even wondered about this place. I knew she was from some place and I never went looking for any of it."

"You were sad for a long time, checked out, in a way. It doesn't surprise me."

When he offered her his arm, she slipped her arm through his and they walked through York much the way they walked in SoHo on the weekends. Wandering from one shop to another through the labyrinth of mews and alleys, she let him lead, because he knew how to lead her. He'd led her through so much that was hard in her life, when she couldn't bear to find her way alone, that even after she'd begun to tread a path of her own, he didn't know how not to lead her.

After bourbon at a pub, they stepped off the curb to make way for others in the narrow passage. She knew some of this would never change: he would always be Miles Paxton, the boy who'd loved her since they were children.

The boy who'd taken her, one day in the spring when she was seventeen, to Rockaway Beach, where he had invited her to get on a surfboard and ride with him. She'd worried that the awkward length and weight of her would topple them, but he had encouraged her to climb on, and she had surfed all day. In the evening, in front of her house, when he dropped her home, all salty and fresh from a day in the sea and the sun, she had wanted him to kiss her. His hair was thick and his lips were round. He had the smartest eyes she had ever seen, and it was the first time she had wanted to be kissed by anyone.

Ahead on the right there was the light of a pub, and Miles led her, but Eleanor saw a bright light filling the night sky and she pulled him in that direction, down another street and around a sharp corner.

"Excuse me, what is that?" Eleanor asked an old woman in a thick coat and sensible shoes.

"Ah, 'tis th' Minster. Tha's not from here? Ye canna miss th' Minster. Walk toward it," she said, "anyone can get ye there if ye lose tha sense of it."

They were now on a wide, busy street with buses and cars that zipped by, people moving with purpose, but they strolled along across the river, stopped to watch a boat pass under the bridge, its flat deck filled with chairs and quiet visitors.

Now she led Miles, and several hundred yards down, just before seven thirty in the evening, their walk ended at the York Minster—a fantastic Gothic building with spires that reached to the heavens—and with their heads tipped back so their throats stretched, they followed the Gothic building all the way around to the south wall, a long stretch of yellow stone in an astounding structure. Lights lit up the building from below. She and Miles followed the sound of people and found them collecting at the west door.

At seven thirty, the Ghost Tour began. The Ghost Trail of York and a delightful storyteller told the thirty people who followed behind tales of ghosts from the Romans and Normans and Stuarts and more. York had grown for two thousand years, he said, it had lived and grown, layer by layer, each century adding dregs, residue, and half-dead remains of scandals, plagues, murders, and hauntings.

The storyteller showed blurry snapshots of ghosts caught just in the nick of time, in the blink of a spirited camera's eye: a photo of a woman floating in a white gown, another of a man in top hat and cane alone in the cathedral.

Eleanor wanted to talk to the storyteller, to ask what *he* made of what she thought she'd seen, what she'd imagined. She wanted to know if he believed in seeing phantoms and phantoms that could hold your hand and tell you about things.

"He likes scaring the pants off of kids," Miles said as they walked away. "Little kids and big kids."

"You don't believe it."

"I've no idea. It might be true, but that guy's a good actor."

The Guy Fawkes Inn was a dreamy place, and Eleanor was tired enough to sleep for two. Their room was blissfully beautiful with a four-poster bed that was draped in curtains they could pull all the way around and close themselves in. The curtains were lined with raw silk on the inside and on the outside an Italian linen printed with red, cream, and taupe flowers on a chocolate brown background. The place was luxurious. The rolled-rim tub was long and deep. There were white linen sheets, soft from hundreds of washings, and everything had the smell of lavender and lilac.

She stripped down to a T-shirt and underpants, lay close to one side of the bed, and reached her hand back to hold his.

She gazed at the dark wood throughout the place, on the furniture and the beautiful well-waxed floors. The light of the Minster was right outside their window. Lit up like a holiday, the church's glow filled the room. It had been a long day, they were tired, and she felt him press his spine against hers. All night they slept that way.

❧

OPEN TO THE SKY WHERE THE RAILS RAN THROUGH, THE train station at York was a modern architect's dream of cable, wire, and steel.

"You'll be back soon, right?" he said.

She closed her eyes and kissed him. Urgently, he wrapped his arms around her, held her so close she could hardly breathe with his mouth pressed against hers and her body not yielding.

She pressed her hand against his chest and took one step away. "Listen, I'm not sure what we're doing. I've no idea what I'm doing. Things have changed, you know . . ."

"Sadly, I do know," he said. Ever optimistic, Miles' heart was buried under layers of plans, blueprints he had for the future. Like his city, where things moved quickly and much went unheard. "But I'm not giving up. I'll call you," he said.

"You won't be able to get through."

"I'll call anyway and when you're ready, you'll be home soon?"

Her wan smile said all she could say.

The train swept by and its engine drowned whatever else Miles was saying and they had no more time. Urgent travelers climbed out of carriages and others climbed in. From waiting, suddenly the place was abuzz with baggage dragged and a hundred hearts stirring. Everyone was going somewhere. They were leaving or arriving or the one to stay behind. It was time to say good-bye and they both had tears in their eyes.

Whatever was coming, things had changed between them.

The train was waiting and he kissed her firmly, so firmly she thought he might not let go, might not let her get on the train before it pulled out of the station. Eleanor stepped inside the train and found her seat by a window. There were people standing on either side of the platform and from inside a group of them, he waved. He got smaller. People do get smaller. With perspective, everything gets smaller. She watched him turn and head inside under the roof where there were ivory stone columns with dark marble at the base and capital. She imagined him on a bench, watching people in the artfully designed station with its receding line of columns and steel. With perspective she saw how the train station mirrored the arc of the river.

HER EYES DROPPED CLOSED THEN OPENED AND HER skin brimmed with color when she saw Mead walking toward her at the station.

"You're virtually transparent," he said. "All the life that moves beneath your skin. It's charming." He took her bag.

"Thin-skinned? That's not exactly me. What are you doing here?" She'd called from the train station to let Gwen know she was on her way back. She was happier to see him than she could have expected to be.

"I'm picking you up and taking you home."

"And what is it you think you see under this skin?"

"I see passion pulling at you." He took her arm and she was surprised.

"Well, that's easy," she said.

"I'm not finished," he said. "I see confusion, too: a divided self, a self deciding whether or not it wants to know its Self."

"That will take me all night to figure out. What you just said. What is it you just said, exactly?"

It was hard not to inhale him. He smelled of heather much of the time, and leather and wood. Eleanor felt soft, walking next to him.

He had no sense of entitlement, and yet the world was his place. When he was around, the world seemed a little more delightful in a nothing-matters-much sort of way, and there was a sound in the air, or maybe the absence of a hollow buzz. She thought she heard it for the first time the first day she went for a walk on the moors. Or maybe it wasn't Mead at all, maybe it was a sound from inside her.

She laughed to herself and he looked her way. "I think the strangest thoughts in this place," she said.

She liked the look of his hand as he carried her small bag. As they walked, she moved just a fraction closer to him.

"So what wild thought was it, now?"

She laughed the easiest laugh. A swing that took her so high she was scared but thrilled, coming down from the swing and feeling it sway to a stop, then twirling the ropes and letting it spin until it spun itself out, and then seeing the world was still there, just the way it always was but better.

"Do you know the Stafford Hotel?" she asked.

"In London. I know it. Is that where he's staying?"

"That's where he was."

"Would he be the reason you left New York?"

"Not at all."

"Methinks you're a scarperer."

"What the heck's a scarperer?"

"One who scarpers. Me, my da. People who know me well call me Scarper. It's someone who runs away from things."

"I'm not running away from anything." Her voice rose. "It doesn't feel like that at all, to me," she said. "How are *you* a scarperer? Hmm? Tell me."

"The car is over here." They walked through the unspectacular train station of Malton.

HE'D WASHED THE CAR AND IT WAS BRIGHTER, THE GREAT lines clearer now. From the back he pulled a thick brown cable sweater and tossed it to her over the roof of the car, suggested she might put it on. The Chanel jacket was tight and not warm enough—the weather was turning frosty—so she threw her jacket in the back and put on his sweater. It was brown and bulky and reached halfway down her thighs, but she liked it.

"You look great in that," he said.

She smiled.

The sleeves of the sweater were long, so she folded them back then rolled down the window. On the floor of the Aston Martin, she found the scarf she thought she'd lost and she wrapped it around her neck many times, tilted the seat back, and watched the sky fly by.

After a while, Eleanor checked her phone. Gladys had texted that now Bergdorf Goodman was also making an offer that would come through in the next couple of days. Eleanor felt satisfied. A lifetime of work had come to this moment with English farmland flying by outside the window, her stocking feet up on the dashboard, her skirt hiked up, and his big brown sweater: something was perfect.

Tabitha had sent a text saying, *Either you've dropped your phone in the toilet of a London pub or it's been stolen by bandits in Sherwood Forest. Either way, you must let me know you're fine. Send homing pigeons.*

Eleanor wrote them back, then turned off the phone. She wasn't ready to head back to New York and was grateful to have a task that kept her tied to Trent Hall. Emily had sought her out, insisted on the importance of finding letters hidden inside a bookshelf in the house. Though it worried Eleanor some, to follow the promptings of an odd woman or ghost, she was going to try to find them. It was all there was left to do, and then it would be time to go.

"Can I ask you something serious?" she said.

"Ask whatever you like."

"I just need a little clarification about something."

"Shoot," he said.

"I've seen a woman a few times, in the house and on the moors."

"You said that. The woman you were chasing that first day."

"Right, her. And some kids, too, and not just outside but in the house, and they don't seem exactly current . . ."

"You think you're seeing ghosts?"

Eleanor nodded.

"You'd not be the first to encounter, to wonder . . ." He looked at her, brought his eyes back to the road, then looked at her again. "I think I can explain a bit of it to you. If you want me to."

"I definitely do want you to."

"It's something like this." She appreciated his hesitation. "Ghosts are a bit last century, fundamentally, but there are things about this place that might make sense of them."

He looked at her, checked to make sure it was all right to

continue in this territory. "It's a fact that things don't decompose in a quite normal way on the moors. Take the peat moss that makes up much of this place: it's rich because it's still living. The stuff that's in it hasn't died all the way. You understand that?"

"I can imagine."

"So consider how long it might take. Whether it were possible, I mean, that in some way these ghosts some people see, maybe what you've seen, are the not-yet-dead spirits hovering, because the body itself isn't altogether decomposed."

Both her eyebrows lifted as high as they ever had.

She was glad to be back with Mead, she realized. It was partly that she loved the sound of his voice and the way he answered what she asked, took her seriously, had so much new to offer in exchange. But it was more than that. As she sat beside him in the car she felt buoyant in her body, as if he'd walked up and taken his place on the other end of her teeter-totter, his weight lifting her up until both their feet were just off the ground, and the beam held in perfect balance.

"Anything left to rot in a boggy place does not ever altogether decompose, so there is living matter still and one wonders if spirit might linger, close by."

"Honestly?" Her foot began to tap anxiously on the dash. "Are you serious?"

"It's a serious subject you bring up."

"There's a physical explanation for ghosts?"

"I think there might be."

"But she's not partly decomposed. She's intact and young and pretty, and the other two are children." As Mead believed her, tried to make sense of what she had seen, the walls against believing collapsed internally and she was left with being a girl who'd walked with a ghost, talked with a ghost, touched one's body, and watched it die.

Anxious with the stirring inside, she changed the subject. "Would you mind if we pulled off the road soon? Stopped for a bit? I've been craving chocolate cake. I can't explain."

"No need ever to explain a craving, least not to me. There are dozens of places with chocolate cake." He smiled.

Soon he turned off the highway. "I didn't mean to upset you with all this. I know it's tricky. I've no idea what you've been seeing, but if you'd like, you can trust me."

❦

THE CAFÉ WAS EMPTY. IT WAS AFTER LUNCH AND before tea.

The waitress brought menus.

"I'll have a glass of red wine and the chocolate cake, please," she said.

"And I'll have some of the apple and cheese pie," he said.

"It's almost more disturbing that you believe me, that you take it seriously, what I think I've seen. I'd rather hear there's a crazy old woman that wanders in and out of the house sometimes."

"You know," he continued, "stories of ghosts are legion in this part of the country. More than anywhere in the world, I'd venture to say. Alice thought Trent Hall was the site of the real-life Catherine and Heathcliff story, and she had things she thought she'd seen, I think, though she didn't confide in me."

"Gwen said something like that. But what does that mean?"

"Well, partly it simply means that Brontë based the book on Trent Hall, or someone in it. I don't really know, but I guess it suggests that."

Eleanor was watching him talk and missing some of what he said. She was studying his face for the Scotsman and the Latina woman in it. His eyes were emerald green and almost too big for a man. She didn't think she'd ever seen a man with eyes so green. She wondered what kind of a gene turned eyes such a deep dark green. His hair was black and curly, but in the light she saw the undertone of red. From Viking ancestors, maybe. His eyebrows were thick and went in different directions. A metro man would have plucked them, but she liked them the way they were. His hands were beautiful.

He was saying that a writer might open a door onto a make-believe world and describe it. Or maybe she would describe something real, something she has known, something she feels. Something she already feels. "That's the thing about Emily Brontë," he went on, "readers then and scholars now have puzzled over how she could write about such a passionate love without ever having had one."

"Maybe she did have one."

"Anything's possible, I suppose, but she's considered a dyed-in-the-wool spinster."

Eleanor recalled the odd wool of Emily's dress. A chill ran through her and she felt suddenly cross. "What difference does all this make, really? I don't get it. What does it matter if Catherine and Heathcliff were real or what Emily based a story on?" Her voice was strident. "And what does it have to do with me?" Eleanor spilled her wine and it ran across the table.

"Shit." She looked for something to wipe it up. Her breath was shallow. There were no napkins and it kept running. It ran onto the sweater and she leaned forward and used it to stop the spill, then took it off. Itchy with irritation, she didn't like him now. It was too much information.

With the sweater off she looked lean and bare in her tank top. Shivering, with their lips blue, the children could swim at the waterfall because they were already dead as ghosts, she thought. She looked at Mead, stood up, and left his damp sweater on the seat. "I'm sorry about your sweater. I'm just going to walk around. I'll be back." She headed quickly out the front door onto the street, where storefront lights were coming on and everything smelled like Christmas. The cold ached on her skin.

There was a general store. The bell above the shop door rang. Behind a counter the shopkeeper perched on a stool.

"Can I help you?"

"I'm looking for a sweater of some kind."

"You must be freezing with nothing on out there."

"Not yet."

"Well, let's get you dressed," the shopkeeper said and went around the counter toward the back of the store.

"I have a man's extra-large and a small left," she apologized. The sweater she held was wool, crewneck, and a heathered gray. "Or these, but they're expensive cashmere."

"Do you have the cashmere in a man's extra-large? I'll take that." Eleanor pulled it on over her head and rolled up the sleeves. "It's warm, it's perfect." She paid for the sweater.

On her way out of the store she noticed a porcelain plate with a familiar profile, brown hair in a smooth bun, a handsome face with pale—almost pale blue—skin.

"Who is that?"

"It's Emily Brontë."

"I thought so, but it's not a great likeness." Eleanor stepped close to a lamp and looked at the cameo on her ring, gave a small wave to the woman inside the shop, headed out and down the street.

Mead was finishing his apple and cheese pie.

She slid in right beside him in the booth.

"I was about to go after you. Where did you get the sweater?" he asked calmly.

She slumped low in the seat. "Next door. Sorry about yours. This one's for you."

"It's just wine. It'll wash out." He leaned forward on his elbows and turned to face her.

"You know the woman I saw," she said, "she was Emily Brontë."

He listened intently.

"It's not true what you say, what they say, about her. I know. I've seen her, I've sat with her, and she's told me. Frankly, I haven't been sure, but"—she laughed—"I saw this silly plate next door. I guess you know it, the painting of her profile, and it's her. It's the woman I sit and talk with."

Mead's face was intensely serious and he suggested they go.

Outside walking, he started, "Well, first you have to know it's a gift, if you've seen what it seems you've seen. If you think of it like facets in a diamond and from each of them there's a view on a world. Right?"

"Okay."

"And maybe caught between the space where light moves through the prism, maybe there are other ways of seeing, other things to see, or, try it this way . . ." He moved his hands as he talked as they walked along on the charming street. "If we assume a continuous range of energy, a continuum"—he was clearly enthused with the subject—"beyond what we commonly understand about space and time, and that it's perception itself that cuts into it, slices it and freezes it, and makes things concrete. Makes it seem real. Something we hold on to as real. That we agree about, between us. We learn to agree about what we see and what we don't see."

"And what we don't *say* we see," she said.

He walked close to her. "I think seeing depends on a lot of things," he said.

"Like?"

"How open the mind, how willing the heart." He paused for a while. "Moisture in the air. If it's anything like a hologram, there has to be moisture in the air."

"If it's moisture they need," Eleanor broke in, "then New York in the summer must be teeming."

"Maybe a bit of quiet is also necessary, but I can tell you what Emily wrote. At one point Catherine says, 'Heaven did not seem to be my home;/ and I broke my heart with weeping to come back to earth;/ and the angels were so angry that they flung me out / into the middle of the heath / on the top of Wuthering Heights; / where I woke sobbing for joy.' "

Eleanor asked him to recite it again and a long quiet settled in between them as she absorbed what Emily had written.

"She knew she'd come back to the moors," Eleanor said.

Mead looked away. "Let's get back on the road and get home."

"I like it when you call it *home*," she said.

With his face turned away, he brusquely wiped a few tears from his face. She wanted to know what had moved him, but didn't know what to ask. She thought of what Jane had said about Mead's quest for his own Catherine, then also what it must be like to speak of ghosts with Alice so recently gone, the hope he might have of seeing her again. She wondered if Alice had ever met the ghost of Emily.

They crossed over a bridge to where the car was parked on the road. Mead opened the car door for her and went around to his side. He rolled up both windows and turned the key.

"What was it like to grow up here?" she asked him.

Mead rolled up the sleeves of his blue and green plaid flannel shirt, ran his fingers through his thick hair, shook it off the back of his neck, and faced her with a boyish smile. She'd never before seen him fuss or arrange himself.

"I grew up around Cambridge," he started. "We came here for weekends sometimes, parts of summer and most holidays. Alice was old-fashioned, so I wore short pants till I was seven. Gwen fought her on it, but Alice tended to win. There's not much to tell, really. We had a flat near her college and she thought I'd grow up to be a scholar, but it wasn't in my blood exactly. I mean, I was good at school." He laughed a nervous laugh. "But I liked the moors, the wild, inscrutable sheep, the enigmatic gaze of a Yorkshire cow, the slosh and slumber of a good pig. I like the quiet, so I can listen to things and hear myself think." He knocked the shift into first gear and moved slowly away from the town. "It's not for everyone."

Mead took back roads, not the highway. The road dipped suddenly and there was again landscape that made her gasp. The black bark of the trees against the wet green land. Along the road were thatched-roof houses that looked like hobbit towns from the distance. The road would wind, whipping like a snake, the curves so tight, with high hedges on either side.

"But you get to know different things living here. See that crimson sea out there." There was a field of autumn grass. "The puffs of white that look like flowers . . . that's cotton grass. You'll see a whole field of it, all white like flowers in the summer, lots of Yorkshire's covered with cotton grass. Where there's heather, the peat is less than five feet deep, but where there's cotton grass, it's sometimes as deep as twenty feet underneath, and that's the richest, liveliest peat. It's like no other place on earth. I'm pretty sure of it."

"You've also got good wool and good cheese," she added, lightly.

"'Tis the depth of it, the stuff in the peat way down there that never fully . . ." He hesitated.

"Go on, say it again. It never decomposes."

"There you are." He slapped his hand on the leather-covered steering wheel. "Only lived 'ere a wee while and already you're larnin'."

As a little girl she would put her head out the window and feel the cold wind on her face. Now, she reached out her hand.

"There's a place I'd like to take you, if you'd be willing."

She was curious, but it was late. "Could we do it another time?"

"Definitely for another day." He smiled her way.

There were many places she could imagine going with Mead, but what she wanted, more than anything, was to find the letters. Emily's face was the face carved on her ring. The letters were real and they would tell her something.

The road was so narrow that Mead had to pull over for trucks and large cars to pass. Eleanor closed her eyes and he talked about his education, friends who had moved to the States or were having experiences on the Continent, but he thought they'd be back, once they wanted to settle down.

She asked if he were looking to settle down and he didn't make a sound.

"Tell me about being a scarperer," she said. "What heart did you break and leave behind?"

"Oh, I left broken pieces behind, I guess, never a dramatic story, but some would say too many. Still, it's not so much someone else's heart I broke, but a tendency to break my own in small ways."

Her eyes wanted to open, but she was sleepy.

"Nothing dark and dangerous. Just an internal scarperin' away."

Before long she was dreaming and his words were like the ocean ebbing, flowing toward her and then away. She dreamed of a little boy with a dirty face picking through rubble and finding pieces of broken ruby. His eyes wide, he'd pick up the jewels one by one, and kiss each of them.

The young crescent moon was high in the sky by the time

she recognized certain trees and stones along the road. She recognized the feel of the long drive up to Trent Hall, but it was the crunch of gravel that she liked most. Mead came to a stop and turned off the engine.

"There's no wind," she said. "It's so quiet."

Mead opened his door and the inside light came on but neither of them moved to get out of the car.

"Does cotton grass grow where the graves are, with the two crosses?" She bit through her lip and let out a yelp. She licked the tenderness where her bite had drawn a drop of blood.

"Here, let me get that." He leaned across the stick shift to wipe the second drop of blood away with his finger. With one drop gone, another came. He kissed her. She pressed her hand against his chest to stop him. He looked down at her lip, and she took her hand down. Another drop emerged, and he kissed her again.

IN THE STUDY UNDER THE STAIRS, SHE PUSHED AGAINST bookshelves, because there might be a false wall. The bookshelves were emptied, so the books that had been there were in boxes. Eleanor could not recall whether Emily had said it was inside, behind, or near a bookshelf, nor even what shape or kind of thing it was she was looking for as she rummaged about. She knew they were letters but letters wrapped in cloth, in a box, buried in the plaster?

She opened one of the boxes stacked in the corner of the study. She hadn't turned on the lights, because she was hiding. If anyone found her, she didn't know what she'd explain. The drapes on the two sets of French windows were opened just a crack to let in a little gray daylight, and she moved quietly.

Each book had a quality of its own. The newer ones had their original dust jackets intact, but the old ones were the treasures: bound with leather or stout cloth and stamped with a gold design or embossed. They were fantastic, and she felt giggles of delight as she sat in the dark corner and pulled them out, one after another. All tones and hues of cloth stamped gold with a design that suggested the story inside: a princess and dragon, a grinning demon, a fat and hungry man. Some had a coat of arms or an Arts and Crafts design, all more evocative than any jacket she'd ever seen, but some pages were brittle, the bindings soft and pliable. She could see why Mead was building a library with glass doors to protect these valuable things. There were piles of books around her, but she'd found no box of letters.

Then Eleanor remembered that Emily had said a children's sitting room. While many of the rooms seemed like sitting rooms, none of them were children's sitting rooms. The children's bookcase would be upstairs, not downstairs where adults entertained.

From the landing halfway up the stairs into the hall to Alice's bedroom, someone had hung a bright floral drape.

There were peacocks and cranes on the sea blue background, orange rosebuds about to bloom. Pulling the drape aside, she saw Alice's room had been emptied. The bed had been stripped and the few pieces of furniture were covered.

With her sleeves rolled up and her hair in a bun, she started up the short flight of stairs that led from the landing to another stairway and then to a hall that was clearly closed off and had been for a long time. There were no bulbs in the sconces on the walls. Out from under the first door, she saw a thread of pale light. Inside that room there was a long uncurtained window and a bare twin bed frame with a painted headboard.

There was something about the room that brought back an unexpected memory of her mother standing inside the open door of a taxi. Her mother was on her way to the airport, that last morning, and she stopped, before climbing in, to wave good-bye. Miles had been standing behind Eleanor, and Tabitha was there, urging her to hurry. They'd be late for the game. Eleanor's mother was going to miss their final basketball game, and Eleanor was cross with her. Her mother in a white cotton blouse with the collar turned up, a beige trench coat tied tight at her waist, her blond hair curling out from under the rim of her hat. Now, Eleanor remembered this image, for the first time. She remembered how pretty she thought her mother was that day, and how much she wanted that pretty being to be at her game. Instead of waving back, Eleanor had turned away, ignored her mother's hopeful wave.

She'd turned away, because her mother seemed excited to be going.

There was no bookshelf in the room. She went back into the hall and there was enough light, with that bedroom door open, for her to see a set of French doors painted a pale turquoise blue at the end of the hallway. She had to kick one door for it to open. The furniture was draped with sheets of muslin. The room was large and oddly shaped. It was almost an octagon, but not exactly. It was wide where the French doors opened into it and had seven pockets or bays, some with and some without windows, and then it narrowed at the far end with one long, sheer-curtained window. From it, she looked out over a meadow with white tufts of cotton grass.

Standing to the right of the window she could see, in the near distance, the broken walls and towers of Trent Abbey. Medieval nuns had stayed silent, cooked simple meals, and prayed there, centuries before. From this height, more than three stories up, Eleanor could see almost everything. Beyond the pink and yellow stones of the abbey, she saw the cliff she'd walked down and the ledge where Emily had sat, then where the land fell away sharply, the smooth spread of deep green rolling hills below and the stand of trees inside which was the pond.

She snapped one sheet and flung it aside. There was an orange corduroy chair big enough for two. Under more sheets, there was a daybed and a long narrow couch. She found a painted closet with an old wood dollhouse on its side, a naked set of dolls, and a small pink leather suitcase filled with clothes for them.

Casually, she turned her head to the empty fireplace. Beside it there was a child-size bookcase. On the bottom shelf were books stacked one on top of another, in three piles. She blew off a layer of dust and read through titles: *Impunity Jane*, *The Railway Children*, *Five Children and It*. All well-worn copies. *Alice's Adventures in Wonderland & Through the Looking-Glass*. Eleanor sank into the big chair with *Alice*, reached out and grabbed *Karoleena's Red Coat*, sat with them in her lap.

Eleanor's mother had read to her from the time she was tiny. Eleanor hadn't wanted to give it up, but her friends' mothers didn't read to them before bed, so she asked her mother if it was all right that they stop, though sometimes they sat together in a chair and Eleanor read aloud to her instead.

She drifted in and out of the books on her lap, looked at pictures and read stray paragraphs. She slipped off the chair onto the smooth wood floor. There was a foot width of old stone that ran around the edge of the room and framed the fireplace. She knelt on the cold stone and tried to open one of the latches on a cupboard door at the base of the bookshelf, but it was rusted shut. She took her barrette from her hair and worked the latch until it opened.

Inside were two cardboard boxes someone had covered in Liberty print paper, and another small, very old wood one.

She pulled them out and laid them on the floor, then worked to open the other cupboards, but those were empty. She stuck her head inside and looked around for secret doors, but there were none.

She looked carefully through the two boxes, found Alice's little girl diary. She found marbles, school report cards, a photograph of Alice as a little girl standing in the courtyard of Trent Hall, in a dress with a frilly petticoat peeking out, white gloves, and matte leather Mary Janes.

In the other box, there were more of Alice's souvenirs from childhood. There was a good pastel picture, which Alice had drawn and signed, of her little sister Anne with her legs draped over the arm of a chair. In the old wood box, there were postcards written back and forth between Alice and her mother while Alice was staying with a family in the South of France for the summer.

From the postcards, Eleanor got a glimpse of what her own mother, little Anne, had done that summer. She'd raced around with her best friend, a little boy whom Mrs. Sutton called "Annie's shadow." Mrs. Sutton described how mischievous they'd been, how they'd carried things from the house to set up a summer home for themselves in a corner of the ruined abbey with squirrels and birds and ghosts of nuns to keep them company. *Annie has got your father to wrap velvet around the rough ropes of the old swing on the hill.* It was gratifying to read. Eleanor could picture it now, every part of it, as if a fine-lined sketch were being filled in, fleshed out, and washed with watercolors.

Eleanor sank back on her heels, leaned against the big chair, and was flooded with locked-away memories of her parents at home: how good they were to each other, how easily they laughed together—watching films, sharing stories, the flush of joy in their faces when they dressed for nights on the town with her mother in a mink jacket, high heels, and blushed cheeks and lips, her father in a tuxedo.

Small things crashed against each other in Eleanor's mind. Here to find letters Emily Brontë insisted on her finding, deep down she had hoped she'd find something to make sense of her own life, her mother leaving home and never returning. Or the way her father had changed so drastically. She remembered how patiently she'd waited for him to return to himself again, but something was broken irreparably inside him and he never did. Still Eleanor had made the best of things. Alone at eighteen she got through his funeral, packed up the apartment where they'd lived, made a home of her own, and got busy washing old wool and making quirky clothing.

Now, she peered into the last empty cupboard. Country air had made her keenly aware of the rhythms of vigor, appetite, and exhaustion. She started to pack things up again and put them in their place. She lifted the wood box and the base of it unhinged. Kneeling, she turned it upside down and saw that the bottom slid out and there was a hidden compartment with a small knob she could take hold of, and her breath caught in her chest as she slid that piece to the side. Inside was a thick package of papers tied with a black satin ribbon.

Eleanor hurriedly put everything back the way she'd found it. With the strange package of papers in hand, she felt an urge to escape the room. She'd found the treasure from this scavenger hunt with clues from a ghost on the moors.

In the hall, Gwen's voice startled her. "Is that you, Eleanor? Are you busy up there?"

The fine, common sound of Gwen in the hall at the base of the stairs.

"I thought you were gone somewhere," Eleanor said as she stepped into the light on the landing.

"I'm just back and just going again. Is everything all right?"

"Perfect." She headed down the stairs. "I was looking to see if I could see the abbey from that last room at the end of the hall."

"My word, that room must be dusty."

"Not really." Her voice too high.

"And there's no light in that hallway." Their sentences crossed each other's.

"I opened windows. Was that my mother's old room?"

"It was, indeed. It was sort of the children's playroom." Gwen had started up the stairs, to meet Eleanor halfway, then turned and joined her and they walked back down.

"Which room was Mead's room?" Eleanor asked.

Now Mead had an apartment in the carriage house. Though Eleanor had never been in it, she'd heard it had an upstairs with two bedrooms and a living room, kitchen, and dining room downstairs. Gwen had moved out of the bedroom she and Alice had shared when they stayed at Trent Hall and was in the old gardener's cottage.

"When I get back I'll show you. You would have gone right past it up there, but all the furniture's in a muddle. I'll be sure to show you." Gwen had a suitcase by the front door. "I filled the fridge, so have at it, won't you?" Gwen's genuinely pleasant smile. "Everything's gone by so fast," she said, shaking her head and looking around at the half-emptied rooms. "You must think this would make a dreadful home, but it's not hard to make cozy. In other times, it has been." She kissed her cheek. "I've got to be off. Do take care of yourself, and promise not to be gone when I get back."

"I think I can promise that . . . ," Eleanor said.

Eleanor walked her to the door and waved and watched and kept waving until the car passed through the gate in the wall.

Standing on the stones outside the front door, Eleanor saw the lights on in the barn where Mead was working with Tilda and Granley. Gwen was gone and would come back soon. The house and all that came with it seemed light and bearable. The winter holidays were coming and Eleanor had an image of the house alive with holly strung on the banister and a Christmas tree near the window in the large living room. Standing alone on the doorstep, it seemed possible that the house could be hers.

The letters gripped in one hand, she went into the living room and sank into a chair. She flicked on a light. As if they were letters from a lover, she wanted to savor whatever lay hidden inside the bundle of papers. She began.

Between two sheets of fragile paper, there was a drawing folded in four. It was a pencil sketch of a woman sitting against the base of a tree and beneath the picture an inscription read, *Here, where courage and passion reigned over the most commonsense and agreed-upon virtues, here where I loved thee, where I found what is truest in my soul and held in thine eyes, myself replete. Know now and for all eternity, I am yours, my sweet Emily.*

The drawing was not perfect, but it was clearly a portrait of the woman Eleanor had come to know on the moors. Right down to the wool dress Emily wore. The dark pencil lines were shaded with blushes of watercolor, which accented the tree's broad canopy, the heather in the distance, a hint of yellow earth, and the flush of joy in Emily's cheeks.

It was a pile of letters. The paper was thin and dry and some were rumpled as if they'd been tossed away. There were no envelopes, but they were ordered by date, and it seemed someone had arranged them, taken good care of them. They were letters from a man named Robert Macaulay.

Dear Sudden Surprise, the first one began. *Just days before I set upon the journey which brought me to find you, I heard a whispering. I knew not whence the whispers came, believed, at first, it to be the wind whistling in the way it can; or whales in the deep distant ocean off the coast of our land speaking to one another in that high-pitched unheard language they have; but the longer I listened the more I was sure that the whisper was meant for me; whether the wind, or the whales, or God himself (though I am not a man God speaks to commonly), the whisper spoke to me and told me, plainly, to begin a walking holiday, a pilgrimage toward I knew not what, but I would walk until I knew I'd found that which I'd set out to find, to discover, to be led toward, a kind of oasis in this world of doubt and fear, an answer to my soul's longing . . .*

Taken aback with feeling, Eleanor dropped the letter to the table. Her heart beat fiercely and her breath was held in abeyance as she picked up the next note and read.

My Fearless Beloved, it began. The bold strokes of his handwriting suggested urgency and zeal. *I shall not be leaving. Have arranged with the inn to stay on in these two rooms for as long as I might, and believe that there is no greater pleasure for me than to spend the rest of my lifetime waiting for the sound of you, then the fragrance you carry all about you, then the feel of your lips on mine, and so we will begin again, tomorrow. I have only to make it through this night.*

You speak of these moors as your one great companion, and I dare to hope, then even to believe, that I have become a part of these moors which you see and touch and allow to flow inside your being, so deeply.

It takes courage, you say, courage and then something more than courage to withstand the passion this land can inspire; and I am a convert, converted by the vigor inside you, by the sublime spirit in the tenderness of your corporality. You are the most courageous being and I the most fortunate man this earth can ever have known. I rush to sleep now, to hasten the dawn.

Tucked between the letters was a tiny book written in an immaculate hand. It was a diary, some thirty pages long and just a few inches square, with handwriting so precise it was like a printed manuscript in miniature. In the first pages of the diary, written months before the notes from Robert began, Emily wrote, *My brother Branwell storms, drunk and sick with love turned rancid; it is all I can do to keep my face above the drowning water of passion he feels and the way he pulls at me, pulling me down like a child fallen from overboard in this wild river raging beneath the placidity of our quiet home, with Father merely watching.*

Some few pages later, the writer wrote, *It is Queen Victoria's birthday and in celebration I have arranged for a respite away from here where I can write in peace on the other side of the Pennines, at dear Julia Enswell's home.*

Eleanor was well through the looking glass.

Eleanor took another and then another deep breath and went back to read the diary. Emily wrote about the moors, about coming to trust and know herself, and then about a man she met while walking up the hill to her favorite tree with, as she put it, *mangled branches so full of leaves that to sit beneath it was like sitting in the shade of a kind mother's watchful gaze.*

Emily described the man named Robert Macaulay.

Come this warm summer, Robert set off on a walking tour as was Wordsworth's wont, but Robert is a gentleman farmer, no poet, he, no thoughts of fancy and love in his head, till the late evening when he found me. We sat together for hours and he managed to bring laughter from inside, this strange new man I feel I have known since before I was born, this strapping man with dark curled hair and deep blue eyes.

He left his home in the Outer Hebrides, for a whisper that maybe spoke my own name before he knew enough to recognize it; perhaps God had a plan we are too mired in sleep to know, but I feel called awake now and though I have asked my heath and the cliffs above the sea for guidance and some word clearly spoken to affirm what I feel, I feel carried. I believe I have been carried toward my destiny and am compelled to accept it willingly.

And on the next page Emily wrote,

Heartbreak! I am called home to Haworth, to care, as I am accustomed to care, for my brother Branwell as he twists and turns in a nightmare of many agonies. Robert will head home.

I cannot go with him. I ran fleeing from my responsibilities and here in the Enswells' home I am resolved to choose what I believe is right, to heal my brother, and if God sees fit, once he is healed, to find my way home to where I know I belong. The Enswells have kept this room for me and now also my secret.

Eleanor's eyes hurt and she was overwrought from the transport to another time. There was not enough light in the room in the afternoon and even that light was fading. She closed the diary and began to tie the letters together, then picked up the last letter from Robert, a short note that read,

The breathtaking sight of you I shall ne'er forget but always carry. Your lovely head bowed in prayer to your earth as you walked slowly toward me until that first instant, when you glanced up and I could see you could not see me, quite, but I saw you for the low sun on your face and also in your bright eyes. You saw the silhouette of me, you say, and were terrified, believing you might be seeing God, my precious and credulous love. I will wait in the Hebrides and will ever be yours, Robert Macaulay.

It was the summer of 1845, just months before Brontë started to write her one novel, *Wuthering Heights.*

Eleanor pushed away from the table and gathered the drawing, the tiny diary, and the letters into a pile, grabbed the ribbon, and went into the hall. The bank of French windows had a view into the courtyard and she saw Mead shaking out his raincoat and heading toward the house.

Her intestines were twisted like a fist till she thought she'd die of the weight of it, and she found herself unable to catch her breath. She tiptoed down the hall, ran up the front stairs, around the landing, and down the hall to her bedroom.

Her tears tasted like salt and her bones felt cold even under the covers. The tree was scraping the window and she picked up *Wuthering Heights* and started to read from the beginning again.

Reading it was different this time. Again, she recognized the room in which she was living. She recognized the cadence of the Emily she'd known, in the writing. She got to the scene where Catherine is dying and cried as she read Heathcliff and Catherine's words.

> "I have not one word of comfort. You deserve this. You have killed yourself. Yes, you may kiss me, and cry; and wring out my kisses and tears: they'll blight you—they'll damn you. You loved me—then what *right* had you to leave me? . . ."
>
> "Let me alone. Let me alone," sobbed Catherine. "If I've done wrong, I'm dying for it. It is enough! You left me too: but I won't upbraid you! I forgive you. Forgive me!"
>
> "It is hard to forgive, and to look at those eyes, and feel those wasted hands," he answered. "Kiss me again; and

don't let me see your eyes! I forgive what you have done to me. I love *my* murderer—but *yours*! How can I?"

Emily was an unmarried woman who'd never been in love, so it said, in so many words, in the introduction to Emily's novel, *Wuthering Heights*. The passion in Emily's novel, the scholar wrote, was based on her inviolable love of God, and readers of the time, it went on to say, were shocked by the cruel and the malicious in *Wuthering Heights*, couldn't fathom how a virgin spinster could be behind such writing.

They hadn't read what Eleanor had read. Emily had been in love. Robert was her promise and life, but her conscience had pulled at her, pulled her home to Haworth to care for Branwell. Torn between two men.

Like a faint sense of the sun before it would rise, it dawned on Eleanor what kind of difference the right and wrong choice might make, in loving.

Branwell died in September and Emily in December 1848. But Robert . . . Eleanor wondered if Emily had ever gone to find him.

TILDA ALWAYS KEPT THE PITCHER IN ELEANOR'S SMALL room filled with clean, cold water. Eleanor poured some into the large bowl and splashed her face. It was late in the evening and she was hungry. Going down the tight back stairwell, her right shoulder bumped the wall and shook the sconce, whose light flickered, and she had the feeling that she had been bumping into that same wall for decades, even centuries, and it brought a sense of faith and hope. Simple things that encouraged her. She continued down the stairs and saw Mead at the kitchen table reading his pink newspaper.

"You've been inside all day," he said.

"I've just come down to make a sandwich. Were you out walking?" she asked.

It sounded bewilderingly like a married couple's everyday exchange. She tried to find something sassy to say, but it wouldn't come. The kiss he'd given her in the car had disoriented her completely.

"I didn't go out today, no," he said, "but the library's nearly finished."

They'd each spent the whole day at home. It was evening and hours stretched before them. She took bread from the bin and slathered it with mayonnaise. The kitchen seemed to her, for the first time, like a common kitchen, a place for making cheddar cheese and tomato sandwiches.

He seemed to sense she was uneasy. "Why don't I open some wine?"

"That'd be great."

Mead put down the paper. "I'll go to the cellar and grab a good bottle." She thought he might kiss her again, but he headed out the door and she was glad.

It was hard not to imagine that Mead might be able to make sense of a lot of things. He had already begun to understand about the woman she'd seen on the moors, and he might be able to make sense of the letters she'd found. Knowing Haworth and how much was invested in the accepted story of the Brontës, she wasn't at all sure she should say something, but neither could she fathom holding on to it all by herself.

Rattling in her mind were thoughts about Emily and her sad choice and the way she died. She couldn't shake the thought that her mother had died, had died young, but she didn't know of any choice she'd faced, except the little boy her grandmother had called her mother's shadow. And Alice had maybe escaped all this, by wearing the ring, in loving Gwen, in loving Gwen well, in staying close to home. Eleanor didn't know how to add it up, what it all meant. Emily had driven her toward the letters without explaining. If there was a curse, Eleanor feared she was somehow a part of it. She had tears in her eyes when Mead came in.

"Hey, what's the trouble?"

He put the bottle of wine on the table and walked around behind her chair. He put his hand on her neck like a friend might, though the feeling he pulled inside was nothing like the feeling a friend might. The knot in her hair loosened and Mead said a swift sorry as he took the loose hair he'd undone and pulled it into a ponytail, tried to help with a bun, as she reached back and his hand was on her hand and she showed him how she twisted it and knotted it in one swift move. He leaned toward her, over the back of the chair, over her shoulder, and he kissed her cheek and tasted what was left of the tears.

He walked around to the other side and sat across from her.

"Tell me," he said. He said it so kindly, so simply, so completely without guile. He opened the wine. Poured two glasses, moved slowly and quietly enough not to interrupt her at all.

Her words tumbled out. "Today, I wandered through that closed-up part of the house, and I saw my mother's room up there. I saw the room she grew up in. Have you seen it? Was it there when you were small, just frozen in time like that?"

He bobbed his head back and forth to say "more or less." He took a great swallow of the rich red wine.

She didn't know how to continue. "I've been reading some letters my mother wrote to my father and there was one she wrote the year before I was born. She wrote to ask him to promise to come back here with her. Here to Yorkshire. She said it a bunch of different ways, but it was the same idea, she just kept asking him to promise he'd come back with her, but even more that he wouldn't let her come back alone."

"Did he answer?"

She shook her head. "I don't think he ever came, but I know she came back alone. At least that once."

Mead's eyes held hers with compassion.

"It seemed like she wanted my father to leave his print on this place. To mark it, make it not just hers but his, too." She stopped and shook her head as if she were trying to shake sense into it. How crazy would it be to tell him she was afraid of a curse?

Mead refilled their glasses and offered her some water to drink, because he knew she liked drinking water.

"Did you know she died here in a car crash?" she asked.

"I didn't know exactly that. I knew she died here. I remember her a bit."

"Shit. I never even thought of that. You knew her." Wispy dismay. "Now, I am spinning."

"I shouldn't have said that."

"No, it's okay." She looked at his green eyes, his dark hair with hints of red Viking underneath, and she remembered how complex it was where he'd come from, who he was, who he might feel himself to be.

"It's great that you knew her," she said.

"I wish I could say I knew her. I just barely remember . . ."

"I didn't even know my mother was coming here. That's kind of weird, I think, right?" Her brain felt heavy with thinking and her body was tired and she realized how long she'd been carrying the weight of mystery around, unasked and unanswered, inside her.

She felt Mead's presence, more conspicuous than ever before.

He could carry some of the weight of it. He already did. He had dazzling eyes and there was something arresting in the way he listened to her, carefully, spoke sparingly, and paid attention to little things. Small things. Important things.

He pushed away from the table, came around again to her, and took her face between his hands and kissed her lips. Deliberately and passionately he kissed her and she felt herself unwinding, disintegrating, and coming back together all at the same time. He kissed her again, this time lightly.

"Take a bite of your sandwich," he said, and she did. The grainy bread and cheese. He sat down across from her.

"Maybe you know more about all this than I do," she said.

"I don't think I do. I know a thing or two, but not more than you."

She sighed. "I want to tell you about something I found."

"Should I be worried?" he asked.

"I don't think so."

"But you're not sure."

"No, I am sure. Up in that strange part of the house. I was looking because Emily told me she'd hidden letters somewhere in this house. That it was important that I find them. And I did. It was a fluke that I found them, but they were in a little box. They were handwritten letters to Emily from a man named Robert Macaulay." Her eyes were glassy as she looked into his.

"I can honestly say you've got my full attention."

"This man named Robert Macaulay walked here, to Yorkshire, from the Outer Hebrides."

Mead's eyebrows rose and fell.

"He walked all the way to the moors, close by here, close to Trent Hall, and out there, by accident one day, he ran into Emily Brontë. She was staying here with friends, and she and Robert Macaulay fell in love."

"This was all in the letters?"

"It was. And more." Again she paused. "Robert wrote about setting out and walking to clear his head, to get away from his life and find quiet . . ."

"Ah, he was a scarperer," Mead interjected.

"I don't think so." He didn't seem to be taking it in. "Have you heard this before?"

Solemn, Mead shook his head.

"They had this place they met where they had picnics she brought and they went for walks and then in the evening . . . it's fancy language but it sounds like they made love out there. He stayed at a pub nearby and she was here, at this house."

He reached across the table and took both her hands in his. "I've heard about some of this from Alice. Not facts and not from letters. Don't be troubled, tell me more," he said.

Relieved, she went on. "Emily told me all of this. Everywhere she found me, she urged me to find these letters in the house, and I found them. I can hardly believe I found them. All these years, letters from him and a diary of hers, a drawing of Emily that he did . . ."

Mead rubbed the side of his face with his hand; there was a burden in what she was telling him.

"Emily's brother, Branwell, was a twisted guy—something wasn't right there. She didn't go off with Robert, because of him. She was scared of lots of things, Emily. But, God, she was passionate. In one letter Robert wrote that she loved like she was dying of it."

Mead was deep in thought. He spoke softly. "I suppose she did die of it."

Eleanor looked up at him with tired eyes.

"You have raw material, Eleanor, real evidence," he said.

Not fully comprehending the weight of this, Eleanor nodded. "Yes, I guess, evidence. She wrote the novel right then, too, in the middle of it all, after she went home to Branwell."

"It would mean a lot, to a lot of people, you know, to know this," Mead said.

"I don't think anyone needs to know." She held his eyes with hers.

"It would become a spectacle." Mead contemplated.

"Emily wanted me to know. No one else has to know," Eleanor said.

His eyes took in the whole of her: spark, ground, wisdom. "Right," he said. "Okay, then . . ."

They both were startled as the kitchen door slammed open and Granley came in, tense and out of breath. "Sorry to bother you, Mead, but Tilda's had a bit of a fright." The old man took off his hat and excused himself to Eleanor.

"What kind of a fright, Granley?"

"She seems to 'ave seen a ghost, she has, and she's unnerved."

Tilda appeared behind him. She was trembling, shaking, and trying to make light of it herself.

"I'm a right idjot," she said, but couldn't stop her teeth chattering. "The wind's bein' its old fool self." She sipped the whisky Granley had poured for her. A wool blanket kept her warm. "That's it, I know it musta been the wind. But she looked at me and wasn't movin', stood there and looked right at me. I feel a fool makin' a fuss this way."

"It's all right, Tild, it's nothing at all. I mean, it's not nothing. I'm sure you saw what you saw . . ."

"Have ye seen 'er?"

He shook his head.

"Ye 'ave seen her."

"I've heard stories," Mead said.

"So she's real."

"I've no idea," he said.

Tilda folded the blanket and placed it on the stool. "Well, I s'pose that's why God gave us whisky, eh?"

THE KITCHEN LIGHTS WERE STILL ON AFTER THEY'D gone. Mead and Granley walked with Tilda back to their place up the stairs, around the back of the stables.

A chill ran through Eleanor when she realized she was alone in the house. Everyone else slept in one of the structures outside the main house. Despite the doors and curtains closing off the rooms that weren't used, the house was stony cold and resoundingly empty.

The kitchen door slammed open and Mead had come back to say, "I'll sleep inside tonight. Just so you know someone's close by."

"Thank you for that," she said. "It's a big house."

"I'll stay in the room across the hall from yours. If you need me for anything at all."

"Okay. I'll see you in the morning." She stepped onto the first stair.

"Right," he said. "Good night, then."

"It is possible I'll get scared in the night . . . ," she said.

"Here's hoping," he said with a stunning cute smile.

AN EDGE OF ELEANOR'S NAIL HAD CHIPPED AND WAS ragged. It snagged the blanket and pulled. With her teeth she tried to file it smooth, but it didn't become smooth. Instead, another part caught between her teeth and ripped down to the quick when she moved it. There was a thin line of blood right at the base. Still the nail was ragged, and now her teeth were set on edge. She curled her thumb into the palm of her hand to keep it from snagging the nightgown, wrapped the blanket like a robe, climbed out of bed, and went to the room across the hall, where she knocked on the door.

It was morning and there was no answer, even after she'd rapped three times. She was hoping that Mead would still be there, but when she cracked open the door he was already gone. It was a pretty guest room with a queen bed dressed in white linen sheets. The walls were painted a slightly grayed orange and the furniture was faintly washed with robin's-egg blue paint. Rows of dark green bindings caught Eleanor's eye.

There were four shelves of paperbacks by a press called Virago. Women writers, every one. To the right of these on the bookshelf there were Brontë works. Cheap paperback copies of *Wuthering Heights*, Charlotte's *Jane Eyre*, Anne's *Tenant of Wildfell Hall*. And there were dozens of books about them: *The Brontë Myth*, *The Brontë Circle*, *The Brontës of Haworth*. Eleanor pulled out a copy of *Wuthering Heights* and one of the studies.

Keeping hold of the wool blanket and the books, with one foot she pushed the big old chair over to the window until it was in the right place. She sat down and curled up in a ball, then opened one of the studies.

An intrepid writer and diarist, Emily seemed to have left no poetry, no letters, no writing at all from her last few years. None had been found and the scholar surmised that either Emily had done something with them or her sister Charlotte had destroyed them.

With private delight, Eleanor imagined that the letters and the diary she'd found had been hidden away to keep Charlotte from finding them. There was a secret Emily had written about, something about the Enswell family at Trent Hall, or about her own family, or both. Now Eleanor was curious about how things had occurred in time, and a picture emerged in her mind.

Emily began writing *Wuthering Heights* in December 1845. Having met Robert just months before, she'd have been filled with the high hope of a sweet love affair when she'd started writing, but then something else must have happened. Apart from having had to make the choice to go home and take care of Branwell, something else had turned the story so desperately dark.

Eleanor dropped the Brontë study to the floor and opened the novel itself to the place she'd left off reading. Her scattered mind held a reassuring image of Mead outside in the barn, still simply building the library. She couldn't hear the brush dipped in varnish smoothing a sheen on the wood, nor the rhythmic whine of the drill making something work, but she knew he was there on the other side of the courtyard, anchoring her.

Determined to finish the novel before she headed out on the moors, she felt an image tugging at her, like a child at his mother's skirt. She kept reading but more images insinuated themselves between the words, so she set down the book and then she remembered.

A dream she'd had in the night. It had to have been a dream. Robert Macaulay, a tall Scotsman with strong limbs, red curls of unruly hair out from under his hat, cheer in his face, and the kindest way about him, walked with Emily on his arm through the seaside town of Whitby. The sun was coming up. Robert and Emily stood in the golden light of the harbor and he turned to her, suggested she choose which of two hands from behind his back. She laughed and tapped one arm and he offered her a small wooden box. Emily's face brightened with delight as she received it, opened it, and pulled out the glistening ring of jet that would grace her hand for just a couple of years and then be passed on for generations. Robert, the tall gentle Scotsman, drew Emily's attention to the carved cameo of her beautiful face, and Emily gasped, tipped onto her toes, stretched up toward him as he leaned down to kiss her, full on the lips and in the bright light of day, that one fine morning.

Eleanor was startled by the vividness of it. Robert's face wasn't clear, but the sense of him was. She picked up the books from the floor and put them back where she'd found them on the shelves. There was a part of the moors she had seen from afar but never been. A high cliff and scarp.

She crossed the hall to her room and dressed for another cold day. In the front hall, she grabbed an overcoat and, moving as if her body were hungry for air, rushed outside, where the sky threatened a storm. It was something Mead had said, something about a writer opening a door onto a real but, to some, invisible world and describing it.

Eleanor went to the mudroom off the kitchen and put on some boots from the collection there.

"You off?" Tilda called to her from the kitchen window.

"Just for a while. Want to get in a walk before it pours."

"Here, take some scones with you." Tilda quickly spread two scones with butter and jam and wrapped them in a paper napkin. She brought them outside to Eleanor.

"Are you feeling better this morning?" Eleanor inquired.

"I am, miss, thank you for asking. A bit of a fuss I made last night."

"Not at all. I'd have done the same." Eleanor thought of saying more, but decided against it.

OUT PAST THE STRAIGHT STONE WALL, ELEANOR PASSED the bending tree and also the tree with the swing and she kept on walking because there was a part of the moor she had seen, but never been. She thought she could remember where it was, from what she'd seen from high on the swing: it was a place with tall boulders and some ragged trees.

Eleanor closed her eyes and imagined if there were ghosts in Manhattan, they were discreet. Amid faithfully recurring Papaya Dogs and pretzel vendors, skyscrapers and siren screams, a ghost would be lost in the shuffle like everyone else and no one would know if nightmares haunted some girl's evening in New York City. If ghosts were there, they would hole up in apartments at the top of stairs and come down only to put out fires set in trash cans on the street.

When, by a boulder, she saw a woman with deep curling

hair, Eleanor's skin contracted with some kind of knowing. Eleanor walked toward her. The woman's knee was bent, with the flat of her foot resting against the slate-gray boulder behind her. Twirling her hair on a finger, she seemed not to notice Eleanor's approach, because her eyes were fixed on a point somewhere below where she stood. An evocative smile shaped her face. She spun her finger around and looped a ringlet of hair, then—barely perceptibly—swayed her hips in a minute, harmonic dance.

Eleanor decided to walk to her right, get to the edge of the rise before moving toward the woman so she could see what it was she was looking at below. At the rim, once she reached it, Eleanor looked down and saw a wild-eyed, dark-skinned man. The young woman was taunting him and he was climbing the crag as fast as he could. He looked right up at Eleanor, not through her but right into her eyes. The young woman danced her wrist and beckoned Eleanor closer.

Real as the wind, the girl's figure curved under her skirts. She wore layers of cotton and at the hem you could count the colors, all shades of brown. She wore a wool shirt and two homespun shawls, one wrapped around the front, another from behind, crossing at her heart and held with a pin. Around her waist she wore something like an apron, this layer the darkest shade of brown.

The young man climbed the jagged scarp, and his breathing was hard. He moved swiftly, seemed to know the handholds as he climbed, barely looked up except to fix his lustful eyes on the girl.

"What do ye make of the moors?" She addressed Eleanor.

"What do I make of them?" Eleanor answered.

"Aye."

"I don't know what to make of them."

"An' what do ye mean by that?" The girl dropped her foot from behind her, placed it on the ground, stood still, stopped the subtle hip swivel, the disordered and shameless seduction of the man.

"I don't know what I mean exactly," Eleanor answered.

"Aye, ye do. Tell me, 'cause you can. Ye can tell me what ye mean."

"I mean there isn't much of anything, but the wind, and I get turned around . . ." Eleanor's head moved in all directions, as if she were looking for something.

"Aye, 'cause the moors they rearrange things," the girl said. "The damp that comes in from the sea"—she tossed her head in the direction of Denmark and Sweden beyond—"can ye imagine there's anything not rearranged by it? Look at that there." Her wrist was small, her bones petite. She pointed to a hare moving through the heather, hopping on long legs, struggling forward against the wind. "The brown hare. He can't be seen so well, no more, yet still he be," she said.

The way she moved was winning, even bewitching. The strength of each tiny muscle and the grace with which she moved against the world. Eleanor wanted to ask her name. Just in that moment, just as Eleanor was thinking of asking her name, the girl called out, "Heathcliff, climb. Climb faster, we've to be goin' now, coom now, or we'll be gone." He looked to ravish her with his eyes, his eyes with a kindness and a rage.

Eleanor was caught in awe when she heard the woman say the name.

"Ye see what ye see and it turns ye," the girl said to Eleanor.

"So, where is it you're heading?" Eleanor asked.

It was about as cold as it had been the whole time she'd been in Yorkshire. The wind was not just blowing but howling in a way she hadn't heard before. Of course, the bluff where they stood was even more exposed than most, and she'd come to it because she'd seen it from the swing, days before. But reading *Wuthering Heights* she thought she had recognized something about this particular part of the landscape. This thought was what had driven her out here.

"Headin'?" The young woman looked to the young man with a saucy, hopeful expression. "There's nothin' and nowhere beyond yonder rigg . . ." She sang a Yorkshire ditty. "We're just pressin' on," she said, "same as always we do."

Eleanor wanted to say the name *Catherine*, wanted to see what would happen if she did. The worst was she'd be wrong, and the girl would laugh and realize the joke and explain how it happened that a boy was called Heathcliff in the middle of the moors. They were young, no more than fifteen years old, both of them, and vivid and evidently real. Still, Eleanor knew they were ghosts.

"I want to ask you something," Eleanor said with a change in tone.

With a wistful look made of mist and breeze, the girl reached out her hand and as she did, Heathcliff got to the top of the climb and took it in his. They stood like statues on the edge of the earth and the air was cluttered with leaves floating around them.

"If you would, if you could, would you choose differently?"

Heathcliff kept his head down, mostly looked at the ground as if he were shy or servile. When he looked into Eleanor's eyes for a second she saw the crazy wild there, but when he looked at the girl, everything went quiet in him. Like she calmed him.

"Why do you stay here?" Eleanor asked.

"We like it here," he said with his eyes on the ground, not even looking out at the heather. "Ah, it's nice enough on the other side"—he squeezed Catherine's hand—"but it's nicer here. Don't ye think?"

"I think I do," said Eleanor. She knew not only who they were, but for a moment she knew why she'd come to Yorkshire. Still, as she glimpsed it, it fled like a firefly. While she spun shadows of thoughts in her head, Heathcliff let go of

Catherine's hand and the two young people started to run and they ran across the rocks without looking down, without a worry about stumbling.

❧

ON THE LONG WALK BACK TO TRENT HALL, A DOWN-pour began and Eleanor ducked inside one of the sheltered coves in the wall of rock. She should have seen the storm coming. Now, inside the sheltering rock, her mind spun. She was worried that the hill might come down around her, or that people back at the house would be looking for her, or that she'd never find her way back and would lose track of north and south and wind up in the Outer Hebrides without Mead.

But that one thought, that last thought, made her smile, and she sat down, feeling the warmth in the stone. The crashing sound of the rain and the wind made her feel small and insignificant in a pleasant way, in a way that brought her relief from the strain she'd been feeling in her brain. She'd decided something. She knew where she was going and she knew Mead would be there. She had the vigor and courage it took to unwind her story.

From inside the rock, she watched the weather change for hours. Inside it was warm as if a hot spring ran through the rock, so she was comfortable sitting with her legs crossed, and by the time the storm stopped, it was lucky there was a moon so she could make her way home without getting lost.

Coming from the dark of the moors, the light in the library shone like a beacon. Thinking Mead might be working late in the library, she stopped there before heading into the house. If Mead were still awake, she would be able to talk with him.

When she opened the heavy library door, Mead was asleep in one of the big chairs. Eleanor leaned down and kissed his cool forehead and as her lips touched his skin, she was grateful.

PART THREE

MEAD HAD INVITED ELEANOR TO GO WITH HIM TO Pickering, a town on the edge of the Dalby Forest where there was an ancient church with the most well-preserved medieval wall paintings in all of Yorkshire. On the way, they were going to stop for drinks with some friends of his, so it was an official date and Eleanor was thrilled to step away from her thorny preoccupations with ghosts and truths and ancestry. She looked forward to a deeper sense of Mead, meeting friends, and feeling like a simple young woman again.

"This Dalby Forest was born in the last ice age on the shore of a great glacial lake." Mead had been telling her all sorts of things about the countryside as they drove along. The houses in town were built of thatched roofs, old brick, and ancient Yorkshire limestone—the geological history of which he'd explained in some detail. He'd told her about the Bronze Age, the Vikings, the Normans, all about mottes and keeps and the structure of medieval buildings.

As the car rounded a bend on a hill, about to drop into the valley beyond which lay Pickering, Eleanor crossed her arms on her chest in a mock moment of pique and interrupted him.

"Did you know that the island of Manhattan rests on a massive bed of Paleozoic garnet? It's what gives them confidence to build those amazing skyscrapers. The earth is so solid underneath them."

He looked at her, hazarding a smile. "You come from a fine city," he said. "Really, you do."

"How about I keep my eye out for roe deer and badgers?" She slid down in her seat and Mead patted her hand.

The road wound around the moors and heathland for miles more before Mead pointed toward a low fortress wall on the top of a hill in the distance.

"That's where we're headed."

The long driveway was cobbled with irregular chunks of Yorkstone, and when Mead stopped the car she saw the house was one story of rambling stone and brick, with no apparent windows or doors.

"It's unbelievable," she said, getting out of the car.

Mead led her through a hardly visible break in the apparently impenetrable wall. Inside, there was a white rock garden with a bubbling fountain and then a pair of glass doors with detailed ironwork. Mead was almost boyish in his excitement as they stood there. Her cheek was at the level of his shoulder and he looked grand in a jacket and loose brandy-colored corduroy pants. He seemed flustered, and she had to remind him to ring the bell.

A friendly-faced young woman answered. She was big with a baby belly, her face was long and lean, and her eyes were limpid with generosity.

"Darling man." Mead had flowers with him and a bottle of champagne. "Eleanor," she said and embraced her warmly.

"More gorgeous than ever," Mead said. "Eleanor, this is my great friend Lucy, and this her hardheaded bloke, Jim." A redheaded man wrapped his arms around Lucy's fine belly and with his chin resting there on his wife's shoulder, reached around to shake Eleanor's hand.

"Come in, come in. Thanks, mate," he said, taking the champagne and flowers. A bouncy short-haired blonde in miniskirt and bare legs came around a corner and took them from Jim, introduced herself to Eleanor. "Kendra," she said, "and my boyfriend, Harry." Coming in from the garden, Harry carried a ladder he set down so he could make it across the room to greet Eleanor properly.

"We're making a baby's room," Lucy said. "Problem is we don't know the color, so we've been mixing paints to find one that pleases, won't offend, whichever she is."

"Whichever *he* is, she means," Jim added.

"We've settled on a slightly grayed green. It looks better than it sounds. Come have a look, won't you?"

Lucy led them in. The back of the house was a wall of windows, from one end to the other, which opened on to a backyard that was flat with a low wall around it and beyond that was the thick of a forest.

"They call the house the Bailey," Mead said. "That out there is like a kind of bailey." He stopped himself. "Do you like it?"

It was sparsely furnished with pieces of this and that, nothing that formed a whole or matched. "It's fantastic. I'm stunned. Can we stay?" Eleanor whispered as they walked a few feet behind the others.

"If we did, we'd have to help clean up. We won't be long. Just wanted you to see . . ."

"He designed this place," Jim said.

Eleanor looked up at Mead's strong, handsome face. He was shaking his head. "Drew some drawings, is all I did." He was genuinely humble.

"It's fantastic, isn't it?" Lucy said.

"It really is," Eleanor said.

The baby's room had a wall of curtains over the wall of windows, but Lucy pulled the drapes open. "In the spring there's a baby field of poppies right there," she said. "It will look nice with the green, I think, don't you?"

"I do." One wall was painted and a crib was half put together. "How long before the baby's due?"

"Any day, we think."

There were too many people in the small child's room, so

they moved into the living room, a pleasant jumble of colorful mismatched furniture that clashed, in the best way, with the perfection of the house itself.

Mead was, as always, relaxed in his skin, but in the company of his good friends she could see more parts of him: how he was a mix of commanding and charming, self-effacing and deeply kind. They'd been at school and then at university together. They were educated and spoke familiarly about an array of things, finishing off the California chardonnay and then opening the champagne. Kendra'd made fudge and some butter cookies, so they feasted on sweets and guessed about names for the baby.

"Did you really design this?" Eleanor asked.

Mead was utterly at home with his long legs stretched out from the chair. He'd finished putting the crib together, had gone into the cupboards for glasses and popped the cork on the champagne bottle, served everyone a glass.

It was different to see him loved by other people. Really loved—one could feel it and it cast a kind of light on his face: like the difference between a postcard and a real place.

"He certainly did." A barrister in London, Harry spoke with a slight stutter.

Mead was across the coffee table from her. "It really was just a drawing," he said.

Jim cuffed him on the shoulder as he walked behind him and Mead dropped his head back. Grabbed hold of Jim and they played at roughhousing.

"He told me he built castles and dreams," Eleanor said, "and I thought he was kidding."

The whole room sparkled with delight at this.

⁂

THE ANCIENT CHURCH IN THE TOWN OF PICKERING WAS modest inside. She and Mead were alone except for a man climbing down a ladder, who invited Eleanor to come have a close look at the medieval paintings. The figures were drawn in thick black lines. She didn't know much about art but she knew enough to be startled. How modern they seemed: beyond a perfect rendering, they were almost cartoons of expression and feeling. Edmund, in the depiction of his martyrdom, was tied to a stake. His feet were turned out and he stood on a small field of cheerful, childlike red flowers. With arrows piercing him, his face looked perplexed, almost ironic, and Eleanor felt him looking straight at her and asking what the heck she thought was going on here. She climbed down the ladder and thanked the old man for letting her up.

They strolled along and looked at the panels. In a low whisper, Mead read to her about how the church had plastered over them long ago and happily this had protected them, once they were restored.

Each picture had a sense of the inevitable in it. Whether Salome danced or St. George pranced on the red belly of a dragon or Jesus tolerated the Passion, they were Bible dramas mitigated by thick, simple black lines, pure colors, and candor.

Outside the church, Eleanor and Mead walked awhile. The fresh air relieved Eleanor and she linked her arm through Mead's. At the top of the hill, so steep you felt you might slide right down and off the edge of it, there was a view of the wildly vast countryside.

"I used to feel in the middle of nowhere, here, but I don't anymore," she said.

He stepped in front of her.

"And you, with those green eyes."

He pulled her toward him. The top of her head was at his chin and he pulled her so close she had to lift her face to see him. "Fact is," he said, "you're only ever exactly where you are."

"And happily so."

"You know the inn's only got the one room," he whispered.

She blessed him with her pure smile. "I am fully capable of behaving myself in bed."

"Well, I like the sound of that," he said.

THE ROOM WAS DRESSED UP IN PINK AND CREAM PAISLEY bedspread and curtains. Eleanor opened the window to let in some fresh air. She sat on his lap. She turned around and unlaced her shoes, then kicked them off. She took off her sweater and wriggled out of her jeans. This left her in a T-shirt and the pale blue frilly knickers she'd bought in Haworth. They were lacy frills from top to bottom, particularly across the bottom.

"Your friends are great, that room she's making . . ."

"You're going to talk whilst sitting on my lap in those lovely knickers?" he said.

"It can't be called behaving if there's nothing at stake, can it?"

His warm hands held her legs. The tips of his fingers moved slightly inside her thighs. Mead took off his shirt and Eleanor shivered with simple pleasure at the sight of him. He gathered her in and they climbed under the comforter. The length of her body was against him.

Mead lifted her chin and kissed her.

There was a knock on the door and Eleanor startled. A kitchen girl called out to say she'd leave the tray and Mead stepped into the hall to get it.

"I ordered us some dinner," he said. "There are lamb chops with greens, the requisite mashed potatoes, and some squash soup."

"Yum," she said.

"Let's start with wine," he said and opened the bottle of a French blend.

"Chocolate and plums," she said, tasting it. "Some tobacco zing and a smidge of dirt."

It was so rich, the wine, she could almost chew it in her

mouth. She tasted the color she saw on Mead's lips, the deep red almost purple stain, and drank enough that her mouth was saturated with berries and ferment, and then she wanted to taste a wine-rich kiss with him.

He stood from his chair and came around the table, offered his hand, and there in the middle of the room she rose on her toes and tasted him, tasted the alcohol and behind that the berries and behind that she felt the warmth of down like a soft pillow it was safe to fall into. And she fell, and he drew her firmly against him so she could feel his blood surge and his heart pounding fast with desire. It was good he was strong, good he had a hold of her, because she'd have dropped to the floor: her knees giving way, her womb contracting.

She tried to think, tried to think about the lamb and the mashed potatoes under the silver domes on the plates on the table, but he moved forward with her. He'd moved beyond the tender kiss to one that suffused her even though his lips were his, and hers were hers, and their tongues were only barely finding each other. The pervasive feeling was separateness, even as she lost herself for moments. He nipped at her lips with his teeth and then his mouth opened just enough that she sensed how great it was.

He lifted her off the ground.

A man had never lifted her off the ground, she'd never allowed it. She'd always pressed her feet into the floor, but Mead lifted her up and she wrapped her legs around him. His hands supported her as he held her in the middle of the room and his fingers moved against her bottom, pressed gently toward the middle point, where she was soft and pliable.

His right hand settled on her left hip bone, his left hand held her hand, and they waltzed in small circles around the room. He was bare-chested. She wore her thin top and lacy knickers. He hummed a Scottish tune into her ear, and it tickled but she didn't squirm away from it, and soon the tickle became an unwinding thrill. With his fingers pressed against her spine, he guided her where he wanted her to go, made it easy for her to follow. Her hand slid below his lower back.

Tension. Taut and tender. Fragile and crazy with vigor. There were things to talk about. Through her brain snapped the thought like a flash of light in the back of the eye: they had things to talk about. They knew enough to be dangerous to each other, enough that embarking on a journey high on that bed, a bed so high above the ground there were three stairs to climb to it, could prove unwise. It flashed through her mind as the dancing became more like dervish swirling and she pressed, climbed up the front of him. He kissed her lips and neck and then at her ear exhaled something with glittery wings that made its way down her spine. She'd never felt so wild, on the inside.

On the outside, he lifted her onto the bed and watched as she pulled the thin tank off over her head. He seemed older, looked at her as if he might be choosing something. The right thing. He tasted one breast and then the other, dropped onto his elbows and framed her face in his hands. He held her still and moved slowly.

IN THE MORNING, THEY'D TAKEN A BATH AND WERE standing in front of the mirror. She watched as he kissed her neck, then draped a linen towel around her shoulders.

She couldn't remember the last time she'd seen herself in a mirror.

He loved the taste of her, he whispered.

They looked beautiful, side by side: her long blond hair and pale fresh skin, his dark hair, tanned flesh, and structured body. Tall and taller, there was something simple and balanced between them. And she felt a wave of sadness inside the pleasure.

In the weeks she'd been in Yorkshire, she'd slowed down enough to feel. And this gesture, draping her with a plain soft towel when she was damp and slightly cold, reminded her how she had coped and set herself to the beat and rhythm so easy to fall into in New York City. Moving and producing and clipping through on pavement with high heels.

"Do you feel like an orphan?" she asked him. As it tumbled out she heard the empty sound of the word, but before she had a chance to explain he answered.

"I am an orphan. A foundling, really. Always have been. My father lives without me in the north, and Alice was more than a mother to me but still not my mother. I am an orphan."

He cupped her breasts in his hands and kissed her again.

She reached her arms behind to pull him closer.

"Sometimes I think we all are orphans, really," he said. He watched her face in the long, cloudy mirror. "But that might be sour grapes in me. My father couldn't raise me after my mother died, but they loved each other deeply, I can feel it inside. Maybe Alice told me, but still I feel it. That's all there is, for me. I've never known it any other way." Mead's breath changed. She felt it through her bare spine against his chest. "Now you," he said.

"My parents were good to me." She caught hold of Mead's eyes in the mirror. "But it's weird not having them. My father disappeared inside himself or something else after my mom died, but I've been making the best of it. Because they were good, they were good to me . . ."

"And the good of it shows on you." He smoothed his hands across her belly and held her hips.

As if the molecules of her flesh and soul had rearranged, she felt open and clear. Though light-headed from a long night of lovemaking, her head spinning with remnant desire, she felt awakened as if some combination of the moors and Mead had stirred the sleeping soul at the base of her spine.

"I think my mother might have had some kind of crazy love," she said.

"This kind?" Mead whispered just below her ear and, as he whispered, his lips brushed that stirring skin at the side of her neck.

Now Eleanor turned and peppered Mead's face with kisses and his eyes and then his neck. "Maybe this kind," she whispered amid kisses, "yes, maybe. Maybe I *am* at a crossroads. Maybe I'm choosing."

In the narrow space between the mirror and the tub they stood. She rested her cheek against his chest. "My mother came back here for a reason. I remember the day she left, that last day. I didn't remember for long time, but I've been remembering things, while I've been here. She was happy to be leaving and I thought she shouldn't be. Shouldn't be leaving and I begrudged her it, that day. She was looking forward to something."

He could see her well-rounded bare bottom in the mirror behind her and the way her spine held strong and stable amid the fall of blond ringlets and curls.

Her skin was still damp. She sat down on the edge of the tub and said, "Emily made a choice to stay with her brother and it killed her. Catherine, maybe she made the wrong choice."

"She never let go of Heathcliff," he said.

"And that killed her." Eleanor was trembling.

Mead started kissing her brow, to quieten her.

"Do you think I can choose and not choose the wrong thing?"

Mead wrapped a robe around Eleanor's bare shoulders and sat beside her. "May I tell you something?"

She nodded, tears on her cheeks and a solid bewilderment in her eyes.

"There's a love here that can be transporting, it's true," he said. "The moors are strong and fierce and wild. And, fine woman, so are you. But it takes more than crazy love to withstand the moors. Crazy love on these moors will kill you. It can't be 'bout choosing the right love, my love. It's all about choosing yourself, finding what's true inside you."

Wiping away tears, she said cheerfully, "I know that. I know what it takes to withstand love on the moors."

"Do you?" He stared into her face.

Her head bobbed with a few short bobs. "Mm-hmm. I do."

"Well, then. That sounds good." He paused between his words, slowing things down, making them last. "Would you mind if I carried you back to that bed and had my way with you?"

IN THE KITCHEN AT TRENT HALL, WHEN THEY ARRIVED home, they found a note Gwen had left in bright red pen on butcher paper so Mead wouldn't miss it. She reminded him of a meeting he had with the rapeseed buyer in Thirsk.

In the aftermath of lovemaking they were floating half-high in air. They'd never got around to eating their dinner the night before, so they scrambled some eggs and ate day-old biscuits, then Mead headed off to get his things together for the day's journey.

Just after the back door slammed, the phone in the downstairs hall rang, loud and shrill, seven or eight times before Eleanor found it and grabbed it.

"Trent Hall," she said into the big old Bakelite phone.

"Is there an Eleanor Abbott?" Gladys' voice was tentative.

"This is me, Gladys."

"Eleanor, my God. You answered the phone. I've been trying e-mails and finally remembered you gave me this number. Just in time. I've got news. Harrods wants a big old piece of you, and I set up a meeting, was just about to cancel it, but great, there you are. Can you make it?"

"Today?"

"I set the meeting for tomorrow, but I can change it. They'll send a car for you, wherever you are."

"No, God, I'll take the train." A wild shift in thinking, she'd lost track of time. "Is everything going okay, there? Production and . . ."

"Absolutely great. You doing okay?"

"I am, actually."

"You sound good. Your voice sounds good and a little English the way you answered the phone. So you'll make it to the city? Listen, I'll make a res at some hotel and text you with it."

"Just overnight. I've got to get back to a few things here."

"Right. Just tomorrow, one meeting. It's not even necessary, but since you're there . . ."

"It's mind-bogglingly great. Harrods, Barneys, this is just insane."

"Just what you deserve."

"Thanks, Glad. I better get going."

"You coming back soon?"

"Hmm, define soon."

It took three minutes to fold her few things and put them in the suitcase. The sky was bright with new winter light outside her windows and the ground had a thin slick cover of frost. She kicked the suitcase closed and went to the barn-library to find him, but Mead's car was already gone.

GRANLEY TOOK HER TO THE LOCAL TRAIN AND IN YORK she changed to an express that went almost straight to the heart of London. She wore the only suit she had, the suit she'd worn in York with Miles, but had the taxi drop her at a shop in Knightsbridge, near the hotel, where she bought some fancy, high-heeled pumps for the meeting the next day.

After touring Harrods' many halls, the buyer took Eleanor to a local stand, where they ate fish and chips in a cone of newsprint. The head buyer was almost as young as Eleanor and her energy was high. She wanted Eleanor to understand that a deal with Harrods was "massive," that her line was "brilliant," and that everyone who'd seen it was "keen" and excited as hell. Eleanor was already unaccustomed to such electrified enthusiasm. Though she could hardly believe it was happening, what she'd dreamed of for as long as she could remember, it was odd to have it come at the exact moment when she cared about it least of all.

She wanted to get back to the house and to Mead, but that night Harrods had planned a dinner at a restaurant in Knightsbridge, where princes and princesses dined, they boasted. She was grateful and gracious, but all through the night looked for a gap in conversation when she might slip away and make it to a late train, but the gap never came, so it wasn't until midday, the next day, that Eleanor finally made it back to Yorkshire.

She found Mead in the library and could see that he was not a happy man.

"Turn your profile to me, will you?" he snapped.

She stopped in the doorway and did.

"You ought to be told you look just like her. The pale white color of the skin, the long neck and sloping shoulders, the upper lip, the urgent eyes."

"Ought to be told? It sounds like a punishment. Who is it I look like?"

"Emily Brontë." It was meant to inflict pain. He went on, "You've got that skin that's sometimes blue, some parts lavender and peach." He walked over to her, lifted her chin, and moved her face like an object. "Sometimes flushed, sometimes just plain white as ivory. I noticed it the first night I saw you." He let go of her chin. "Though yours is also like very milky coffee, after some sun on it."

"You're mad," Eleanor said to him and pulled her face away.

"*I'm* mad?"

"You're mad at me," she said.

"I am not." He sat down across the table from her.

She stepped out of her high heels. "I didn't think about a note till we were on the road. I don't have any numbers for you." Numbers all people had, in the modern world, for everyone. "But I asked Granley to tell you. I thought . . ."

"You suddenly had to go to London, that's what he told me."

"Oh, my." She started around the table, approached him as you might approach an irate grizzly. "It was nothing to do with Miles. He's not in London."

Mead's scowl disappeared.

"Seconds after you walked out, the phone rang and it was my assistant, Gladys."

"You have an assistant?"

She nodded. It sounded as strange to her as it must have to him. "I went in to Harrods for a meeting she'd set for the next day. I stayed the night and then they arranged a dinner and I had to stay another. I tried to figure out a way to reach you but you were already gone to Thirsk, when I came to find you." Her shoulders said, "What should I have done?"

He emerged from his man-pout before her eyes.

"The meeting went pretty well?" he asked.

She nodded.

"So what is it you do? In New York City?"

"I make things. Wool clothing with beautiful buttons. I buy old used sweaters—well, not so much anymore, but that's how it started. It was quirky stuff, at the start. Now it's a little more polished."

"I'd no idea."

He invited her to come closer. He unbuttoned her jacket.

"It was exciting, London. They took me to a small Italian place for dinner last night, a place I guess Diana used to go. And Harrods is massive. Have you been there?"

His smile was gracious love.

"They're buying my things. A line I'll design for them, for spring."

This was a part of her he didn't know. He unzipped her skirt and it slipped to the floor.

"I was a young girl when I started this, you know." She stepped out of the skirt, peeled off her jacket, blouse, and stood before him in the bright colored prettiness of the underthings she wore.

"You feel like a young girl, right now."

"I'm happy."

He kissed her bare chest and one finger moved along the lace of her bra. His other hand was wrapped right around her hip and she could feel how lean and strong she'd become from all the walking.

"You're not mad at me anymore," she said.

"It was a misunderstanding. Truth is, it's thrown me to be

falling this way." He put the flat of his hand on her belly. "But, I'm happy to . . ."

He kissed her navel.

She leaned back against the table and tried to get the problem that she had been working on, the whole train ride home, right out of her mind. She'd decided she had to go into Scarborough and find the boy who'd been her mother's shadow, once upon a time, but Mead's hands were warm on her inner thighs and his tongue pressed against the fragile nerves around her hip bone.

He lifted her onto the table and held her with his hands along her spine, so the lovemaking was tender and deeper than it had been, her head bursting from where he hit her within.

❧

ELEANOR REACHED FOR THE WHISKY BOTTLE AND A short glass, which wasn't clean but wasn't dirty. She poured them a few fingers and took a sip before giving him the rest.

She took the glass back and refilled it then slid onto his lap sideways, her legs dangling over the edge of the chair. She kissed him.

"There's just one last thing I need to do," she said.

"There's something I need to ask you." He poured a little more whisky and drank some. "I'm the son of a Brontë scholar, and you've found material that the world has no idea about, material that would change things for Brontë scholars."

"It's not just the letters," she said. "There's the family tree, Mead. It's not just Brontë family—she's related to me. She's my great-great-great-grandmother or something."

"I think I've missed something." He pulled a strand of her hair and wound it about her ear.

"Emily had a baby she left here at the Enswell house. Raised by the Enswells after Emily died. Alice had the tree—she knew all this and she didn't want to do anything."

She straddled him. "I understand it changes something, really, I do. But I don't think it's necessary for the world to know. It'll upset everything for nothing. It just doesn't matter that much. To me anyway, does it to you?"

He kissed the hollow at the base of her throat and gazed at her. "You're right, I know you're right. Blimey, she's your grandmother. Alice would be stunned speechless she'd be so proud of you. So what is it you're going to do? This one last thing you have to do?"

She rubbed the tip of her nose against his. "I wondered if I might borrow your car for the day, or the day and the night?"

"Now where are you going?"

"Scarborough's not far, is it?"

"No, not far."

"There's an old address of a man who wrote my mother, and I want to see if he's there. I'm pretty sure he's a friend from childhood, and I just want to see if I can find him."

"You don't want me to drive you?"

"I think I want to be on my own, in case I do find him. Because you're kind of distracting."

He ran his hands all over her bones and flesh and burrowed his face in the side of her neck in a flurry of puppy love till it tickled and she giggled and pushed him away. She stretched her arms into his cotton button-down shirt and looked around.

"It's done," she said.

The shelves were in place and filled with books, some arranged by color. There were wood-framed, clear-glass doors protecting the books from damp and dust and insects. On the floor, an orange and blue floral design in a Persian rug.

"It is."

"Wow, what does that mean for you—what's next?"

He shrugged. "I suppose soon, I'm off to face my father. He's a Scotsman and a scarperer, and I've got a home up there I need to investigate, in case he leaves this earth one day. An island with a yurt he's built on it."

"Really?"

"They call it something else, but it's a yurt."

"Don't go away . . . ," she said and kissed him.

"I won't go while you're gone."

"I mean, don't leave this place. I think Gwen wants to turn half of it into a hotel anyway, so we can all live here. Sometimes, anyway." She gave a nervous laugh. "Promise you won't leave before I get back."

"You're taking my car." He reached forward to grab his keys off the table and dropped them onto her belly.

"Oh, right." She blushed happy. "Perfect."

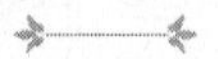

THE ROADS WERE PAVED. GRIMSTONE, SCAGGLE-thorpe, a road to Pickering she didn't take. Even to find her way around Brooklyn, on foot, Eleanor needed a GPS. Scampston, Willerby, a turn onto Spital Road. She was sometimes on the A64, sometimes on a back road, but she'd stopped for a map and every so often pulled over to read it or ask for directions.

When in the town of Scarborough she found a café where she rested with a dish of something warm to eat, she relaxed into the adventure. She drove along a sandy beach and a beautiful stretch of shore on the North Sea, turned down Queen's Parade, and drove past a cluster of small hotels directly across from the bay.

The road turned at the end of the bay, took a left onto Castle Road, and ended at a castle gate. She found a place to park her car and went through the high arching gate, past a sign that announced *Three Thousand Years of History*. The castle wall ran for miles. The castle itself stood in a sensational spot on the headland between two bays, and as she headed down toward it a guard approached to say the castle was closed for the day, that she should come back tomorrow.

Melancholy hit her like a wave. She thanked the guard, asked him some questions about the place, questions Mead would have known how to answer. When she walked back to the car, she still felt a mix of dread and sorrow. Dreading time. The grand hopes of the humans who had conceived that castle, and the ones who had taken the time and labored hard to build it, without comfort even at the end of arduous days. The knights who'd fought and died, the babies who'd been hungry and cold and left alone to cry.

The lady at the reception desk of the hotel she chose on the North Bay was polite, but it wasn't like where she'd stayed with Mead in Pickering, it wasn't like the Guy Fawkes Inn, in York. It was synthetic, antiseptic, with artificial flowers and a spray to take all natural smells away. It was for tourists and as it wasn't tourist season, the place was dead.

A young man led her up to the room and opened the curtains to show her the view of the sea. "The North Sea with Denmark there and Norway there." He pointed. "From where the Vikings came," he added proudly—a strong strapping kid with a shock of unruly reddish blond hair.

When he left, she felt old. She was not even thirty, but she sat down on one of the twin beds and felt like a traveling spinster. A woman alone on the edge of the world, knowing no one, no one knowing where she was, just a solitary wanderer. What felt exciting not a half hour before, suddenly sank. She felt the drone of sameness and continuity. All the women who'd come to this room might well still be looking for the something that had brought them to this seaside hotel.

The bed was hard. She pulled off her boots and walked to the full-length mirror that stood in one corner of the large room and looked at herself. Standing in Scarborough on a dingy rust-colored carpet, in a room decorated with teal and rust polyester quilted coverlets and pillow shams, she undid her bun. She looked at herself from all sides and wasn't sure what she thought. She was thin from the side. Her stomach was flat in the wool dress she wore—a simple black cashmere sheath that fit her nicely—not too loose, not too close to the body. She held both breasts in her hands. She pulled her dress off over her head and then peeled her tights off her legs. For a quick moment, she glanced at her naked self.

In the nightstand between the two beds was Scarborough's phone directory and in the lean book, she found the name Garrens. There weren't as many as she feared there might be, and she began calling. When someone answered, she asked if there was a Martin and when there wasn't, she asked if they knew a Martin, which without exception led to a curt no at the end of the line.

It was a waste of time, she realized, as she punched the third in the list of phone numbers into the phone by the bed. She'd picked up the idea from some film: a scene of a woman with one meager clue who makes phone calls from a hotel room. And the one she's looking for is the last one she calls. Eleanor heard a man answer, saying, "You've reached Edgar

Garrens." His voice was high and cheerful. Feeling ridiculous, she hung up without leaving a message. She put on jeans and her thick sweater, slipped her bare feet into Ugg boots, and went out for a walk.

Across Queen's Parade, over the rail, and down the side of the hill, she must have looked a bit wild, from out in the country where people climbed and trudged, didn't bother with paths and roadways. She crossed another road and climbed another rail and dropped onto the beach below. The only person on the sand, she left her boots against a rock wall and headed south.

The wind was calm. It was nothing like the wind on the moors. This wind was smooth and soothing. It was gentle on her face. And it felt almost warm, where her toes sank into the cold wet sand. Bare under her thick sweater and jeans, she had an urge to dive in, to swim, though the water must be freezing. She wanted to be naked in the North Sea. She rolled up her pants as far as they would go and went in as far as she could bear the cold.

The bay was not wide and when she got to the end of the sand, she walked on the promenade and then the rocky shoreline. The sea was grittier at this end, with barnacles and weeds. She'd picked up a walking stick and a handful of shells. They reminded her of her buttons, and she put them in her pocket thinking she'd drill tiny holes in the strongest, prettiest ones and sew them on her next batch of clothing.

It was dark when she got back to the hotel, night falling

early in Yorkshire. In the uncomfortable twin bed, she decided it didn't matter about finding Martin Garrens. He might live in one of the Carolinas or in New York City, for all she knew. She was tired of hunting without a clue. There were four more people named Garrens in the book, but it was embarrassing to be on the prowl, to hear the suspicion at the other end of the line, to have no way of explaining herself.

Still she dialed the next number on the list. J. Garrens. As the phone rang she glanced and saw it was almost ten o'clock. She was about to hang up, when a woman's voice answered.

"Hello," said Eleanor. "I didn't realize it was so late."

The woman cleared her throat.

"I'm looking for a man named Martin Garrens."

"Who is calling?"

"I'm sorry."

"You have the right number—who's calling?"

"My name's Eleanor. Eleanor Abbott. Eleanor Sutton?"

There was a long pause. "Well, which one is it?" The woman's voice was almost playful. "This is a pleasant surprise. Are you in Scarborough?"

"I am."

"It's late tonight, but might you be able to come for tea in the morning?"

❧

ELEANOR CHECKED OUT OF THE SMALL HOTEL AND drove along Marine Drive, below the headland. She drove up to the castle and walked beyond the ruins to the castle walls with a view of two beautiful bays and she thought how wise the kings and queens of medieval times had been, to choose this piece of property. Now, there was Luna Park with a Ferris wheel to the right, the harbor below, and a garish strip of awnings along Foreshore Road that looked like Coney Island. She felt the ominous gray of the day inside her, but then the sun popped out from behind the clouds and this seemed like a good sign.

Mrs. Garrens lived where Craven Street met Albion Road, at the junction, in an ordinary house. The interior was all grays and browns, nothing like the colorful dress, scarf, and shoes Mrs. Garrens wore. There was an umbrella stand and a coat stand and then an unlit staircase up to an even darker hall.

Eleanor didn't have a coat and was still wearing yesterday's jeans, but she slipped off her dusty Ugg boots and left them by the front door. Mrs. Garrens led her into the sitting room where there was a piano with a few framed photographs and a bay window but no view of the bay. On the settee in front of the window, she sat while Mrs. Garrens went into the kitchen to make a pot of tea. It seemed that no matter how recently tea or coffee had been taken, when a fresh moment came, there was more tea poured and with the tea there was always a plate of biscuits.

Eleanor fidgeted and felt anxious. If she'd felt old the previous afternoon in the hotel, she felt ancient that morning, sitting in a colorless room on a gray day with an elderly lady. She took a chocolate digestive biscuit and nibbled at the edge of it.

"You came all this way."

Eleanor nodded.

"Have you had a good stay?"

"I've just been here one night. I stayed at a little hotel across from the beach."

"The North Bay. Have you visited the castle?"

"I did. Yesterday the gate was closed, but I went up there this morning."

"It's true, it would have been closed yesterday, but you had a chance to see it. I'm glad." Mrs. Garrens looked like a parrot the way she moved her head, the tightness in her mouth like a beak, the gaudy clothes she was wearing. "I think it's good you're here," she said to Eleanor. "I think it's a good sign."

It sounded like a bad sign.

"I'm sorry I called so late last night. I didn't realize. I came here looking for Martin Garrens, but I don't know him, didn't know how to find . . . I looked in the phone book. There were seven or eight, actually."

"Oh, my." Mrs. Garrens tugged at the string of pearls around her neck. "I thought maybe Alice had said something."

"Alice, no, she didn't say anything. Then you know Alice . . . Are you Martin Garrens' wife?"

"No, goodness no, dear." In an instant something softened in Mrs. Garrens' face. "You must have come to visit Alice."

"I don't know if you knew that she was sick recently."

"I read it in the paper, that she passed. I'm sorry."

Eleanor knitted her fingers. "So, I'm here in England because I came to visit Alice, to meet her, really. I live in New York." She heaved a sigh of exasperation.

"What moved you to call me?"

"Coming to England, I found some letters in my mother's things and some of them were from a Martin Garrens, from Scarborough, so I came."

"I see."

"I have to admit, I'm really at a loss here."

Mrs. Garrens went to the piano, picked up one of the frames, walked slowly back across the room, and handed it to Eleanor.

The frame was heavy, old and made from silver. The picture was faded. The young woman in the picture had curled blond hair that reached the top of her jeans. A thick leather belt was cinched tight at her waist, and she wore a loose paisley blouse. Next to the young woman stood a clean-cut, handsome man fat with joy. They both looked filled to bursting. That was all she saw.

"Do you recognize your mum?" Mrs. Garrens said.

Eleanor looked more carefully and her heart jumped seeing the unmistakable eyes and the way her mother always stood with her right leg akimbo, a familiar self-conscious smile on her face. It was almost the face Eleanor remembered.

She looked up at Mrs. Garrens, but didn't like what she felt in the room. All confused, in Scarborough, on a Wednesday morning.

"I do," Eleanor said.

"It's your mother and Martin."

Eleanor looked more closely at the picture.

"That's Martin Garrens."

"It is." She sat down beside her.

It was an uncomfortable sitting room. All the chairs were a little too far from any table, so you had to reach to pick up or put down your teacup or reach for another cookie. The chairs looked as hard as folding chairs and the couch was not only firm, but the material that covered it made Eleanor's skin itch right through her clothing.

The couple in the photograph leaned against a convertible car that was parked in a wide driveway. There was a stone house in the background, and it looked like summer, because there were flowers in pots and the man was dressed in a short-sleeved shirt and shorts. The man wore sandals.

"My mother lived here in Yorkshire, I know." Eleanor was trying to find a story in the picture. "I assume that's Trent Hall behind them," she said. With a shallow layer of tears on the surface of her eyes, she looked at Mrs. Garrens.

"I assume you came because you want to know."

Eleanor nodded.

"Your mother and father . . ."

"I don't think my father was ever in England. I mean, I'm sure he wasn't, unless he didn't tell me. He'd never been to England, and my mother wanted him to come here." Eleanor felt a sense of panic rise.

Mrs. Garrens now looked like an owl. Her fat face became the most pleasant face Eleanor had seen in a long while. It was a yielding face and now it was broad and Eleanor saw the round, brown eyes—clear and unaffected as a child's. She smelled of talcum powder, lipstick, and Yardley perfume.

"I should go," Eleanor said.

"You can certainly go," said Mrs. Garrens. Eleanor didn't get up. Mrs. Garrens offered her another biscuit. Comforting and nourishing and sweet, all in one round cookie.

"You're a dear girl. May I say that?" Mrs. Garrens waited.

Eleanor's almost imperceptible nod.

"Put your feet up." Mrs. Garrens seemed to know her. Eleanor tucked her feet under herself on the couch.

Eleanor hadn't noticed how deep was Mrs. Garrens' voice, and when she spoke, it was as if she had candies in her mouth that she moved around without letting them get in the way of her well-enunciated words.

"I don't know which place to begin, because I suspect now you've managed to work it out. More or less."

"I don't know what you mean. I haven't worked anything out . . ."

Mrs. Garrens looked around the room as if she were looking for something more to give to Eleanor. She sat forward, turned her body, her hands folded in her lap. She had a sad and hopeful thin smile on her face as she went on, "Your mother and my son Martin, they knew each other as children."

"Right. That part."

Mrs. Garrens took Eleanor's hand, as if it were the most natural thing to do, as if she had comforted Eleanor's confusion since she was a small girl.

"Martin loved your mother with all his heart and there was a time when she loved him, too." She waited a bit. "I see him in you." Now, Mrs. Garrens' eyes welled with tears. "I'm your grandmother."

Eleanor turned away. She studied the face of the man in the frame, the man who stood, casual and at ease, beside her mother. "I came here looking for him, because I found some letters from him to her. I never had reason to wonder, to ask her. My mother died when I was young." She looked at Mrs. Garrens. "I think I wish I hadn't come. This is more than I was prepared for."

Tired beyond words, she thought of her own father, John Abbott, who had loved and raised her. "I never met him, did I?" Then Eleanor remembered a memory, a fragment that held itself at the edge of her sight almost all the time, a puzzle she'd just set aside.

There had been a man at the pier in Los Angeles. A friend

of her mother's, who had watched her on the Ferris wheel, and then taken them for tacos. She had tasted the salty rim of his margarita.

"God, I did meet him, didn't I? I did." From one edge of her eyes to the other, both eyes let forth a smooth wash of water on her cheeks, around her nose, over her lips, and dripping from her chin onto the sweater.

With hardly a sound, she cried, except she kept repeating, "I did, I did."

He had stood watching them ride the Ferris wheel. The ocean was behind him and seagulls were everywhere, screaming. Every time the wide chair came down and swept close to the ground and then back to go around again, she saw the man watching them. There was a lost look on his face and he frightened her a bit, until when they climbed off, her mother introduced him as a friend and pretended it was a strange coincidence he should be there. Eleanor had known she was pretending.

He had taken Eleanor's young hand and bent forward in a gentlemanly bow. He might have said she was pretty or lovely or called her a princess, and then he had suggested they get Mexican food somewhere, and there was a place right at the end of the pier.

Her mother had been happy on that trip to California. They had seen him again. He'd invited them to the opera *Carmen*, and they'd dressed up. That night her mother had slipped out of the hotel room and come in very early in the morning, but Eleanor was too young to think anything of it till now.

Eleanor's face was wet, but she'd stopped crying. Her mouth was open so she could breathe as pictures streamed through her mind like she was watching a movie. There was nothing Mrs. Garrens could do but witness it. A mountain of silent compassion, she held Eleanor's hand.

"Well." A deep inhale and the handkerchief wasn't adequate to the job, so Eleanor dabbed her face with the arm of her sweater, which made both women laugh and broke up the awfulness. "Well, some things make more sense now." Eleanor had a good enough heart that she could laugh.

"I've been reading letters, meeting . . ." She decided against telling Mrs. Garrens about the ghosts. "Learning things from every direction, and all the time, this is what I came to find." She sniffled and stood. "I think I should go now. I'm going to walk to my car and drive home now, but maybe we can meet. Another time." She was drenched in sadness. "You know, the craziest part of all this is that I'm going back to that big house that's supposed to be mine. You know the house, right? You must have known my mother for a long time." Eleanor sniffed and ran her fingers through her hair, wrapped it into a bun, and looked for her glasses. Mrs. Garrens handed them to her. Just after another sniffle Eleanor said, "Well, I suppose I'll stay long enough to meet him."

Mrs. Garrens' bust rose and fell and her eyes closed in a sad, slow way.

"Oh, God, I shouldn't meet him?" Eleanor said.

"I think you should sit for a bit more. If I may say, I think it would be better to stay a little longer."

⁂

ANNE WENT ON IMPACT. MARTIN WAS GONE BUT DIDN'T die till almost a week later. His heart was strong, the doctors had said.

Went and gone and passed. The impact intense. It was a lorry that had hit them. A runaway lorry. None of the words made any sense as they rattled in Eleanor's head like a lurid chant.

Mrs. Garrens sat still and asked nothing of her. She let her be silent and in the silence Eleanor remembered being in her family's living room when she was twelve. Her homework page, she could see it as if it were present. The grain of the wood table made her pen stick, so she put a book underneath the page and eavesdropped on her parents' conversation. He was irritated that Anne had to go. There was a concert and a reunion of people who'd known each other, but her father, John Abbott, was not being asked to go. "You said not to let you go to Yorkshire without me," he reminded her. Eleanor remembered the strange tone in her mother's voice when she said, "It's different now." And he didn't go.

Coming out of her reverie, Eleanor asked, "What was the concert they were going to?"

"The concert?"

"My parents were talking about it, before my mother came here."

"Ah, that, yes, it was the reunion of a concert they'd been to thirteen years or so before. They all got together that summer, friends from years ago. They came from all over, but Annie came the farthest, and there was a small concert, in memory of the great Free Festivals at Stonehenge. That's where they were."

"Right," Eleanor said, "that's what they were talking about. They were going to a reunion of what—what were the Free Festivals?"

"They were something like your Woodstock," Mrs. Garrens said. "Music and young people roamed around amid the ancient stones. It was a great big concert. Your mother had come back to visit—she hadn't been back since she left at fourteen—and it was the last concert they let them have there at Stonehenge, before they closed the place to protect the stones. Anne was already engaged to your father, to John, by then. They were young still, little more than teenagers. She had been in America for a long time, but for Martin, Annie was his only love. His whole life, Annie was."

"His soul," Eleanor said without inflection.

Mrs. Garrens got up and walked in small circles.

"That summer when she came back from America, they ran about, almost like they were running from something. They'd both been to college, but they played like kids, like puppies. They swam in the ocean from here to Whitby, had picnics with friends, went a little crazy with the feeling that something important was ending."

"How do you know I'm his?"

"They knew you were theirs," Mrs. Garrens said.

"Did my father know?"

"John? I don't think so, no. He didn't know."

"I think he knew, at the end." Eleanor's voice was frail.

"Yes, he might have known then."

"Why didn't she stay here and marry Martin?"

Mrs. Garrens hesitated. She wanted to get it right though she wasn't certain of the answer. "She loved John. I don't think she knew she was pregnant when she left. She went back and married him, just as they'd planned."

Her mother had had a choice between two men. Her mother couldn't inherit the house and didn't wear the ring. Eleanor's head was spinning with superstition, facts, and nonsense. What she'd lost and what she'd gained. She wiggled the ring off her finger and held it in her fist, slipped it in the pocket of her jeans.

"Eleanor, you know it was heaven for her, being a mother to you. She talked about you all the time, that last time she came, all about you and what you were doing, that last summer. You were just a young girl then."

Eleanor chewed the inside of her cheek, nodded. She felt cold creeping through her as the facts fell into place. "So what happened, exactly?"

"Well, as I said, there was the reunion. Anne and Martin

decided to drive together, just the two of them in his car, down to Stonehenge. It was a crowd of them that went, but Anne and Martin went in his car. I don't know what they were doing. I don't know what they were thinking. I wasn't privy to most of it."

The room had turned as dark as a thundercloud, but a heater close to Eleanor's legs glowed with red stones. There was something about England that held her, not in a warm way, always, but still it held on to her even when tossing her about. She'd found one father, lost a vision she'd had of her mother, and lost her true father in some way. She'd grown stronger, not just physically, not just from the exercise of walking against fierce shifts in wind on the moors, but psychically, she'd grown more vulnerable, accessible, exposed.

Even though it was gray and cold, even with awful things coming and going, she felt something balancing. Something moving in the right way, unstuck and unwinding like the swing on the hill with its arc all wild and uncanny.

"After the reunion, Anne and Martin decided to stay the night in Bath. The next day, they went for a picnic, went back to the place they'd been to all those years before, a picnic up on Solsbury Hill. A beautiful field where they'd been together, when they were still young, when your big soul first stepped into the world."

With tiny movements, Eleanor shook her head.

It might have been the first time Mrs. Garrens had had a chance to tell the story, and so, after clearing her throat again, she went on, "It was late afternoon. Your mum had a flight out the next morning. They were on their way down a narrow road, the one that leads from the gate where they'd parked and walked up the hill to picnic and take in the view. The top was down on his car and she had a scarf around her hair. I imagine they were happy. Anyway, it was then, right there around the bend"—it was clear she had a vivid picture of the geography—"at that crossroads where they would have turned left to head home, that a lorry came barreling down that hill and lost control."

They called it a runaway, because it was out of control.

The front of the lorry was taller than the top of Martin's convertible—the car small and the couple inside even smaller.

Mrs. Garrens took a deep breath.

Eleanor wasn't breathing. "They'd gone back to the place where they made me?"

Mrs. Garrens' eyes were complicated with feeling. "Yes."

"And it killed them," Eleanor said.

"You mustn't think of it that way," she said, quiet and firm. "It was an accident."

It killed them, Eleanor thought. The wrong love or the right love gone wrong, it killed them. "But why didn't they stop? Why did they keep seeing each other?"

"They didn't. I don't think they did. That last visit . . . it happened as it did . . ." Mrs. Garrens didn't have an explanation.

As much as Eleanor wanted to screech, *They kept seeing each other,* like a teenage girl in a warranted rage, *They wrote letters and visited each other. She let him see me and didn't let me see him. She never told me about him. I don't know how many places she went to be away from us and be with him*, she didn't say anything.

"Excuse me a moment." Mrs. Garrens tucked her hair into place as she left the room and went up the staircase.

Eleanor poured herself a cup of cold tea and added some milk, then she got up to leave. She was stepping into her boots in the hall when Mrs. Garrens came back down the stairs. "I wanted to give these to you. I tried to find some ribbon and collect them. They're pictures. They're for you."

She handed Eleanor a box wrapped in flowered paper tied with a bit of twine.

"Thank you."

"We won't say good-bye."

"No," Eleanor agreed.

"Let this settle. Come back and I'll make you a meal. We'll have a meal together." They pressed their cheeks against each other, first one side, then the other.

ELEANOR HAD PULLED OFF THE A170 AND WAS LOOKing for the posted gas station when her cell phone rang. In searching for it, she reached under the passenger seat and scratched her arm on a piece of metal. Finally she answered, exasperated.

"Yes."

"It's me. Hey, I was wondering about you."

"I'm on my way"—Eleanor slowed the car and pulled over, parked on a grassy patch on the side of the narrow road—"back."

"That's good. I've missed you."

She didn't say anything.

"Did it go well?"

"Not so well."

"Disappointing. Are you all right?"

"I don't want to . . ."

"Okay." There was a touch of gentle awe in his tone and nothing was said for moments. "But you're on your way back here."

"I don't know where else I'd go." Her words were clipped and her heart knew it wasn't fair. Still, she had nothing to spare.

"You're not all right."

"I'm not, no." Hard and dry was what she felt inside.

"You made it to Scarborough, though." He waited, but she didn't answer. "Eleanor, let me come get you. Can you stay where you are?"

"You don't have a car." An inhale and exhale to try to change her mood.

"I'll take Granley's car."

"Mead, no. I'm fine. I just pulled off to fill the tank, and I'm starting out now, on my way back there. I'm almost back, and I'm fine to drive, really."

"It's pummeling rain, are you sure you're safe?"

"It's not raining here."

"There should be a phone connection the whole way back, if you want to talk. Almost all the way, until you're almost here, we could keep talking."

"I don't want to talk now. It shouldn't be long, from where I am."

"You sound odd."

"Don't worry."

"And you don't want to talk?"

"I don't, not now, not later, really."

"But you're on your way."

"I am." She didn't say good-bye when she turned off the phone.

Later, on a small road, she redialed him. "How is it I sound odd?" Having him at the end of the line began to melt the iciness in her belly and around her heart.

"I dunno. Lonely, angry."

"Are you packing to leave?"

"I'm not. I'm waiting for you."

She smiled. "Where would you go if you were packing up to go somewhere?"

"I'd take you to Patagonia."

"Seriously?"

"Not terribly."

"Ah."

A close-knit family of sheep stood in the road and she slowed to a stop.

"There are sheep in the road," she said.

"In Patagonia?"

"No, there are sheep in the road and they're not moving." She swerved a bit to the right and stopped.

"Honk and keep honking till they budge."

"I don't want to. I'd rather wait for them to go. Where are you?"

"I'm at Fiddleheads. Having a lager here and reading the news."

"Can I meet you there? I'd rather not go straight to the house."

"Get back on the main road when you can. It'll get you here faster. The back roads might take you a couple of days, if you don't lose your way. Call me when you're almost here, if you need directions to the pub."

"There's a man coming now," she said. "Through the bushes, where the sheep came from. He's got a dog with him and they're moving now. I'll find the highway and see you soon, okay?"

"Yes, it's great."

She didn't hang up and neither did he. "You know, you're a fine lass, an astonishing fine lady." She listened. "Whatever's spinning you about, nothing in the world will change that, ever."

❧

THE DEPTH OF HER ANGER SURPRISED HER, AS SHE DROVE through the rain that had started to pound so hard she could barely see through the windshield, and was all tangled up with knowing she would never know what it was her mother had chosen, much less why.

Mrs. Garrens was a lovable kind of grandmother. Yet more family, in this world of families she had found, after living so long without family. Eleanor Sutton Garrens Abbott. No orphan should have so many names. Something had been explained. There was some way in which a mystery was solved, but she experienced this one, this secret that had shrouded her life, as a taint. There was something dangerous in what she'd uncovered and though facing truth seemed, all in all, a good thing, she felt jangled and desolate and raw.

She called Mead again and he directed her along the road to the pub at Fiddleheads. As she passed through Flatfields, the rain stopped, and a distinct double rainbow arced from one side of the valley to the other. It should have been a good sign, but it seemed like a mockery.

Mead was outside waiting for her in a peacoat and black corduroy pants. As was often the case since she'd been in England, Eleanor was wearing the clothes she'd worn the day before. She checked in the rearview mirror, but there was nothing to do about the way she looked: she'd been fretting and desperate since the morning.

Mead stepped up and opened the door for her, took her in his arms, and held her close, held her long enough to break her heart open. She took his hand and led him away from the pub. Holding hands and walking, the simplest thing in the world and it felt like heaven and gold.

She told him the full length of her story from the beginning to the end, from the awful sheets on the bed at the inn to the feel of Mrs. Garrens' cheek against hers. In telling it, the story began to make a different kind of sense to her, and she knew that sometime she would want to look carefully at the pictures Mrs. Garrens had given her. Find her own features in his face. See what Anne Sutton and Martin Garrens looked like when they were in love.

A waxing gibbous moon in the sky, as she and Mead walked back to the pub. She went straight to a man at the bar and asked if she could have a cigarette. His silver lighter snapped open and she leaned in, watched the end catch fire, and thanked him. She inhaled deeply, blew a stream of smoke into the air. Popped a few perfect circles. She hadn't made smoke circles since she learned how to make them when she was sixteen, but the nicotine went straight to her head and calmed her like a magic blanket. Made the world fuzzy around her.

They sat on a couch by the fireplace. "Did you know about this?" she asked Mead.

"No, I didn't. Not exactly."

"All in all, it's not the worst thing that's happened," she said, feeling worldly. "If I get myself out of the picture. All my feelings and stuff like that. Think about it," she said to Mead as if persuading him, "how was my mother going to tell a little girl all that?"

She went back to the stranger at the bar to ask if she could possibly have another. "I guess I'll have a whisky with this one," she said to Danny, the bartender. She waited for the drink, and for a moment at the bar felt she had all the time in the world and nowhere she had to be, as she watched Danny pour her drink.

She thanked him and ambled back to the couch. Spent from the day. Worn out from deep inside. She sat as close to Mead as she could.

"She didn't mean to have that crash. Right?" She offered him a sip of her whisky and he took it. "Maybe she was going to bring him back with her, change their lives and be together." Her open palms against her face, she folded forward and cried for a moment—silent and shaking and all of a sudden, as if out of nowhere—and then she sat up and wiped the tears away.

"Did you know that I met him? When I was a kid, I met him. She brought me to meet him. That was bold of her, wasn't it?" Eleanor felt manic. "We took a trip, just the two of us, my mother and I. I think they were there together and I didn't know it, but he did things with us. Just sort of showed up. And at night she'd go out after I was sleeping." Then she asked him,

"What did you mean, 'not exactly'? A little bit ago, you said you didn't know, at least not exactly."

He took a sip, sat back, stretched his arm along the back of the chair so it wrapped around her without touching her. "I meant I knew there was something. It didn't mean much to me when Alice talked about it, but when she was ill she started thinking about you taking on the place and she said a few things about your mum and this man Martin. She was mulling over some responsibility she had, because she pulled at Anne to come home, to come back to Yorkshire, and felt responsible for all of it.

"But then she talked about your dad, John, and the way he loved you, and the way Anne loved him."

Eleanor's mute nod.

"She said he lost every ounce of brightness when your mum died."

"But it wasn't because she died," Eleanor said. "He must have found out about Garrens then. He must have pulled away because he knew about him. Jesus, it must have been awful. Alone with me every day, and all of a sudden a stranger to him."

Mead leaned his forehead against her forehead. "Your mum cherished him, your dad. He was a hero, to her. That's what I mostly remember, from what Alice said. She talked about how fiercely your mum loved him."

"That she loved him." Eleanor sat up straight, turned to look Mead in the face to make sure she was understanding. "My dad, John?"

He nodded and Eleanor's spine bent with softness, as Mead continued the story.

"Alice said you and your dad would put on plays for your mum, that he took you everywhere he went on Saturdays, no matter what he had to do. I think she said he taught you bunny ears for how to tie your shoes."

Her upper body was trembling with remembering.

"He made a puppet theater for you," his face smiled, "and cobbled together some puppets, too."

"You're making this up."

"I'm not."

"Well, it's true, every part of it's true. I can't make sense of this, this new thing, but I know who my dad is." Her words were hiccups as she tried to speak through silent sobs. "He walked me to school in the morning, ripped off Band-Aids without any pain." She swallowed and her voice squeaked and Mead held her close. "He taught me to swim and to dive and not be afraid." Eleanor managed to inhale a full breath. She took Mead's hand in her hands and turned her whole body toward him. Like a hungry flower, she'd been watered and with gratitude she kissed him.

ELEANOR WALKED INTO THE STUDY WHERE GWEN stood, looking into the courtyard. Gwen turned toward her and said, "Mead told me at breakfast this morning. I am sorry beyond words, Eleanor. I wish I'd been the one to tell you. I wish I'd said something. I know Alice meant to, and I should have but didn't know when, with all that was happening." Gwen's eyes teared up and she slapped the tears away with the backs of her hands.

Eleanor stepped in and wrapped her arms around her.

"It's all pretty simple," Eleanor said. "It's just the way things are." She stepped back. "When are you going?" she asked.

"Not till tomorrow."

"Why do you have to go? Why can't you stay here?"

"I've got to get back to Cambridge. It's where we live. I suppose it's where I live now. It's where our friends are. But you'll come, for a visit. Not now, I know, but you'll be back, you'll come and visit the house there. It's very different from here, you know. I think you'll like it."

"Gwen, someone has to stay here. I can't stay. I can't take all of this on. I've got a whole life in New York City and I really can't stay, now."

"A whole life" sounded insincere and pale and small.

"Don't let this change anything," Gwen said. "This world is yours. Unequivocally yours, whatever you do."

It was the room where everything had started. That first night when she'd sat at the edge of this couch.

Gwen pressed her cool hand against Eleanor's face. "You have my numbers. When you need me, when you've decided what you're doing, whether it's now or much later. Nothing will change. As you can see, this place survives in spite of everything. And you belong here. Whether you stay or go, it will always be yours."

Tilda walked by with a bowl of carrots and peas and a platter of roast beef on her way to the dining room to serve Gwen an early supper.

"What will happen with Tilda and Granley? Will they stay?"

"They live here. They take care of the place. I know it seems like everything's topsy-turvy, but they'll be here, I'll be back," Gwen reassured her. "And Mead . . ." She stopped herself. "You'll have a bite with me?"

"I'm not hungry." Eleanor looked past the long hall through the front windows toward the moors as if they called to her. "I'm going to go out for another walk soon."

"Is that a good idea?" Gwen looked concerned. "It's going to be dark in an hour."

"There's a full moon. I won't go far."

"Please stay and have a bite with me."

Eleanor wrapped her arms around herself. "I will. I'll sit for a little bit."

The sound of Gwen's knife and fork against the porcelain plate, the whistle in the chimney—Eleanor spoke softly so as not to disturb any of it. "Did you always know Martin Garrens was my father? Did Alice always know?"

Gwen placed her knife on one side of the plate and her fork on the other. She pressed her napkin against her mouth and set it back on her lap. "I believe we did," she said. "Alice wanted to say something: it was one of the reasons she had me call. But once she saw you, seeing you moved so many feelings inside her. Your face seemed so happy, for one thing. She kept saying so, and she didn't want to take that away. Every day, when the night came, she resolved to tell you the next day. We lay beside each other and she spoke of nothing else, nothing but the bittersweetness of having you here, of not having known you for longer, having to leave you . . ."

Something hard had hold of Eleanor. "But why didn't she say something to me sooner, tell me years ago?"

Gwen held Eleanor's eyes and Eleanor knew, she knew inside, she was old enough to know the truth. "It would have taken too much from you," Gwen said. "How could anyone take John from you?" Gwen didn't need to take hold of Eleanor's hand. Her voice held her, her eyes held her, her love moved inside her till it softened what was hard. "When, dear heart, when would we have broken in and insisted on the truth being told? I'm sorry, dear, but when exactly? There was never a right time."

"I know." Eleanor pushed her chair away. She got up from the table and stood behind Gwen's chair, put her hands on her shoulders. "I'm going to go walking, but I promise I'll be okay."

"I expect I'll see you in the morning." Gwen's hands were folded in her lap and Eleanor knew she wouldn't finish her dinner but would walk around the fountain for a while before heading back to the gardener's cottage for one last night without Alice at Trent Hall.

Eleanor kissed the top of Gwen's head. "See you in the morning."

She put on her coat in the front hall, heaved open the heavy front door, and started in the direction of the pond and waterfall.

⁂

SHE TOOK OFF ONE BOOT AND STUCK IN HER TOE, HER big toe, and the water was icy cold. But she pulled off her other boot and then dropped her old jeans. Her coat was already behind her on a stone. She pulled her sweater over her head and her two shirts came with it.

"Don't be silly," the young and healthy Emily said. "It's freezing in there."

"I'm going in," Eleanor said. She took off her pink and red lace bra and stepped out of the matching underwear. She dove in.

Emily walked into the water in her long skirt and stood by the side with her shawl open to wrap around Eleanor when she came out.

"You're blue. You'll make yourself sick," she said.

But Eleanor turned on her back and moved her arms through the water to keep herself moving, her body afloat.

Emily wrapped herself in the shawl again.

"You know the whole confusion began because I should have gone home with Robert. I should have known not to turn away from him. Ah, if only we could know." She spoke in a very small voice. Everything about her, though she stood five feet, six inches tall, seemed contracted and small.

"I'm going to walk to the Outer Hebrides. If Robert can walk from there to here to find me, then I can walk." She looked north.

Eleanor sank under the water, blue and shivering with cold.

❦

ELEANOR SCANNED THE COUNTRYSIDE WITHOUT TRYING to find the children. It was no longer lush green as it had been when she arrived. The bite of winter had come and there was frost over everything. Her throat was sore and she could taste a change in the air that tasted like snowflakes.

With her sweater, she dried her hair briskly, then pulled on layers of shirts and the damp sweater on top of them. The coat would keep her warm. There were fewer small animals to rustle the grass, in the winter, and more of the chimneys in the distant village were smoking, but other than that it was the same as it had been the day she'd arrived. If she were on the swing, her toes would have had no chance of touching the leaves on the branch, let alone the sky.

Hurrying, she slipped and fell on the damp ground, fell on her knees and the palms of her hands. She wiped her muddy hands on the back of her pants then went to the tree and rubbed her muddy pants against the bark to get the chunks off, to get it down to a thin smear of mud that would dry quickly. She might pass by the graves on the way, but she wanted to get back to the house and she couldn't remember which direction she should take.

When she came on the gravesite, she imagined her mother and father buried beneath. Together, like Catherine and Heathcliff, wandering forever in love on the moors. A childhood love that wouldn't let go, didn't know how to let go. Eleanor wondered why her parents' ghosts were children, wondered where in the world was John Abbott's ghost. She made a wish, with her hands in prayer, that she might see them again. All of them. She tried to remember what it was that the children at the pond had said to each other, that first day on the moors. What it was she'd wanted to ask them.

She didn't feel sad. Mead was right. It was an old grave, an old untended grave, and maybe there was nothing beneath the crosses; maybe they stood only in memoriam. It might have been two beloved animals buried there, or children, from another century, she thought, and that was a sad thought, but she didn't know. Alice might have known, but Eleanor herself didn't know and maybe there were certain things that would be lost and never known. Maybe there were things that didn't need to be known.

PART FOUR

THE SHELVES WERE STAINED, THE BOOKS WERE ARranged, and Mead had placed the furniture close to the bookshelves, so there was a lot of space in the middle of the finished library. His long desk was cleared of books and papers, but now there was a telephone.

Eleanor dialed Gladys. She told her she was finally on her way back, and Gladys hesitated. "Miles is still in England," she said. "He's arranged to work at his firm's London office, so he's still there, waiting for you."

Eleanor took it in and felt confused. How much time had passed since their visit to York? How strange it would be to see him.

She was leaving Trent Hall, and she hoped that in continuing to move, something would come clear. There were things in New York she had to get back to: her clothing line in production without her oversight, the most important time in her life as a designer. Her apartment going as dusty as her mother's room at Trent Hall, she felt if she didn't touch ground in New York soon, none of what she'd learned here would ever make sense to her.

Eleanor climbed up the library ladder and sat on the top rung. From this point of view, the library was even more beautiful than it was from the ground. Sun shone through the stained-glass window and the place felt like a medieval cathedral with the colors of alizarin crimson and lapis lazuli dancing around.

She sat on the top stair of the ladder and watched sunlight sparkle on the glass, light move across the books' bindings. There was also the shadow cast from the branch of a tree just outside the stained-glass window, doing something interesting.

She missed Emily.

She was wearing the ring again.

She smiled at the memory of her day with the ghosts of Catherine and Heathcliff. How would she tell anyone what had happened here in the Yorkshire moors, where she'd found herself and her family?

With the courage it took to know one's self, she'd undone the curse. Facing truths and opening doors that led down dark halls, she'd started the journey.

Love was powerful, childhood love with its innocent hooks could be enthralling, love on the moors wild enough to kill you, but with feet on the ground and a lofty soul, there was nothing but right love to choose. There was nothing to fear.

Mead would come eventually. He had to come eventually.

And he did. In a matter of time, he came through the old barn door and took her in. He walked to the base of the ladder.

"So, you're going back," he said. "You've decided."

"I haven't decided anything." She attempted a smile.

He climbed one rung and then one more, and he recited Browning as he climbed toward her. " 'How sad and bad and mad it was—But then, how it was sweet!' "

" 'Grow old along with me!' " he went on, from another piece. " 'The best is yet to be.' "

She scrunched up her nose and he climbed higher to kiss her freckles, then he kissed her lips fiercely and grabbed her so tight that it hurt and she squealed of it, so he let her go.

She sucked her upper lip where it felt like he'd bruised it and his eyes filled with words that even he, a fine Scots storyteller, couldn't tell.

Eleanor took a deep breath and was trembling. So she couldn't stop it.

It was one of those things. It was one of those moments of awe and dread and desire, inevitably.

She'd curled her hair and it was thick and tumbled around her face.

He stood just below where she sat on the top of the library ladder and he looked at her carefully. She knew that he was seeing a girl all dressed up and curled for a boy.

"Miles is still in London," she said. "I made a call to Gladys just now, on your new phone." She tried a smile. "She told me. I didn't know, but I'll see him there, on my way . . ."

Mead ran his fingers through her hair, mussed it, pulled it back into a ponytail with his hand and tugged gently.

"Is there something I could say?" His accent was more pronounced when he was in a certain mood, and she loved this in him. "I know it's what I didn't say, or what I did say and shouldn't have said."

"Shh . . ." She reached toward him, to put one finger to his lips, and lost her balance for a second, but he was right there in front of her and kept her from falling.

His eyes lit up. "Do you remember when you fell from the tree in your mum and dad's backyard?"

She was startled.

"Do you remember my catching you?"

Puzzled, she smiled an unfathomable smile.

"It was back then when Alice and I went to Manhattan, for the funeral. That day or another one, and you'd let me come play with you and some friends of yours. You were climbing a tree and you fell from a branch of it, and I happened to be there when you fell."

"I've never forgotten it," she said. "It's almost the only thing I've always remembered from that time, but I didn't know it was you."

"It was like you were falling in slow motion and I just opened my arms."

Now the world gave her more. It never stopped giving her more. If it was Mead who'd caught her in his arms, was he her childhood love? She inhaled his peace and knew there was nothing to be afraid of.

Mead backed down the ladder and Eleanor followed him. He held her hand and walked her to the other end of the library, to another ladder. He fixed her eyes with his. "Ready to climb again?" She climbed ahead of him and he kept his hand on her the whole time, on the back of her legs beneath her skirt to the swell of her bottom, till they were up in what once had been the hayloft, where the floor was now hardwood, finished and stained, and there was a woven rug and pillows on the floor, like a home in Morocco.

He lit a fragrant candle and she thought they could just live there, where long ago an owl had made his family. They wouldn't have to come out even to eat, but could live off the light and air in the loft; and she wouldn't have to go anywhere, she'd be home.

There was a zipper on the back of her skirt. He was harder than she'd ever felt him. In all ways harder. Angry and insistent and suffocating so she kept gasping for breath and her mind was blown, through the top of her skull, he pressed so deep inside her, lifted her so she was upside down, inside out, and he touched something that hit her physical heart.

She was crying and all she could think was she'd fallen from a tree.

Neither could he breathe. They were wet with sweat and

panting like angels in the loft till he started laughing. And she didn't know why he laughed, but she started laughing as well, and she thought, it was you who caught me.

❧

MEAD WATCHED AS ELEANOR DRESSED AGAIN, TO GO. Back in her pleated miniskirt, she slipped into one black boot and then the other. Her opaque-black-stockinged legs. He picked up her satchel and carried it outside. She walked slowly, behind him. There were leaves all over the gravel ground and there was frost on some of the branches. Mead put her small satchel on the seat inside. "This all you're taking?"

She looked up into his face, bit her lower lip, and gave a few nods. Her eyes fell shut and she took a deep breath, took in the fragrance of him, then the leaves in midair, the horses not far away in the stables, so she'd never forget. It seemed a lifetime ago she had just arrived. She felt her jaw chattering. He stepped close to block the wuthering wind.

"I don't know what you're doing, but I know you're the lady of the manor here and you always will be." He looked about the courtyard. "I wish I had some flowers to weave into your hair." He took her face and kissed her long again.

She looked up at the tree whose branches had scratched at her window and saw that now it stood without bending an inch to the wind.

"You know there's much more I will say to you one day."

She nodded mutely.

His hand on her back, he urged her into the taxi and closed the door before she had a chance to say good-bye. The taxi drove away from him and she sank back in the seat as Trent Hall disappeared behind the hill. The taxi passed the wisp of a village called Flatfields.

❧

WHEN SHE SAW THE NORTH SEA, SHE THOUGHT OF THE selkies. Seals that swam up close to the shore and slipped out of their skin to be human, on land, and then slipped back in again. But if a man stole and hid the skin, he'd keep the selkie forever as his human wife. The world was full of puzzling stories.

The woman beside Eleanor on the train had nicely shaped calves and wore a pair of sensible shoes. She offered a lap blanket and Eleanor received it happily, pulled it up to her shoulders, and tucked it under herself, wrapped it tight around her legs so no cool air might slip in.

The woman wore a felt hat, her hands were delicate, and she wore a beautiful emerald ring on her wedding finger. Her hands moved quickly as she knitted blue and green yarn with nubs and ribbons into the shape of a carpetbag. She had one like it sitting beside her on the seat, out of which she pulled a package of thin sandwiches made with pumpernickel bread, cream cheese, and chopped cucumbers. She offered a sandwich to Eleanor, who took it gladly. The train cut through the familiar green of the moors.

When the train slid smoothly into the station, Eleanor dried out the tin cup the woman had given her with tea and milk. She handed back the blanket she'd loaned her for the ride and thanked her. The woman finally slipped off her hat to straighten her hair. She looked into her reflection in the train window and smiled a big smile with an excited wave of her hand as they passed a handsome man and two blond children.

Without a hat, the woman looked quite young. The man and the children ran along beside the train smiling at her and waving until the train stopped. She made a bun of her pretty hair, tucked in some stray hairs, then placed her hat carefully on her head and pinned it there.

Miles was at the end of the platform when Eleanor stepped off. He came toward her, took her bag, and put it down so he could take her into his arms. He rubbed her back with vigorous encouragement and she buried her face in his chest. When he pulled away to get a look at her, she clung tight for an extra moment, then tossed her head, tossed her curled hair, let him see how she was doing. She unbuttoned her overcoat and offered to take back the bag. Side by side they walked through the station and then to the curb, where Miles hailed a taxi to the Stafford Hotel.

On the vinyl seat, her skirt didn't slide easily, so Miles went around the other side and met her in the middle.

"You must have things to tell me," he said. "I know you do." His arm went to its natural place around her shoulders. "You can start now or save it for later." His hand moved briskly up and down her right arm, as if he were trying to warm her. "They didn't feed you," he said, "you're thin."

At home, this would be an unequivocal compliment. "I'm strong from walking." She watched the streets of London go by.

"I can't believe you've been here all this time," she said. "I had a meeting at Harrods and you must have been here. What have you been doing?"

"I sent you loads of texts."

She remembered seeing them, but had only just read them on the train.

"I've been learning about the market here. We've got offices in London, so it hasn't made much difference. I could easily live here." He craned his head forward to read her face as he spoke, then sank back against the seat again.

"Is Harrods making an offer?" he asked.

"Looks like it, yeah, I think they are," she said.

"That's great."

Conversation between them had never before been strained.

On Regent Street, she noticed top-end shops and elaborate Christmas decorations. Piccadilly Circus with throngs of people and unlit neon lights. She caught a glimpse of the Mall and Buckingham Palace. He kissed the back of her head, and she sensed him smelling her hair.

The hotel was like an elegant home. Velvet upholstery and floral wallpaper, lovely rooms and halls. Their suite's sitting room was blue and tan velvet with a bay window in front of which a table was set with flutes for champagne and a bucket of ice with a bottle of Cristal.

Eleanor slid out of her overcoat and peeled off her sweater.

Miles stepped back another step and walked backward toward the table, where without looking he reached for the bottle of champagne. He unwrapped the foil and deftly jimmied the cork free. He poured two flutes and lifted one toward her, without a word.

She walked toward him and happily took the glass and a sip.

Miles was saying that it worried him, when he thought about it, that she hadn't made a scene when she saw him, at least when she got alone with him. "You never got mad at me," he said. "I thought maybe that wasn't such a good thing. Not a good sign, right?"

"Please." Enough of signs, she thought. She touched her temples.

He undid his tie and sat next to her.

She rubbed her temples like she was rubbing in a stain. "You can't imagine how much has changed," she said.

"I don't want things to change." He knelt on the floor in front of her where she sat on the edge of the bed. "I want to tell you about why it happened."

"I don't want you to." She didn't want to talk about the girl, who she was, and what had moved him to want her in his bed on that evening, or on many evenings about which she'd never heard.

She rubbed her temples again.

"You're going to hurt yourself," Miles said and he pulled her fingers away from the sides of her head.

Miles knew much about her life, but he didn't know that her father was not her father, that the man who'd come to her basketball games was not her blood. He didn't know that her true father had lived in a small living room on the edge of the North Sea and had loved her mother since she was a little thing. He didn't know that her father had eyes like hers—eyes that changed so in some pictures they looked shuttered and secretive and other times appeared as generous and open as when the sun reaches down with its fingers through the clouds.

"Of course." She looked into his scared eyes. "You should explain to me if you need to, if you want to, you should."

"Maybe you're right, maybe we should just go home and talk about it once this is behind us more."

"No, you should go on," she said.

So he explained the way it had felt to love her since childhood. The blind faith he'd had in himself through her love and what it had felt like, after so many years of seeing himself through her, to feel other women's eyes. To feel the power of his own attraction. To feel himself desired, how little it took to seduce a girl who liked him—once he started with a most natural smile.

It sounded like there was more than one girl, but Eleanor didn't ask. She let him continue.

He explained that he'd never wanted anything but a life with her, and the closer it came to being true, the more he felt he owed it to them, to himself and so maybe to their life together, to be a little wild before embarking on forever, because he imagined them together forever—from the beginning to the end.

Eleanor's bones felt less cold. She sipped the champagne. She looked at Miles' face and she liked him. She always had, she had loved him. He was telling the truth, and she liked him for that, that part of him that felt he needed to tell her the truth and get it all on the table.

She knew he had a life planned for them, one that started on their school playground and would end on the playgrounds of their grandchildren. It included a diamond ring and a white dress, a house in the country for the weekends, with swings, and children on the swings one day, and Eleanor opening her own store in the city and then one in the country.

"Let's go out and find the river," she said.

He stood and put on his jacket.

"You look good," she said. He looked handsome in his navy jacket and gray slacks.

The cab dropped them near Westminster and they walked on the Victoria Embankment.

"It's magnificent, isn't it?"

"It really is," she said.

"You know, I've been talking a mile a minute since I got you back, up close again."

"I know."

"I guess I don't really want to find out what happened over here." He shrugged. "I've got a bad feeling about it."

She sighed the sigh of resolve. "A lot happened."

She told him about some of the things she'd found. The clues that seemed to have been left for her like crumbs to collect on her way out of the woods. She told him about the letters she'd found by accident in the cupboard of one of the rooms, how she'd gone into Scarborough looking for an old family member, but she was changing things and leaving things out.

The Victoria Embankment was beautifully shaded with trees, though they'd dropped their leaves, and the sky seemed very high over the river.

She looked at him and laughed at herself.

"What?" He didn't understand what was funny. "Really, what?"

"Nothing. It's all so awful." She was smiling.

He seemed lost and she was sad to see him lost and to feel so far away from him. His hand held hers. Their fingers fit perfectly together in a fist. She remembered noticing it and thinking they were meant for each other when he first took her hand like this.

"You're my best friend," she said. "Really, my best friend."

His sad face brightened.

"It's not the girl, or even the girls, if there were many of them." She noticed he didn't object and her heart did one small flip before she continued. "It's something else. Maybe something that's been happening. Maybe you noticed something before I did, or maybe you sensed there was something more in store for each of us."

"Eleanor, it wasn't that."

"I know. Let's sit down." Her voice was soft like a fine mother's can be. "I'm saying that maybe what happened, happened because it was time for it to happen. Time for something else to happen. At the root of things. Maybe?"

He started to object, but she saw him decide against it.

She knew she was being a coward, not saying what she was afraid to admit. "And anyway, I've not even told you the half of it here."

He stiffened.

"I mean what it's been like to find out so much about myself in such a short time. And without you." She looked at him with great earnestness now. "Right? I mean, I've never done anything without you. And it's strange that it happened the way it did, because if the call had come any other night, or if I hadn't run up there and used the key, you'd have come with me."

"Eleanor."

"That's wrong. I don't mean that. I'm not sure I believe that. I don't know. I like what I've found over here, on my own."

"Let's get a drink," he said. It was all he said. "Let's get a drink."

They got a cab and pulled up to a pub, but Eleanor suggested they go back to the bar at the Stafford. The American Bar.

❦

MILES CROSSED HIS LEGS AND KNOCKED BACK THE LAST of his mojito, caught some ice cubes in his mouth, and chewed them. They hadn't said words to each other in ten minutes or so but had been chewing on the salted mixed nuts from a bowl.

Finally he said, "I understand it's the end now, I do, but I'm glad I'm here. I'm glad you didn't fly home alone. I'm glad I didn't come with you, and I'm glad I stuck around. You're the best of everything there is." He gestured for another round of drinks. Eleanor's heart heaved in her chest.

With the courage it took to become her full self, she was free to do anything at all.

After their second mojito, Miles kissed her. She felt the kiss of the man he had become. The man who had learned how appealing he was.

"You deserve everything, everything good in the world," she said to him.

Outside the Stafford, the cab pulled up and it would take Miles to Heathrow.

"I'm going," he said.

Eleanor put the back of her hand against her mouth, and the fact that her eyes welled with tears, she knew, gave him a treacherous moment of hope.

He said, "I shouldn't have come. I should have waited for you at home." He looked at her the way he always had, with frankness and kindness. He waited and her clear eyes held him for an eternity.

"You're the most wonderful girl." He pressed one long kiss on her cheek and walked toward the big London cab. He never walked awkwardly, but he walked awkwardly now. She watched him throw his suitcase in, then he glanced back and held his hand up for a wave, climbed in, and the cab drove away.

She changed at Trent Hall before heading to Fiddleheads. Stepped out of the black wool skirt and put on jeans and the sweater she'd forgotten to give to Mead.

Mead was talking with Danny when she came in. Danny saw her and, without saying anything, stepped away to pour a glass of whisky with a drop of water to wake up the flavor. Eleanor slipped onto the seat next to Mead at the bar.

Before he'd seen her, she started speaking. "I figured out that with my Self in place, I have everything I could want."

Danny set her whisky in front of her. "Welcome home," he said.

"You surprise me," said Mead.

"I surprise myself, I guess."

They were alone in the Fiddleheads pub.

Mead reached around for the back of her head and pressed his forehead against hers. "May I?" he asked her, all gentlemanly. He slipped his arm under her knees and felt the gorgeous heft of her lovely body.

He lifted her up off the stool. "I'm glad you're not a scarperer," he said.

He spun her around and kissed her face madly, then set her down.

"I guess, so am I." She was breathless.

He took her hand and led her past the pictures to the small bedroom.

"I wasn't sure when I'd see you again."

"I don't know what I'm doing," she said as she slipped the sweater over her head. "I can't make a promise of anything. I want you to feel free."

"Right, I will bear that in mind. But in the meantime . . ."

She flipped on her stomach and kicked off her shoes, slid up to the top of the bed, and lay back on the pillows. He smelled fresh and clean and she couldn't believe she'd almost walked away from this feeling.

"You're my heaven," she whispered, and he lifted her up while he wrapped his arms around her, beneath her, his body on her and his weight not a burden but a relief. He didn't kiss her for the longest time. His lips brushed her lips and his wild hair smelled of smoke and chocolate. The bedroom window was open and the breeze blew the curtains so the sheer silk brushed her face and she flinched for a moment, but he brushed it away. His eyes smiled, when he saw that for a second she'd been afraid. She felt the horse beneath them and the wind carrying them.

EPILOGUE

If Emily had wanted Eleanor to make public her great love and the daughter she'd left with the Enswell family at Trent Hall, she would have said as much. The world didn't need to know what Eleanor had come to know about her family. It was a secret to keep and to hold. The ghosts had come to heal her soul.

Mead made room for a dishwasher in the perfect old kitchen, and they transformed Trent Hall from a shadowy place to a brightly lit home with guest rooms, a great master bedroom, a grand dining room, and an easy one for their quiet dinners. There was plenty of room for friends and they had lots of parties.

The good sheep on the land had provided wool forever, but now Eleanor engaged the finest weavers and the sheep were shorn of their fine thick coats early in the spring. Fleece, rich with lanolin and oil, was washed then picked and carded, divided into pencil rovings and spun into a twist on winders and skeins, and cleaned and dyed and ready to be blocked into all kinds of clothing.

In cities like Paris, New York, and Milan—each one so much like another—Eleanor and Mead drank champagne in hotels where they'd stay, but most of the year they lived at Trent Hall with books and buildings, swings on trees, and roving dreams.

Parts of summer and all of August they visited the island of Rory, in the Outer Hebrides, and Mead's father grew fatter and happier every year.

In the beginning, Eleanor had resisted changing anything at Trent Hall, thinking Emily would get lost trying to find her. But after a while, she realized Emily had gone. She might have walked all the way to Scotland on her own, or maybe Robert had met her halfway, in the shadow of a tree on the moors.

Occasionally, Eleanor glimpsed the children at the pond, heard their giggles over the sound of the waterfall, but only vaguely. And she imagined that forever climbing on that craggy scarp were young Catherine and Heathcliff.

By the swing, Mead sat against the trunk of the orange-barked tree with Eleanor's head on his lap. They'd walked clear across the moors and back again and were resting before a dinner of roast lamb, onion mash, and gooseberry pie. It was the height of another summer and the sun was still up at nine in the evening. The world was shaded lavender and while they lay there a rare brown hare skipped by, then suddenly stopped and seemed to look at them. He looked Eleanor in the eyes. Then his head twitched first to the left and then to the right. Mead placed his palm on Eleanor's belly and felt the foot of their baby kick. As if pleased, the hare dropped onto his forepaws and scurried down a hole into the quiet earth.

ACKNOWLEDGMENTS

My deep gratitude to Sarah McGrath for her guidance and skillful editing. To Pete Harris, for persuading me. To Elaine Markson, a rare and wonderful agent, and to her assistant, Gary Johnson. My thanks to Candace Cotlove, Diane Golden, and Marion Rosenberg for starting me on this adventure. To Nancy Wyler, for my love of the written word. Crazy deep thanks to the great crew and fellow writers at Peet's Coffee and Tea in Westwood.

To Glenn Holland, for reading everything, and because I couldn't have done this part without you. To the many good friends who've read countless manuscripts, especially Aline Smithson, Danni Greenwalt, Jennifer and Howard Bulka, Ninaya Laub, Jennifer Miller. To Anne and Tony Campodonico, for their laughter and their love. To Kim Baxter, for abiding support and grounding. To Suzie and Mike Scott, for being on the road with me, particularly the virtual ones in Yorkshire.

Thank you to Jack Grapes for teaching me; to Lori Grapes for layers of insight.

Deepest thanks to Deb Marlin for the care she took in reading endless drafts of Eleanor's story, for her sage advice and friendship.

To Dimitri Logothetis, for collecting my poetry, when we were young, and for our son.

Heartfelt thanks to Nancy Furlotti, for being Beatrice and Virgil as I walked through the rings of hell, for giving me back the life I was born to live, through some combination of truth and courage.

Above all, to my son, Timothy Logothetis, because you stepped into my office one Halloween night and suggested I write a new novel, one I hadn't yet started. You turned the light on in my world, from the day you were born, revealed love to me and taught me its magic.